A HERO'S DEATH

Morris shut his eyes against the image of the kid, startled by the sideswiping of his car and the crash into the bridge, free-falling, smashing into the canal, stunned out of all reason, water rising up over the car plunging, sinking to the bottom, terrifyingly aware, tearing his own muscles and fingers to free himself without hope, the girl conscious, sober enough to scream. . . .

She was flailing the shrinking air in the car. The kid was unsnapping her seat belt, deciding in an instant, rolling down his window to the dark, cold, unbreathable chill of the water, dragging the girl, pushing her over him out the window, himself down there left alone forever. Trapped in the dead silence.

The sheriff knew Morris's thoughts as if he'd said them aloud.

"Poor bastard."

"I'm thinking he was as far as you can get from that," Morris said.

Morris and Sullivan Mysteries by John Logue:

Follow the Leader

Murder on the Links

The Feathery Touch of Death

A Rain of Death

On a Par with Murder

ON A PAR
WITH MURDER

John Logue

A Dell Book

Published by
Dell Publishing
a division of
Random House, Inc.
1540 Broadway
New York, New York 10036

ISBN: 0-440-22400-4

Printed in the United States of America

Published simultaneously in Canada

February 1999

10 9 8 7 6 5 4 3 2 1

WCD

To Philip Spitzer
and the good life on the
eastern tip of Long Island

. . . Captains courageous whom death could not daunte.

—MARY AMBREE, *"The Ballad"*

CHAPTER ONE

A light rain fell, tapping along Broadway among the early-evening traffic as if it might dance up the steps into the Plymouth Theater.

A black limousine with dark-tinted windows came to a pretentious stop. The driver stepped out with an umbrella. John Morris expected him to usher to the curb the entire traveling squad for the New York Knickerbockers.

Out stretched the long legs of a young woman in a black skirt so mini, it was marvelous.

Julia Sullivan dug her elbow into Morris's vast side.

"Even the President of the United States is allowed to lust in his heart," Morris said.

"You remember what happened to him in his last election," Sullivan said, now recognizing the young woman's face. "You realize who the legs belong to, Morris?"

"I guess the guy getting out of the limousine looking like Al Capone."

"He's nobody. She's Tenney Bidwell. Her photograph was in the business section of this morning's *Times*. She just inherited most of the Upper East Side from her grandfather."

"And she already had the legs. Life is unfair."

Morris did not question how Sullivan managed the up-front seats for the opening night of this "musical," *Chronicle of a Death Foretold*, but he had a sinking feeling it was the audience who'd be doing the dying. There was some hope. Director-choreographer Graciela Daniele described the play as involving those great dependable human verities: "sex, obsessive love, and machismo." Morris thought maybe "machismo" was the middle linebacker for the Chicago Bears.

Funny thing. Hardly anybody in this "musical" sang—anything. It was mostly dance, and Morris found himself wondering if the writer of the original novel, Gabriel García Marquez, was sitting among them—and if he remembered how it came out.

It seems a rich stranger stopped in this South American village and was taken with a young woman. Not surprising. She had the legs to catch your attention. Too bad the stranger in the village didn't catch the legs that got out of the limousine. Al Capone would have taken care of him in the street and spared the whole damn village the trouble.

Well, the stranger marries the young girl, but on their wedding night he figures out he didn't get there first. This *innocent girl* has been around the village square. So what? This is no big village. But the stranger takes it personally and returns the girl, in disgrace, to her family. Morris thought, *In America you would have to return the population of uptown Manhattan. Gabriel García Marquez had something going with A Hundred Years of Solitude. The Mets still suffer through it at Shea Stadium.*

But here he's gone a hymen too far. Morris was careful not to say this aloud with Sullivan as she wept into her handkerchief.

The young girl puts the blame on a local village playboy. Her brothers swear to kill him. They do not keep this decision a secret; the whole damned village knows it. Nobody does anything about it. Just like in *High Noon*, but Gary Cooper is not dancing in this cast to save the day. In the end, the brothers kill the sonofabitch, guilty or innocent—and this, Morris thought to himself, is not even Texas.

Morris hoped Gabriel García Marquez and Graciela Daniele were satisfied. The eighteen heavily perspiring dancers seemed plenty glad to get it over.

Morris stood and applauded with Sullivan and the entire audience. The dancers hadn't sung much, so there was little fear of an encore.

Sullivan was drying her eyes as they stepped out of the Plymouth Theater.

Morris said, "You just have the one sister, you don't have any brothers, do you, Sullivan?"

She tried to be angry, but she couldn't help laughing. Taxis were scarcer than virtue along Broadway. Morris was pleased to unfurl his huge green umbrella with the "The Masters" logo. Sullivan and half of himself fit easily under it. What would the golfing godfathers of Augusta National think of their logo drifting past the sex shops—themselves an endangered species—of Times Square? They would probably think nothing of it. After all, sex is a diversion of the masses who do not have access to that grand erotic experience—money.

"What are you thinking?" Sullivan asked as they picked their way among the theatergoers, street musicians—one of whom played an old-fashioned washboard in the New Orleans manner—panhandlers, young toughs, jaded cops, tourists lashed to their cameras, tubercular dope fiends, hotdog vendors, con men, off-duty strippers, a Salvation Army team deep in enemy territory, and hot-eyed teenagers clinging to one another—all passing in several languages, giving the city its wonderful, restless, dangerous air.

"I was thinking I prefer this Times Square to the one Walt Disney is bringing," Morris said.

"You can join the Southern Baptist Convention and boycott it."

"That's a thought," Morris said, dropping a dollar bill into the cigar box of a tiny black woman who seemed older than the sidewalk she stood on.

The rain increased and the crowds thinned as they pushed along, glad to be alive in the closing years of the twentieth century, when a miracle occurred; a taxicab dropped its fare at their feet, and they climbed inside, taking refuge from the rain and the ever-moving feet and eyes of the city.

Morris remembered when many of the taxi drivers were veterans of World War II, and hearing his accent fell to passionate recollections of the lush country girls they'd known pulling duty at Maxwell Field in Montgomery, Alabama, or at Fort Benning in Columbus, Georgia, or at Randolph Field in San Antonio, Texas, or at a hundred other southern bases and airfields of that great war. Or maybe they would ask if the Green Derby was still alive and in business in Jacksonville, Florida, and maybe tears would come to their eyes to hear that it was.

Now the drivers came mostly from third world countries and the wars they remembered were unknown to southerners or even to the New York locals who fought their way into the backseats of the cabs they drove. This driver was proud to be able to find West 67th Street.

Café des Artistes, their favorite New York eating joint. It was always crowded with talk and hustling waiters, the city particularly alive inside it. Their longtime friends, Edwin and Lib Gower, were already waiting with a captured table. Edwin, with his large, intelligent, irreverent eyes behind his black horn-rimmed glasses, was the ultimate New Yorker, born earlier in the century in Brooklyn when there were still farms on the outskirts of the borough. There must have been someone in Manhattan who wrote, or painted, or photographed, or edited some magazine or publishing house, or ran one of the great museums with an iron heart, who did not stop and gossip at any table at which Edwin Gower was sitting, but John Morris had never seen it happen, including with The Lady herself, his old friend Jacqueline Onassis, for whom he had designed several books.

Edwin loved to claim "one thirty-second" of the Pulitzer prize won by a pictorial history of the Civil War he had designed. He saved his greatest admiration for the project for the late self-taught historian who wrote it—wouldn't you know, an old ex-sportswriter, thought Morris—who could knock out a sixty-three-word cutline on any Civil War personality without opening a reference book.

All things for John Morris and Julia Sullivan were moving toward the coming week of golf on Long Island, even the conversation at Café des Artistes.

Ironically, Edwin and Lib kept a farmhouse retreat on Long Island, which was as near a golf course as you were ever likely to find either of them.

"So who is going to win this golf tournament?" Edwin asked with the terminal disinterest of a longtime—and terrible—tennis player, nodding in approval at the fish on his plate and the wine in his glass. Edwin, being the ultimate New Yorker, was of course the ultimate gourmet.

Morris said, "Whoever can drive it straight and keep it out of the hellish rough at Shinnecock Hills, and land it and hold it on the slick greens will win the U.S.

Open. The Australian-American, Greg Norman, would seem the likely choice."

Sullivan rolled her eyes in dissent.

Morris ignored her, "The 'people's choice' might be the young phenomenon Buddy Morrow. Whoever wins it will hit it straight. The penalty for hitting it in the Shinnecock rough is only slightly less traumatic than the penalty for fornication in *Chronicle of a Death Foretold*." (It was an unfortunate comparison that would resonate through events to come.)

"I believe it was our friend Bob Wynn who first published *A Hundred Years of Solitude* in America," said Gower, happy to abandon the mystical subject of golf. Gower enjoyed telling of the particularly difficult children's encyclopedia he once designed and produced for editor-in-chief Wynn. They had gone to lunch after it was published, and Wynn barely mentioned the book, prompting Gower to ask him if the finished product hadn't pleased him. Wynn, a man of few words and faint praise, answered, "Yes, I liked it. What did you want me to do, *lick it*?" Ah, New York, New York, the city of ever-sensitive commerce.

Morris said, "A young friend of mine, Mort Chilton, and I once tried to sell Wynn a book idea titled *Hitler's Daughter*. I can't imagine why he preferred to publish Nobel prize–winner Gabriel García Marquez. There's no accounting for taste."

"Do you have a place to stay on Long Island?" Lib asked. Lib was always the voice of reason in the Gower household. When they came into a bit of money with the sale of *American History* magazine, all of Edwin's grandiose Wall Street banker friends pitched this and that investment at him, but Lib had insisted they simply buy their three-bedroom West Side apartment, which turned out to be a golden idea.

"Oh, Sullivan has rented a modest beach cottage near Mecox Bay," Morris said.

"That's an oxymoron—a 'modest anything' near Mecox Bay," Edwin said. "Well, here's to golf that 'good walk spoiled.'"

It was the perfect thing to drink to under the marvelous nude nymphs painted on the restaurant walls in 1934 by Howard Chandler Christy. *With a name like that, he should have been a pitcher in the National League,* thought Morris. *By God, he had the eye for it.*

CHAPTER TWO

Morris was asleep, Manhattan traffic be damned, before Sullivan even pointed the rental Ford over the George Washington Bridge.

"Some lover," Sullivan said into the lonesome blues music she'd found on the radio dial. She patted Morris on his bad knee, causing him to deny something aloud in his dreams.

"Don't think you can get away with anything, just because you're asleep," she said, fitting the Ford in among the traffic restless to escape the city. Impossibly far down under the bridge, the Hudson River had never shone more brilliantly since the Dutch sailed into the harbor.

After crossing the less spectacular Throgs Neck Bridge, where the East River merges into Long Island Sound, Sullivan pushed the eager Ford onto the busy lanes of Interstate 495. How could so many people, on a Wednesday morning, be abandoning the great engine of

New York City? Didn't anybody have to work? She was careful not to say the word *work* aloud; she did not want to contaminate Morris's dreams, even if they were a fantasy of girls he had never known as a young man. With all the traffic blasting along the four-lane asphalt in both directions, it was impossible to know they were fleeing east on an island.

Sullivan waved a kiss when she passed the turnoff to MacArthur Airport, where she'd parked her precious Gulfstream jet among the fleet of company planes on which dedicated CEOs, always ready to sacrifice, had flown greedy executive customers to a week of perks at the U.S. Open. Ah, American business, you had to love it.

She did not wake John Morris as she turned south on Highway 24, passing through the beautiful Sears Bellows County Park, a refuge for marine life and wildlife as untamed as a thousand years ago.

Sullivan had to smile at the five-story-high Suffolk County sheriff's office rising up on the west side of the highway, with SHERIFF OTIS HAGGARD up in one-foot-high letters. *With luck, we'll never meet ol' Otis professionally*, thought Sullivan. But that wasn't the sort of luck fate had in mind.

Highway 24 quickly emptied into Highway 80, and Sullivan shook John Morris as she neared the Shinnecock Canal, connecting Great Peconic Bay with Shinnecock Bay and linking Long Island Sound with the Atlantic Ocean.

"My God, where are we? What happened to New York City?" Morris said, rubbing his eyes, then reaching for his cane as if to steady himself inside the moving automobile.

Sullivan, turning left at Hampton Bays, slowed just past the huge Spellman's Marine Boat Storage, so that Morris could look down on the Shinnecock Canal. Private yachts and sailing boats and little runabouts were tethered to their moorings on the west marina like bright floating toys waiting for a child's eager hand to set them free.

"Good Lord, we're almost to Shinnecock Hills," Morris said.

"The man's all journalist," Sullivan said.

On the eastern side of the canal, Sullivan turned north to "Old 27," as that Mississippi icon, Willie Morris, loved to remember the original highway, from the years when he held forth in Bobby Vann's saloon in Bridgehampton. John Morris had first met him in those "days of wine and roses." Ironically, he and Willie and Edwin Gower, that ultimate New Yorker, had collaborated on what turned out to be a significant pictorial book of the American South.

Morris was now very much awake. "Do you remember the first time we ever visited the Shinnecock Hills Golf Club?" he asked.

"Oh, yes," Sullivan said. "It was 1986, in the early spring. Two months before that year's Open. You wanted to see the 'grand old course before the assault of commercial television and the unwashed thousands.' Unfortunately, you were driving, Morris. The last time I remember you driving anywhere. Of course, we were lost."

"We were not lost. You were talking. And not looking. It slipped past us."

"Just like that: the oldest golf club in America 'slipped past us' without a sound. Oh, no. You missed it. You were looking for a grand entrance. Guards at the gatehouse, that sort of thing."

"True," Morris admitted, pleased to remember, having turned around and headed back west on Old 27, catching a glimpse of a red flag and a swatch of golf green. Then turned north between a modest conifer and a clutch of yearling maples—up a humble asphalt road that looked like it might lead to an aging farmhouse. And then a short way along, and there it was—high on the hill: Stanford White's original clubhouse.

It had been late on a Friday afternoon in April 1986. Only a few cars were parked in the small, unpaved lot for "members and guests," just off the practice range. They'd climbed a couple of hundred yards up the hill, past the free-standing pro shop on the left and the large, rolling practice putting and chipping green on the right.

Morris knew only one member, the erudite sportscaster Jack Whitaker, but he was unlikely to be on the grounds late on a Friday afternoon in April, with a cold, damp wind blowing off the Atlantic Ocean.

The long, narrow, white-shingled country house looked like a steamboat sailing on a green sea, with its flying columns and famous veranda and the club flag blowing in the breeze over the eastern bow, where a tiny clutch of serious men were dealing cards behind the glass walls of the foredeck.

They'd gone up the five steps past a low privet hedge, a stack of common cordwood, and in between the formal line of white Ionic columns onto the wooden veranda, which supported modest green pots of old-fashioned red geraniums.

Unchallenged as interlopers, they'd stepped inside the main sitting room, entirely empty save for the prints on the wall and the furniture on the floor. The room ran the width of the clubhouse and opened onto the northern veranda, looking down on the 9th green. In its understated elegance it might have been the quiet lobby of a small, very expensive British hotel, complete with a tiny opening for an unmanned "front desk" in the eastern wall.

In the southwest corner was an old grand piano, left carefully unrefinished, that Chopin might have rehearsed on as a young man. Green wicker chairs surrounded a scattering of low, glass-topped tables for four. A sofa, backed by a long table under a sunburst of cut flowers, divided the wide room.

A fireplace promised a warm winter nook in the western wall. Down from it, on a low table, stood a two-foot-high silver Founder's Cup, a relic from the nineteenth-century competition among the USGA's five founding golf clubs: Shinnecock Hills, Chicago Golf Club, Country Club of Brookline, St. Andrews Golf Club of Yonkers, New York, and Newport Golf Club. On the wall behind the cup was a black and white photograph of the Shinnecock Hills clubhouse, taken in the spring of 1892, a simple view of the first golfing clubhouse in America.

Hung plainly on the walls of the main room were antique prints of legendary golf holes from the Old World: Walton Heath, Old Course, 16th hole; St. Andrews, 5th and 18th holes; Sunningdale, 4th green; The Royal St. George, Sandwich.

Opening off the northwest corner of the main room was the bar, with its round marble-topped tables and green iron chairs of Chinese Chippendale. The end of the bar looked out over the first tee and down onto the western half of the course. A splash of Peconic Bay caught the sunlight like a distant mirror. To the west stood the signature windmill of the National Golf Links, which touched Shinnecock Hills, as did the Southampton Course, a remarkable golfing triumvirate for one narrow peninsula.

Morris learned that golfers standing on the high 13th tee of Shinnecock Hills could see, from the only spot on the course, Peconic Bay to the north and Shinnecock Bay to the south. The great Atlantic Ocean rolled unseen some three miles farther south.

On the wall of the bar was a whimsical black and white photograph of Centennial Day in August 1991, with the Shinnecock membership posing for the world in hats and long dresses and knickers, like a summer's day in the last decade of the nineteenth century. And there was a true image of one James Foulis, in bow tie and cap, having just won the second U.S. Open, played, of course, at Shinnecock Hills.

A century passed in the distance of a few feet on the bar wall to the shining face of forty-three-year-old Raymond Floyd, being hugged by his wife and daughter, having won, June 15, 1986, the U.S. Open, over the historic links of Shinnecock Hills.

The bar opened onto the northern veranda, looking down onto the 9th green, which washed like a green wave high above the 9th fairway. Unseen from the veranda, with its low boxes of red impatiens lending a quiet cheer, was the finishing 18th green, which sprawled below the great height of the 9th.

Morris had counted. There were five steps down to a possible immortality.

This Wednesday, the eve of the 1995 Open, presented a much more formidable presence at the entrance to Shinnecock Hills than had the lone conifer and yearling maples of April 1986. Security guards waited with serious frowns on their faces, too aware of the limited parking spaces even for members, not to say the thousands of fans expected each day.

Sullivan guided the Ford Taurus among the guards, lifting her precious pass for inspection. Morris was sure that she would have parking privileges by the time the feast was laid for the Second Coming. They were to be rarer here than sub-par rounds over the rolling wind-blown Shinnecock Hills course.

The club itself included just over three hundred members, requiring the U.S. Golf Association to conscript a small army of volunteers to carry off so huge and complex a production as the U.S. Open. Tickets for the Open had to be restricted to the lucky thousands, because of the limited grounds for viewing on this the oldest incorporated golf club in America.

It was a gay sight, the final Wednesday of practice before the tournament proper, the people in their colorful hats and bright shirts, sitting in temporary bleachers and walking the steep dunes, even posing on the grass over beer and sandwiches as if it were the last of the nineteenth century and the elite of the great city had been let out for a June picnic.

Of course, Sullivan also had cadged clubhouse passes, which were rarer than double-eagles. Morris, his scotch and water in hand, felt as endowed of wealth and power as the richest club member, standing again on the long wooden veranda, looking down on the fearful 9th green and across the sandhills over which long waves of brown fescue rippled with a fatal beauty. There were even patches of true Scottish thistle, planted inadvertently in the early years by the hobnailed soles of golfers from mother Scotland. He and Sullivan might have been standing on the balcony of The Royal and Ancient Clubhouse looking across the Old Course at St. Andrews. It was links golf come to America, though the Atlantic Ocean, in truth, lay out of sight to the south.

The New York Times, in a rare, giddy emotional burst, wrote, "There is a genuine sense of the auld sod at this special place where the 95th United States Open will be played. You can breathe it, see it, touch it. This is American golf with a heavy burr."

Oddly enough, though Shinnecock Hills has a decided "links look" to it, as if it had been shipped by boat from Scotland, the club traces its origins to France.

It seems William K. Vanderbilt, of the Vanderbilt Vanderbilts, was on holiday in Biarritz, France, in the winter of 1891. He was in the company of a couple of pals, Duncan Cryder and Edward Mead, all of them members of Long Island's Southampton summer colony.

The Scottish professional Willie Dunn was designing a golf course in Biarritz. Vanderbilt and his friends were curious as to how the game of golf was played. Dunn took them to a par-3 hole of 125 yards that he had laid out across a deep ravine, and lifted a few iron shots onto the green, several of them near to the pin.

Vanderbilt was impressed. "Gentlemen, this beats rifle-shooting for distance and accuracy," he said in a burst of hyperbole. "It's a game I think would go in our country." Here he did not overspeak. But he could not have imagined that twenty million Americans would be playing golf, and millions more watching it on something called television, by 1995.

However, it was Duncan Cryder and Edward Mead, and not Vanderbilt, who convinced Samuel Parrish and General Thomas H. Barber and other friends, to help transplant the game of golf to their own Southampton, Long Island.

Scotsman Willie Davis, golf pro at Royal Montreal, came down from Canada in 1891 to design a modest twelve-hole course for Shinnecock Hills. Davis and Samuel Parrish chose a stretch of land between Shinnecock Bay and Peconic Bay—close, in fact, as events would prove, too close, to the Long Island Rail Road line. Although it was not on the Atlantic, it had the rolling sandhills of linksland, dear to the heart of Scotsman Davis.

Nearly all of the construction work for the course—using horse-drawn road-scrapers—was done by 150 Shinnecock Indians of the Algonquin Nation, who had lived since the fifteenth century on the eastern end of Long Island. A tradition of employment of Shinnecock Indians to maintain the Shinnecock course survived on into the 1990s, with one Peter Smith reigning as course superintendent.

An early hazard for golfers at Shinnecock Hills was a family of bald eagles that would swoop down on the course and pluck up golf balls off the fairways and greens. Many years later Jimmy Demaret and Jackie Burke would build Champions Club in Houston, with trees full of fat squirrels who would race across the practice putting green and grab up golf balls and carry them to their nests like round pecans, to the delight of Demaret and Burke. Morris had seen the squirrels and wished he could have seen the eagles.

In 1892, Stanford White designed the Shinnecock Hills clubhouse. It sat on the hill, a classic white-shingled country house. Four years later railroad mogul Harry Kendall Thaw shot White dead on the roof garden of Madison Square Garden (which White had designed) for allegedly having an affair with Thaw's wife.

Morris thought, *Better White had been golfing and rocking on the veranda at Shinnecock Hills.*

In the 1890s Shinnecock men played their golf in white knickers and red coats with brass buttons. Private golf clubs were to become bastions of male exclusivity for generations. But America's first golf club permitted women members from the first day until now. Shinnecock's Beatrix Hoyt, playing in a long skirt with a wonderful mass of dark hair piled on her head, won the U.S. Amateur in 1896, 1897, and 1898. Her fellow member Mrs. C. S. Brown had won the first Women's Amateur in 1895.

Women could play on the main course at Shinnecock Hills, but they also had their own nine-hole "Red Course." Modern Red Tees for women very likely spring from this course.

Morris loved the old black-and-white photograph of Charles Blair MacDonald, swinging in his knee socks, wool cap, and coat and tie, winning the first U.S. Amateur championship in 1895 at Newport.

The first U.S. Open was won the same year—in fact, the next day—at the same Newport Club, by Horace Rawlins, sporting a full weeping mustache. He defeated longtime Shinnecock Hills club pro Willie Dunn, the same Scotsman who had demonstrated the game of golf to Vanderbilt and Cryder and Mead in Biarritz. Rawlins's prize money was $150, tax free.

In 1896, Shinnecock Hills hosted the U.S. Amateur, won by H. G. Whigham, a foreign newspaper correspondent from Great Britain and the son-in-law of Charles Blair MacDonald, who was reportedly felled that year by ptomaine poisoning. Shinnecock hosted the U.S. Open the same week in '96, won by James Foulis, who turned thirty-six holes in 152 strokes. In those days the big news was the Amateur. The Open was a casual affair dominated by rather anonymous professionals.

In 1896 John Shippen, the son of a Presbyterian minister and schoolmaster on the Shinnecock Indian Reservation, became the first black man to play in the Open.

His presence was not universally appreciated. Several British professionals protested playing in the same tournament with a black man and with an American Indian—Oscar Bunn of the Shinnecock tribe. Shippen had helped build the Shinnecock course, and he and Bunn had caddied there and learned to play the game there, being taken under the wing of club pro Dunn.

The USGA's first president, Theodore A. Havemeyer, founder of the Newport Club, told the British protesters: "Gentlemen, you can leave or stay as you please. We are going to play this tournament *with them—and with or without you.*"

Morris knew it to be a tragedy that this democratic resolve died with the 1896 U.S. Open. It would be *eighty-five years* before another black American, Jim Thorpe, played in the Open at Merion, where Morris saw him shoot a splendid opening 66 before falling back in the field.

John Shippen scored a solid 78 to tie for the first-round lead of the 1896 Open. Unhappily, he took a fat 11 on the 13th hole, in the second and final round. But finished in a tie for fifth place.

In 1928 Suffolk County ordered a highway built parallel to the Long Island Rail Road, dooming Shinnecock's original golf course, which had been expanded to eighteen holes by Dunn.

Shinnecock member Lucien Tyng personally bought land for a new golf course north and east of the clubhouse and donated it to the membership.

William Flynn laid out the new course. He is also remembered for having designed Cherry Hills in Denver, a favored Open venue, not to overlook his timeless creation, Merion East.

Flynn designed a par-70 course, playing to 6,749 yards, an immediate classic and a marvelous test of golf. The par-3 holes were of a great variety and much admired by first-rate golfers lucky enough to test them. The long par 4s played with the prevailing southwest wind, and the short par 4s played into it. The course was completed in 1931 and was very much ignored by the high priests of the American game until long after World War II.

In 1967, on a nostalgic whim, the USGA held its Senior Amateur, a decidedly low-profile event, at Shinnecock Hills. The course, with its linkslike beauty and classic windblown challenge, lingered in the mind. Then came the 1977 Walker Cup matches. America's amateurs and Britain's amateurs were impressed—with the golf course.

After a mere ninety years, so was the USGA. Frank Hannigan first suggested Shinnecock for the U.S. Open. He convinced other USGA officers and Shinnecock president Virgil Sherrill. And the Open was on at Shinnecock Hills—for 1986.

Even Ben Hogan himself approved, and he was not

an easy man to impress, but once he traveled to Southampton to play the course. Hogan was never an easy
man to impress. He found, ". . . each hole different
. . . requiring a great amount of skill to play it properly
. . . one of the finest courses I have ever played."

Ben Crenshaw, in a friendly round long before the
'86 Open, scored an unprecedented 65 at Shinnecock
but declined to claim the course record, having taken
two tee shots at the first hole. Ever the historian, Crenshaw called Shinnecock "blessed golf terrain." And later
he said, "If they broadcast the Open from there, it
ought to be on the radio."

Morris could picture the last round of the 1986
Open, and the aging iron-willed Raymond Floyd, lashing an approach shot dead into the wind to the par-5
16th green for a birdie putt to give him a two-stroke
lead with two holes to play—becoming at forty-three
the oldest man ever to win the Open, until Hale Irwin
won his third Open in 1990 at age forty-five. Rarely has
there been a more popular American champion than
Raymond Floyd.

"John Morris, where are you?" asked a voice just to
the side of him on the veranda, a voice otherwise known
as Julia Sullivan.

"Lost in the past. That I never saw, and only read
about. Sometimes I think that's where I belong."

"I don't care where you *think* you belong, Morris, so
long as it's in my bed."

"Scandalous," Morris said, lifting his glass to drink
to that warm proximity.

The years passed in their four seasons, and their own
lives followed. It seemed longer ago than a generation,
and only yesterday, to Morris—when the automobile
crash had killed Monty Sullivan and left him with a
ruined knee. It had been a tie as to who loved Monty
the best, his own young bride, Sullivan, or Morris him-

self. All these years later, the two of them often lifted a toast to Monty, and they never practiced guilt for being together. Marriage? *Who said that?* Morris thought, smiling to himself.

CHAPTER THREE

Stepping out on the veranda was a tall, rail-thin figure of a man, his hair gone entirely white as if it had turned in the winter of the year.

"*The Times*'s own man," Morris said, taking his slim hand in his own huge one.

Tom Rowe, the vintage cowlick in his hair like shattered snow, ignored the greeting to kiss Julia Sullivan on the lips.

"Don't bother the man, Morris. Can't you see he's busy?" Sullivan said, returning the kiss with equal vigor.

Rowe had written golf for *The Times* of London for thirty years. He seemed a threat to overtake the record for tenure by the late great Bernard Darwin—grandson of Charles himself—who loved anything written by Trollope and who had very nearly invented the writing of golf for *The Times* over the last forty-six years of his life.

Rowe had been a friend of Morris and Sullivan since

his hair was as brown as a thrush's wings, and he had been helpful in their prying into several murderous tragedies that had afflicted the world of golf in past years.

Rowe turned reluctantly to Morris. "I've come to the Colonies to buss Ms. Sullivan and to see for myself this wunderkind golfer, Buddy Morrow. Have you seen him on exhibit, Morris? Are his skills equal to his sudden reputation? And does he have a proper given name?"

"No. I can't say. And I understand his given name to be James. But I haven't seen his birth certificate, which I mean to see," Morris said. "*Golf Illustrated* shares your inquisitiveness. I've accepted a vast advance—equal to an afternoon's pay on the famous *Times* of London—to answer such questions." Morris could not help taking on a fake formality when talking with his old friend, the very aristocratic Thomas Carleton Rowe.

"You missed seeing this young man win the Greensboro Classic? And the Houston Open? My! How could golf stand up under such an absence?"

"Barely. Just barely," Morris said. "I was snowbound in Denver."

"The truth is, he broke a leg skiing," Sullivan said.

"Snow skiing?" Rowe said incredulously.

"It might better be described as a *human avalanche*," Sullivan said, laughing so that she was at risk of falling off the veranda.

"It's a thing that has happened to Olympic champions," Morris said, leaning on his cane for emphasis and for support to his old stiff knee, on the same left leg that had the bad luck to be broken.

"I tried to talk him into something less . . . challenging," Sullivan said, "such as skydiving. But then, we didn't seem to have sky enough in Colorado." She ducked as Morris reached for her handsome neck.

"Well, I first heard of this young Mr. Morrow a year ago—actually, from Gary Player," said Rowe. "Gary was a special guest at the World Cup. I don't believe I saw you there, Morris." With his gray eyes Rowe accused him of a dereliction of duty.

"I believe I was a special guest that week at the White House," Morris said.

Sullivan rolled her blue eyes and offered the sign of the True Cross for them both.

"Gary warned me to look out for a young golfer—he believed his name was Buddy Morrow—didn't know his actual first name," said Rowe. "Seems this Morrow was playing in the Dimension Data Pro-Am in Sun City, South Africa. I've walked the course, Morris. It's one Player designed. Quite a challenge. Gary said this lad reached the 18th green with a *seven-iron*. Takes a bit to impress Player. The hole plays to 422 meters—that's 461 yards to you Yanks."

"Did he make the putt?" Morris said with a straight face.

"In fact, he did. Finished back in the field. But he cashed a fair whack. Gary didn't know the lad's nationality. Seems he'd played all over the world. He's a chap from everywhere—or nowhere. Player's own son saw him the year before at a tournament in Jakarta. Turns out, of course, he's a Yank. But he speaks snatches of many languages—not excepting the true king's English."

"Don't hold your breath to hear it spoken on Long Island," Morris said. "Supposedly, Morrow is indeed one of us Yanks, poor bastard. But his PGA biography reminds me of how MGM used to invent romantic lives for young starlets, who maybe flipped burgers in Queens. 'The daughter of a Russian countess killed in the 1917 revolution'—that sort of thing. It takes a bit of swallowing: Morrow growing up all over the world, the son of a military officer. His mother dying young and buried at Verdun. His father disappearing on a hush-hush military mission to the Arctic. Teaching himself golf out of Hogan's book, *Five Lessons: The Modern Fundamentals of Golf. That* I can almost believe. Nobody ever wrote more wisely on how to play the game. Finishing high school in Ontario, while living with a bachelor uncle who was killed on a deer hunt by a grizzly bear. Give me a break."

"His tournament record in Asia and South Africa, and in the lesser tournaments of Europe over the last three years, is real enough," Rowe said.

I wasn't in Greensboro or Houston," Morris said, "but I doubt the PGA gave the winning check to an impostor. Still, just who is James 'Buddy' Morrow? He's supposed to have accepted a golf scholarship to Florida State University."

"One of your chaps asked him about that in the press tent Monday," Rowe said. "Morrow admitted he never made it past the first weekend at Florida State. That he was startled to learn the golf coach had actual drills for putting and chipping and ball striking. He said if he'd desired drills, he'd have 'joined the ROTC.' One of your chaps explained to me that that was a form of military training."

"He's told that story before," Morris said. "I called the golf coach at FSU—he's been there over a decade. He has no recollection and no record of offering a golf scholarship to a James 'Buddy' Morrow. But he insisted I *not* quote him. He recently got a check in the mail for $25,000 for the golf program. From—you guessed it— James 'Buddy' Morrow. The coach sees him as the hottest poster child for recruiting the golf team ever had."

"Tom, you've known the young phenoms of the last thirty years. How does he strike you?" Sullivan asked.

"I watched him on the practice tee. He strikes a lovely ball. A bit of a lash—that would remind you of vintage Hogan. The downswing beginning just an instant before the backswing is completed—a terrific flexing of the shaft—and a resultant explosion through the ball. Provoking even the soft fade of Hogan. Don't know about the nerves and the intelligence. I'm not prepared to say he's the Second Coming of Mr. Hogan."

"How does he seem to you, as a person?" asked Sullivan.

"Handsome bloke. All that dark hair and dark eyes. A ready smile for the birds, who flock around him. Might auction him off and reduce the national debt. Heard him tell a young thing, seeking *him* and not his autograph: 'Let the good times roll, dolly-bird, but don't count on time itself to hang around for the sun to come up.' Rather dry wit. More mindful of a Brit than a Yank. No offense intended." Rowe bowed to Sullivan.

"So you like him," Morris said.

Rowe thought. "Yes. He's full of energy. Never be anything but a kid. I only knew Walter Hagen when he was an old man dying, and even then he was nothing but a kid. The lad loves everything, even four-foot side-hill putts. He doesn't understand you can three-putt four or five times in one round the way Palmer did at Oakmont in 1962, losing the Open playoff to Nicklaus."

"All that optimism—after all the deaths in his young life?" Sullivan said.

"If there were deaths," Rowe said skeptically.

"If they were true deaths," Morris said, "maybe he learned early—dying is what you do. And nothing terrifies him. So then you die. So what? And who can worry about a simple three-putt? Assuming you believe any of it."

"I don't know what to believe," Sullivan said.

"One minute I'm sure he's faking everything," Rowe said. "Then I think perhaps his nerves run through steel cords, and he conceals all fear and doubt."

"It's good to know we understand him perfectly before we ever meet him," Morris said.

"John Morris, we don't know the first thing about him," Sullivan said.

"When did that ever slow down America's grand media machine?"

"Oh, you'll find him quite the interview," Rowe said. "Then he's gone. Vanished. No idea where he's boarding. Doesn't pal with the other lads."

"I hear the industry guys are shaking the money tree over him," Morris said.

"God save the Queen, yes," Rowe said. "Representing himself, is he. *No bloody agent.* An insult to American free enterprise. Driving the money boys mad. Hasn't signed with any of the manufacturers, has he. Plays the most mixed bag, Morris, since Bobby Jones. Wedges, short irons, midirons, long irons, metal-woods—that ghastly oxymoron—all of different makes, some of the irons as old as thirty years. I've done a piece on his 'bag of anonymous clubs' for today."

"Bully for you—but I want a copy," Morris said.

"Of course you do. You follow Hemingway's old proven counsel: 'Steal only from the best.' "

"Modesty, thy name is Great Britain. I hear club manufacturers are talking ten million dollars to sign."

"They're talking twice that. Morrow simply smiles and listens. Says, 'See me after the Open.' "

"I love it," Morris said. "I've never met this boy, and I know him to be innocent like a wolf."

"Oh, yes. His cavalier attitude has the retail peddlers drooling all over themselves. And agents the length of Long Island are howling at the moon."

"Let's find the young bastard and find him out," Morris said, turning to Sullivan.

"I'll pretend I'm a one-time dolly-bird."

"That won't be hard to do."

James "Buddy" Morrow stood at the far end of the practice range, lashing wedge shots you might throw a lampshade over. He was as lean and tall and dark as a young Hamlet, seemingly without the darker disposition. He smiled at every shot as if it were an original invention, his teeth a flash of health and strength.

"Hold me up, Morris. I'm losing it," Sullivan said.

A gaggle of young girls, who didn't know a wedge shot from Wedgwood, panted behind the ropes after the sight of young Mr. Morrow.

"I believe you are outnumbered by the competition," Morris teased.

"I would like my chances at hundred-to-one odds."

"Dream on."

But it was good that she was only fantasizing. John Morris would never make a bet of honest money against Julia Sullivan. Many were the bookmakers with bare pockets who had.

Morris was pleased to see that Morrow had no "golfing guru" watching his every muscle twitch as he lifted one perfect wedge shot after another. He was obviously his own man. Morris laughed to himself at the thought of some self-appointed swing doctor bending over, correcting Ben Hogan publicly during his practice routines for a U.S. Open. Plenty of the other professionals on the practice tee were being assaulted with advice from their personal coaches, one of them sticking an actual golf club between the locked knees of his famous pupil, who tried to swing and maintain some modicum of dignity, as other young girls giggled behind him.

Sullivan timed her approach perfectly, stepping with confidence over the restraining rope to catch the arm of Buddy Morrow as he passed, having left his clubs for his caddy, a local teenager, to gather up.

"My name is Julia Sullivan," she said, flashing her illicit press pass.

He shook her hand, looking directly down into her blue eyes with his startlingly deep green ones. His handshake was as firm as his gaze. He wore no hat. The sun had burned his face as dark as weathered mahogany.

"And this . . ." Sullivan turned, just able to breathe.

". . . is Mr. John Morris," said Morrow, reaching for the big wide hand that Morris stuck out in some amazement.

"I read your book on the Ryder Cup. In fact, I have it with me. It's terribly good—the way old, long-forgotten matches burn on the page, as if you could hear the rush of air as the players swing their clubs with fear in their throats."

Whatever nasty, iron-hard question Morris might have asked went down his own throat as he swallowed.

"Flattery will get you somewhere with Morris," said Sullivan. "Have you got a minute?"

"I'll stand for a round of beers, if we can find a quiet place to sit," Morrow said, looking with some pleased alarm at the gathering of young girls around them.

Sullivan lifted her precious clubhouse pass and smiled.

Morris loved it, the sight of her—light brown and graying hair, recently cut fashionably short—for once, speechless.

Buddy Morrow stood on the practice tee until he'd signed an autograph for each of the young girls and anybody else who wanted one.

Shades of Arnold Palmer, thought Morris.

Shinnecock members, even those Lords of Manhattan Commerce, turned their heads to see young Morrow take his seat after inspecting the Founder's Cup. Not that they would interrupt him for an act so plebeian as signing an autograph. Plenty of famous faces sat regularly in the room. His was just the newest and youngest.

Damned sure the handsomest man in the room, thought Sullivan. His lean, hard figure, his green eyes, his dark widow's peak, his skin burned dangerously terra-cotta, he was as drop-dead handsome as the young Tyrone Power.

Morrow lifted his glass of draft beer and touched it against their own. "To the United States Open, God save the man who wins it." His voice was a soft baritone with no detectable accent.

"Hogan says no man ever wins the Open, it wins him," Sullivan said, not taking her eyes off his green ones.

"Who would be fool enough to argue with Hogan?"

"Did you truly learn the game reading Hogan's book?" Morris asked, not bothering, not needing to take a note after thirty years of ten thousand interviews. Answers lingered in his mind years after his questions had been asked.

"Yes. I still have my original copy in my room. In the same bag with your book. I'll thumb through it tonight. It always seems like a private conversation—Hogan talking to Herbert Warren Wind, with the damnedest drawings by Anthony Ravielli. You know the book, Morris?"

Morris was pleased that he had dropped the "Mr." without being asked.

"Oh, yes. It's the one book Wind wrote with someone else that sounds like the man he wrote it with. His book with Jack sounds like Herbert Warren Nicklaus."

Sullivan laughed. "I can't wait to tell him you said that."

"You're incorrigible. Of course, Wind already knows he and the late Ed Miles of *The Atlanta Journal* were the two grandest American golf writers of their time."

"I doubt I'll remember to tell him that."

"You're trouble, Sullivan."

"I try to be."

Morrow laughed at their jousting, seemed even to envy it. "I always learn something from Mr. Hogan—or

I remember to trust something he already taught me to believe. I've read his book a thousand times since I bought it as a kid in an army PX in Panama. Many's the night I've lain in a bunk in the dark, even at sea, and visualized Hogan's description of the correct swing."

Morris surprised himself. He liked the damn kid. He'd been prepared to dismiss him as This Year's Phenom, full of himself and bound to be forgotten by the next. Of course, the book titles he carried around didn't damage his image with an old, failed sportswriter. That he carried a book bag at all separated him from ninety-nine percent of the pro golfers, excepting probably his fellow Texan and golf historian, Ben Crenshaw, who had surely read every word Hogan had ever allowed into print under his name.

"Any one thing Hogan believed that's made the most difference to you?" asked Morris.

"The most important thing: the grip. Get that right, and the rest of the swing becomes possible. Get it wrong, and you must pervert the swing for a good result. One thing among the pros on the PGA tour has amazed me: how many of them handicap themselves with poor grips. Let's see if I can quote Mr. Hogan on the 'Left Hand.' " Morrow closed his green eyes: " 'Place the grip so that the shaft is pressed up under the muscular pad of the heel and also lies across top joint of the forefinger. The main pressure points are the last three fingers and the heel pad. The V should point to the right eye.' I always wondered why Hogan—or Wind—left off the 'the' before 'top joint.' He used it before other nouns in the paragraph. But it does help me remember it."

Morris was more surprised at the quality of Morrow's own spoken language than at the great clarity of Hogan's book, shaped by the genius of Wind. "Pervert the swing" was a rare phrase for a golf pro to use. Young

Morrow did not think or speak like a predropout from college.

"Buddy, I love your biography in the Open program," Sullivan said. "Is any of it true?"

"Oh, yes." Morrow grinned a flash of teeth. "Most of it's true. Or *some* of it. Or *nearly* true. Or *ought* to be true. At least my name is real enough." He pulled out his Texas driver's license: "James B. Morrow."

"What does the *B* stand for?" Sullivan asked, noting that he was born July 7, 1968, making him twenty-seven, almost twenty-eight. He was fit as iron, but his green eyes had seen a lot and seemed older. The sun burned these golfers as dark as bedouins and made them seem younger and older at the same time. Those with light skins peeled and suffered; all of them risked deadly assaults of melanoma. She bit her lip, so as not to caution him to wear a hat.

"Just say that I prefer 'Buddy,'" he said, grinning his bright grin.

"You grew up an army brat?" Morris said.

"Absolutely. All over the flippin' world. Cuba, Panama, the Falkland Islands, Japan, the Philippines, France, Israel, the United Arab Emirates, South Africa, England, Canada, countries and military bases I can't even remember, and Washington, D.C. And San Antonio, of course, that being home country." Morrow raised his glass. "To the Alamo." And they drank to Travis and Bowie and Crockett and their doomed, merry band of 187, all of whom lost their playing cards to the Mexican army, March 6, 1836.

Sullivan couldn't help herself. "I know the sun doesn't burn you with your dark complexion. But you should wear a hat and sunscreen. You're in it so terribly much."

"Must be my lucky tournament. To be advised by so beautiful an adopted mom. I can just remember my own." There was no way he could have affected the sudden melancholy in his voice. Tears came to Sullivan's eyes. Morrow touched her hand, as though sharing every lonely moment of his motherless, vagabond boyhood. In that instant she meant to keep him as a friend for good, one of their tight circle of pals reaching back to Monty himself, long dead but alive on the tips of their tongues.

"I hate hats," Buddy said. "Seems I grew up under blazing suns. Often in the tropics. If I go out by the Tropic of Cancer, so be it."

The turn of phrase, Henry Miller's old illicit book so ready on his tongue, made Morris eager to know the young man and catch his life in his own words.

Sullivan decided on the spot what she would give him for his upcoming birthday: a huge straw plantation hat like the one worn by Australian Greg Norman, of the blond hair and fair skin.

"How did you come to golf?" Morris asked.

"I was ten years old," Morrow said. "There was a golf course on the base in Panama. I used to hunt up lost balls in the high rough—careful of the snakes—and sell them to the club pro for ten cents apiece. He gave me an old club to bang balls around with. But he didn't take me seriously. Didn't offer to show me how to use it. I found the book by Hogan in the PX."

"When you were *ten*?" Morris said.

"Almost eleven. From then on I lived at the golf course, wherever my father was stationed. When the base had one. Usually it did, or there was one not so far from the base. I didn't have to worry about making new friends. Just find the golf course. My old man never played. Never picked up a club. Never picked up anything, off duty, that wasn't bottled." There was more amusement than regret in his voice.

"Let's see—that would have been sixteen, seventeen years ago," Morris said.

"So many countries ago—it seems like another lifetime," Morrow said.

"Your father was lost on an expedition to the Arctic?" Sullivan said, wincing, though she loved the high cold in the Colorado mountains.

"True." Morrow offered no further explanation.

"I've got an old Air Force pal in the Pentagon," Morris said. "We lift a glass a couple of times a year. I was with him last week. He's a pretty good amateur golfer, about one-third as good as he thinks he is. He was curious about your father. He found too many Morrows in the Army records to know which officer he might have been. And he ran into a glacier when it came to any lost expedition to the Arctic. The Army ain't talking."

"No," Morrow said, offering nothing else.

Morris changed tactics. "Do you think you have a legitimate shot at winning the Open?"

"Yes." Morrow never hesitated. "First, the wind. Remember, I was born and have lived from time to time in Texas, home of Hogan, home of the wind. Second, Shinnecock Hills tests your game, your ability to drive the ball into position to play the second shot. No loose drives tolerated here. And so many raised greens, your approach shots must hold, or you find yourself in collection areas chipping blindly up to flags you can't even see. It's a course you have to *feel*. Cold-blooded yardage on a card means very little. You have to *feel* your way across Shinnecock Hills—with these." He held up his long, callused hands, only for an instant.

"Third," Morrow said, "I've played on five of the seven continents. Under every imaginable condition, but not against so strong a field. And I've held my own—and drowned some of them in their own sweat when I didn't own a pot to piss in. Excuse me, Sullivan." He said it all with no bluster. He might have been talking of old military campaigns and not golfing tournaments.

"If you ever need a pot in an emergency, call me," Sullivan said, laughing at this splendid young man who seemed wise beyond his years.

"The wind can damned sure blow across the eastern end of Long Island," Morris agreed. "The first round at the Open here in 1986—the tournament won by Raymond Floyd—the wind nearly blew the field away. Nicklaus shot 77. Lost his first ball ever in Open competition. Said, 'It was the most difficult day I have ever seen in American championship golf.' It's not in the weather forecast, but it could happen again before the week is over."

Morris finished his own beer and then confessed, "I'm doing a piece on you for *Golf Illustrated.* It won't come out for several months. Would you talk to me about your father, his background, his military service record, etc. And your mother? How did their deaths affect you? Or are the family tragedies too intimate or too painful for you?"

Morrow finished his beer. He set the glass gently down. "No. It's an old pain. Comes to everybody, if you live long enough."

Morris kept a careful grip on his enthusiasm. "I'd like to know a bit about the bases you lived on, the countries you lived in growing up. How you made the transition from self-taught amateur to professional golfer. Your increasing success on the Pacific and South African and lesser European tours. The life of the international bachelor. How you decided to bring your game to America. The shock to the PGA of your wins at Greensboro and Houston. That sort of thing. I don't mean to open any old wounds," he said honestly.

Morrow blinked his understanding, in no way ill at ease. "It's not pain I'm avoiding. It's the absence of mystery, Morris. *Just who am I*—is an advantage in the marketplace, even on the golf course. You'd be surprised. I love the inventions that have been said and printed about my life. I can't say I haven't encouraged them. I also haven't signed any long-term contracts. But I will, I think, soon. I'm only waiting, not for the best offers but for the *best choices* among offers. Then I'll be as candid about my life as you like. With you, Morris—and Sullivan. I promise you that." He raised his empty glass in salute.

Morris nodded his own agreement but said, "If you win this golf tournament, the media—*The New York Times*, CNN—won't let you up. They'll know your blood type before the sun goes down."

Morrow laughed and tapped his glass lightly on the table. "I hope I do. I hope they try." He looked at his watch. "Got to run. One last party to make, and early to bed." He winked a green eye at Sullivan and was gone from the room, vanished, every head turning to see him go.

"What do you think, Sullivan?" Morris said.

"I don't think God would cut me but ten percent for that," she said lewdly.

"I must say I like the books he reads."

"I like *him*, Morris," she said seriously. "I like everything about him. He reminds me of a young man who has aged overnight in the war. He's seen the world, and the tragedies in it, from the time he was a kid. Even his eyes seem tired."

"But I wouldn't say jaded."

"Green enough for jade," Sullivan said. "He makes me laugh, Morris."

"God, he swings a lovely club. I wonder," Morris said, "if he can sing?"

Wednesday, June 14
3:00 P.M.

CHAPTER FOUR

Sullivan disappeared to find a telephone to check on her jet plane, the way a mother would check on her child. Morris took one step down from the clubhouse veranda.

Jack "Speed" Wallace reached up and grabbed his cane. But it never left Morris's tight grip.

Wallace was a big thick-chested man from North Carolina who played a solid tight end for the New York Giants at the close of the Gifford era. He got the nickname "Speed" for his notable absence of it. He'd earned his way as a jaw-to-jaw blocker in the trenches of the NFL, where there was no quality of mercy at one-thirty in the afternoon. His weight had shifted downward. But he still thought of himself as the eternal jock.

Wallace had sold his way up to executive vice-president of Wargo Golf, Inc. Loved to say he got started "selling balls in a eunuch colony." He should have been a peddler in the Eisenhower years before everything went high tech, including his company's three-piece, two-piece, solid, wound, surlin, zyulin, ballatta-covered golf balls with dimple configurations to make them fly high, low, far, straight, or stop on the back of a box turtle, with liquid, metal, rubber, titanium-to-come inner cores.

"Well, shit, friend, it's round with 332 dimples, and if you catch it in the screws, it will do what you ask it to—the same as your women," Wallace liked to say, and laugh obscenely.

Wallace held on to Morris's walking stick, deliberately threatening his balance on the steps on his bad left leg. Morris didn't speak but put his large, not-terribly-clean left shoe sole on Wallace's hundred-dollar sports shirt. One or both of them were about to go down the steps of the veranda.

"Goddamn, Morris," Wallace said, releasing his stick, his own face burning quickly red, then gradually, reluctantly subduing his anger while brushing futilely at the dark smudge on the front of his shirt.

Morris knew Speed to have an evil temper since his football days at North Carolina and in the NFL. He once threw a rival sales rep through a Wargo display at a trade show in McCormick Center in Chicago. Cost the company a quarter-million dollars to settle out of court. "I got a million dollars in laughs and sales out of it," Wallace said, "and saved me a workout at the goddamned gymnasium."

One look at the soft-bellied Speed, with his already-swinging jowls, and you could see he had not been working out at anybody's gymnasium. Morris never liked him and never pretended to.

"Saw who you were knocking back beers with, Morris." Now Wallace slid into his good-ol'-boy voice, which was entirely fake, as he'd grown up the spoiled son of a rich furniture manufacturer in High Point, North Carolina.

Morris only nodded.

"You think he has a chance to win the Open?" Wallace sounded like a man who'd bet heavily on a favorite horse.

"I've never seen him play in person," Morris said. He did not say he'd seen him on TV and rehearsing wedge shots just now on the practice tee like Hogan used to nip them.

"Not seen the bastard talk to anybody for as long as he talked to you, ol' buddy, and your girlfriend. Better watch her. I hear he's been in every pair of pants from here to Paris, France."

"Don't see him wearing a Wargo cap," Morris said, not hiding his smile or his satisfaction.

Wallace flinched in spite of himself. "What kind of kid is he? What does he want? I can't get to him. At Greensboro and Houston, he just said, 'See me later.' Hell, *this is* later—the United States goddamned Open. I'll be honest, Morris. I'm here ready to write him a check with seb'en zeros."

Morris leaned on his cane without comment.

"Gimme a break—what did you two talk about? Never saw him sit that long with anybody. Not even a dame. What the hell does he want? I told him the one time he gave me three minutes: 'Now, son, sign your goddamned name, *Buddy Morrow*, right here, and you'll never have to worry about another unplayable lie under some goddamned bramble bush.' And that was just our first offer. Morris," Speed plunged ahead, "you're freelance now. You can work for anybody. There'd be a helluva lot in it for the man who helped Wargo get next to the kid."

Morris said nothing, which encouraged Wallace to keep plunging ahead.

"I see you driving that Ford with the rental plates. You'd fit better in your own goddamned Mercedes. I know I'm big as you, and I do. I can have one delivered right here today. You interested?"

"No," Morris said, stepping down off the veranda. He and Wallace were almost exactly the same height. Morris was equally wide but, despite his size, carried very little fat. He could swim two miles with the bad leg, and often did. He'd never been able to tolerate low-rent guys, and luckily, working for the independent Associated Press and afterward on his own, he'd never had to.

"Ford's a straightforward vehicle," Morris said. "I especially like the *honest* smell of it."

Speed Wallace's thick face burned summer red. "Careful, boy. Don't let your mouth overload your ass."

"Cliché stuff, Speed," Morris said, stepping past him. "I expected more from a Chapel Hill boy, but I don't guess Thomas Wolfe went down there to play tight end."

Morris headed for the practice tee without looking back. He didn't go far before being stopped by Edgar Spencer IV. *Or was it the fifth?* Morris thought.

"I say, what was that about?" asked Spencer, as tall and thin as the eastern-born, Princeton-educated counterpart to Speed Wallace ought to be. Spencer Sporting Goods had been founded by his great-grandfather in the late nineteenth century. Edgar, president and chairman at the age of thirty-five, was far and away the most severe and the most successful chief executive in the company's history. Not three months went by that *The Wall Street Journal* failed to publish a rumor of some huge corporation making a run at Spencer Sporting Goods. Edgar, whose family controlled seventy-five percent of the stock, refused ever to comment on any alleged offer, fueling the market's perpetual interest in the company.

Morris had a weakness for the Spencer name. The

old grandfather and father before Edgar had been true gentlemen, the father dying unfortunately young in an automobile accident. Young Edgar was a cold piece of work but undeniably talented in a precarious business.

Morris said, "I believe the competition is heating up for the name and goodwill of Buddy Morrow."

"I saw you and Julia Sullivan sitting with him," Spencer said.

Morris nodded.

"He's an elusive young man. Declines any formal business discussion. Someone's giving him volatile advice. Would that be you, Morris?"

Morris shook his head. "I barely know my nouns and verbs. Endorsement contracts are 'not a game of which I am familiar,' if I may pervert a quote by the late Bobby Jones, having first seen Jack Nicklaus strike a golf ball vast distances."

"Were you discussing any aspect of his business future with young Morrow, if I may intrude on your conversation?"

"Hardly," Morris said, offering no hint of the actual conversation, which only provoked the interest of Edgar Spencer IV, in his coat and tie and buttoned-down shirt, despite the June day.

"Morris, you've known the best golfers of the last generation. Do you regard Buddy Morrow as a major talent?"

"I've only seen him practice a few wedge shots," Morris said. "I did catch him on television in Houston. Hard not to like the way he maneuvers the golf ball. Favors the fade, not unlike Hogan, a bit unusual among today's kids, who prefer the raw power of a draw. Sorry I missed him at Greensboro and Houston. We'll see how he adapts to the punitive rough and slick greens of the Open."

"I followed him at Greensboro," Spencer said. "He thrived on the bent-grass greens."

"We'll know in a few years if he is, in fact, the true goods."

"I don't have the luxury of waiting him out," Spencer said. "American golf is of the moment. It has little regard for the timeless and the proven. And the young man has already won the first two American tournaments in which he's competed. Who else has done that, Morris?"

"Good question." Morris could only shake his head. Even Gary Player hadn't won his first two American tournaments.

Spencer, as if giving himself an intellectual pep talk, continued, "The public imagines it can purchase a sound game of golf—which, of course, it cannot, regardless of what all of our advertising might claim for all of our clubs and balls—"

"Don't suppose I can quote you on that?" Morris interrupted, with a wicked smile.

"Indeed, you can. So long as you identify *our* playing equipment as 'classic and timeless and proven.' "

"But it would be much more lucrative, if Buddy Morrow was doing the *proving*," Morris said.

Spencer nodded, yes. "This young man—handsome, well spoken without benefit of a college education, and more than a little mysterious growing up all over the world, the son of a soldier lost on duty in the Arctic—this young man has caught the fancy of the public."

Spencer paused. "I'm prepared to offer him more money than we have ever paid to any golfer to play our line of clubs." He looked up at Morris as if he might be empowered to speak for Buddy Morrow.

"Good luck," Morris said. "He's an appealing young man, aware beyond his years, I think. If you should miss out with him, don't neglect the other, even younger kid in the tournament—the Amateur champion, Tiger Woods. I *have* seen him play. I'm not sure he has an equal in talent among the players in the game, young or old."

Spencer opened his mouth as if to propose something important but bit his bottom lip shut.

Morris feared some unseemly offer for his own influence with Buddy Morrow—which was nonexistent—and was glad that it had not come about.

It felt good to Morris to prop himself up behind the practice tee and watch the boys go about their daily ritual of rehearsal. Not even Old Tom Morris, were he alive, could judge only among the variety of swings and separate the few great players from the merely mortal.

Most of them launched the ball improbable distances, some with the grace and balance of a Steve Elkington or a Payne Stewart, a rare few with a corkscrew motion, giving the appearance of trying to screw themselves into the ground. Young Jim Furyk, who did not make this year's Open field, carved figure eights in the air with his backswing but was an artful man with a putter and a threat for Opens to come.

Only the young Phil Mickelson swung from the left side and with the natural grace of a Bobby Jones. He struggled with a tendency to take his driver—however gracefully—beyond the parallel on his backswing and too often missed fairways—disastrous on Open courses. He commanded every chip, pitch, and flop shot imaginable around the greens and was the last player to win on the PGA tour when he was still an amateur.

The three-time British Open champion and twice Masters champion Nick Faldo took his stance, made his shoulder turn, and delivered the clubhead with a robotic consistency, dominating the wide arc of his rare height with the mechanical preparation of a soldier saluting. He was the greatest tall player who ever played.

Greg Norman, the people's choice with his blond mane and the narrowed eyes of a hawk hunting, delivered artillery shots into the far reaches of the practice grounds with his steep swing—but always with a deadly tendency to slide his hips a mite far in the backswing, threatening the firm brace of his right knee and sending rare fatal shots to the right of the target under great pressure. Not to discount, please, his many tournament victories around the world, including two in the oldest of Opens presided over by the Royal and Ancient Golf Club of Great Britain.

Another few players, such as wee Corey Pavin and Jeff Sluman and Loren Roberts (the ultimate putting machine), did not command huge length with their tee shots but won tournaments with sheer resolution—the dogged consistency of their play. Pavin had proved himself in the Ryder Cup to be one of the most tenacious competitors in the world and was perhaps the best player not to have won a major tournament since Tom Kite won the U.S. Open at Pebble Beach, taking that onus off his own career.

Watching them swing their clubs through the inanimate balls, lifting them into the Long Island air as if they had taken flight of their own volition, was to Morris like smoke to a tobacco addict. The silly thought made him cough to clear his lungs.

"Don't go and die on us, Morris. This ain't but Wednesday. It's Sunday them golfers lay down and die like strangled dogs."

Morris knew without turning his head it was J.C. Stroud pounding him on the back with his gnarled hand. Ol' J.C., the true country boy, not the manufactured version, with his red flyaway hair and big splotches of freckles across his wide sun-blasted face, and with a great brown belt with a huge, gold buckle of a dollar sign holding in his considerable gut, and with his walking boots and his wide smile and big horse teeth. J.C., though a country boy, was the mayor of good times.

"J.C., you're looking fit and ready for the Open. How about your lad, Roy Bream? Is he on his game?" Roy hadn't won on the PGA tour in three years. He hadn't contended in the Open in five. He was pushing forty and looked ten years older. If you counted the days and the nights, Roy Bream, golf's emissary to life-after-dark, would be nudging eighty.

"Don't go askin' me, podner," said J.C. "Roy don't know I'm alive. And I almost ain't." He patted his vast stomach. "I'm fired, Morris. We up and lost the deal with American Express. And Wargo's dropped us—they want their damned clubs back outta his bag, I guess. Roy blamed me. Got him a hotshot kid outta Berkeley, some kinda dopehead, representin' him. Roy dudn't need no new agent. He needs a night's sleep—by his-self—and some birdies and eagles. Me? I need a meal ticket." He put both gnarled hands on his wide stomach to be sure it hadn't vanished.

Morris had seen J.C. eat twelve dozen oysters at one sitting, with a mountain of hush puppies and a key lime pie, not to overlook the considerable pitcher of domestic beer that went down with the oysters.

J.C. grew up on a hardscrabble farm outside Nashville. As soon as he found his way into town, he never went back to the farm. He got started as an agent for a country singer who not only couldn't read music but couldn't read or write anything.

"My kind of client," J.C. had recollected to Morris late one night in Augusta during The Masters. "If that gal coulda quit marrying up with ever' cowpoke she met in the sack, we woulda got richer than John D. Rockefeller. When I met up with her, she was playin' grammar school auditoriums for what she could make passin' a wool hat."

Morris knew that his singer, "Little Nell" Lambert, busted at least twice for controlled substances, had died of the disease that is an occupational hazard of country singers: small plane disease. It took down the great Patsy Cline, and nobody has successfully covered the lyric "Crazy for Lovin' You" since. Jim Croce, that crossover music star, fell straight out of the sky. As did the Van Zandt brothers of Lynyrd Skynyrd, maybe singing their famous "Sweet Home Alabama." Not to forget Little Stephens and his magic guitar picking Stevie Wonder's "Superstition." Or the immortal Buddy Holly, who took country into rock 'n' roll and came down in flames over mournful America.

Little Nell crashed twelve years ago in the Smokey Mountains. J.C. said, "High on whiskey and run outta gas." J.C. swore she was wanging out the Hank Williams favorite, "Long Gone Lonesome Blues," on the airplane radio when they hit the mountain. (Hank, of course, died of an overdose in the back of a Cadillac car, private planes not having come into vogue at the time.)

Morris had written about the colorful J.C. Stroud since he switched to representing athletes rather than entertainers, and oddly enough a great deal of what he swore happened turned out to be true. Morris even talked once with Little Nell's little sister, Vicky Sue, whose own singing career never got off the ground, maybe a blessing since she was still alive. But she was supposed to have been on the plane that night over the Ozarks and fell sick with the flu. She was engaged to the young pilot and never got over his death, or the fact that it was his responsibility the plane's gas tanks be full. She swore he was the most responsible young man she ever met and poured herself another in a long line of drinks, which along with her thin voice did not help her failed music career, despite all the hustle and bustle J.C. could manage.

"Then along come Roy Bream in the Tennessee State Amateur Golf Tournament," J.C. told Morris. "Boy could hit a one-iron two hundred yards through a outhouse knothole. So I took up representin' him, and

then that se'ben-foot basketball player who got hisself
locked up for life for rape. Now ain't it a wonder the
young waitress picked *him* outta the lineup? Them
Nashville *Po*lice had five little turds standin' up with 'im
'bout to his kneecaps. Then I had the quarterback from
Vanderbilt—so damned smart investin' on the market,
he gave up the game."

J.C. could keep you up all night laughing until your
ribs hurt with tales of the string of athletes he had rep-
resented. Morris knew the past tense—"had repre-
sented"—was J.C.'s current problem. The big country
boy had fallen on thin times, and now he'd lost his longtime meal ticket, Roy Bream.

Morris got a kick out of J.C. The persnickety world
of professional golf, as elitist as its reputation, also responded to him. Despite his hardscrabble growing up,
J.C. was the first sports agent to insist that his client,
Roy Bream, be given stock options to buy a nice chunk
of Wargo Golf, Inc., at a favorable price. That he made,
and frittered away, some $5 million was not lost on
other agents for money-loving golf pros.

Of course, J.C. "married off" his share of the stock
deal. It was one of two lethal habits he couldn't kick.
Like Little Nell, he got himself married every twenty-
four months, and it always cost him a bundle to bundle
off the ex-wife.

And J.C. loved to bet. On anything. How many golf
balls would roll into a lateral water hazard on a Thursday was a wise investment to J.C. Only, of course, it
wasn't. If J.C. bet on a horse at Belmont, it was a race as
to whether the horse would die on his hooves or the
jockey would faint and fall off. J.C., in the good times,
made hundreds of thousands of dollars and spent the
better part of millions. Certain brass-knucks bookies
were always giving him "until Friday, old buddy" to
come up with his end of a lost bet. Morris had learned
not to bail him out, much as he enjoyed him.

J.C. said, "Podner, I hear you're tight with the new kid, Buddy Morrow."

"You *hear*?" Morris said, always amazed at the warp speed of golf's grapevine.

"Tha'ss right. Now cut your old buddy in on what he's lookin' for."

"He's *lookin' for* to win the United States Open Golf Championship," Morris said.

"Godamighty, Fort Knox wouldn't hold the gold I could make 'at boy. You know what I mean. He come up tough all over the damned world—his daddy dyin' a hero in the military. He don't need no Harvard College agent."

"Let me guess. He needs—"

"J.C. Stroud, hotamighty, I'd—we'd—be back on top."

"Have you talked to him?"

"One time. Not two minutes. He did know my goddamned name. Maybe, Morris, he—"

"Knew you too well," Morris said, unable not to laugh.

J.C. laughed with him. "Hell, 'cause all the racehorses has gone crazy and I'm broke—temporarily, don't ya know—don't mean I ain't made some stiffs in steel-spiked shoes some millionaires. Just cause a ungrateful sumbitch I made rich twicest over—who took him on when he didn't have a dime for a pay toilet—an' he drops me ain't my fault. I can't go to bed for him at night."

"J.C., if you both had tried going to bed alone, or with the same human being you were married to, you'd still be together and living the good life," Morris said piously.

"Maybe you better take up preachin' on the television," J.C. said. "A man can he'p a lot of things, but he cain't he'p where he wakes up in the mornin' after a wet night out."

"There's no cure for you, J.C.," Morris said, laughing. "Maybe old age is the only antidote for what you've got under that wore-out brown belt."

J.C. said seriously, "Lord, I'll never see sixty. I just don't mean to starve before I die naturally. He'p me with the boy, Morris."

"I had one beer with him," Morris said. "Like you, I was amazed he knew my name. Seems a good kid, wise beyond his years. Just be yourself, J.C. God knows I've never seen you any other way. If he ever asks me, I'll put in an honest word for you. I mean that: *an honest word*," Morris said.

J.C.'s smile was about to break the splotches of freckles in his wide face.

Morris said, "I know you to shake rattle and roll in the marketplace. And the guy who ties up with you had better be ready to look out for his own life. And I don't mean you'd cheat him. I never knew you to cheat anybody, J.C., not even American's soft-hearted bookies."

"Those bastids? They'd take the blanket off the Baby Jesus in his crib. You're a good man, Morris. I can't ask more than that. But if he don't bring my name up—you know how to say it."

"Go away, J.C. I've got to poke around the golf world. You got me talking country as Little Nell Lambert."

"Now them was some good days," said J.C. as he turned his wide body toward tomorrow.

Morris had seen enough of the practice tee. And he'd save the great golf course for tomorrow, when every stroke against it was recorded in The Book of Doom. Now where would a Julia Sullivan go in the fading hours of a Wednesday afternoon? Of course, the northwest corner of Stanford White's clubhouse. Wasn't that where he put the bar?

Amongst all the swells, no Julia Sullivan.

"Hello, Morris."

The flat, understated voice of Jason Everett was unmistakable. It might have come from the Yale Law School. In fact, it did. Everett was not a young man to use the English language at all when a check of seven digits would speak for him. His clients were top-of-the-line athletes. If you weren't certain to be a lottery choice in the NBA draft, you wouldn't hear from Jason. The only Olympic medal he recognized was the gold medal—and only in the sexiest events, beginning with women's gymnastics. He would represent you in *any* round of the NFL draft, so long as it was the *first* round. Only one of his clients was a golfer. Of course, he was the playing captain of the American Ryder Cup team.

"It must be the National Open," Morris said, "the flesh merchants are coming out of the woodwork."

Everett squeezed his thin lips into a narrow line of silence. "Flesh merchant" was not a title he answered to. But he lifted his hand for a limp shake, business before station.

An unspoken shadow lingered over the agency of Jason Everett, the ghostly form of his late partner and Yale classmate, Edward Jemison, who had committed suicide on his twenty-ninth birthday. One week before he shot himself, presumably alone in his old office, Jason had dissolved their partnership—on honorable terms, of course. Or so the courts ruled against Jemison's young widow two years ago.

Morris knew Everett's business dealings to be low key. Deadly, but low key. He hustled no one with sound and fury, least of all his clients.

Of course, he's not above tapping the bottomless knowledge of aging, overweight golf writers, Morris thought, smiling as he said, "Well, Jason. Anything out here in spikes appeal to your instinct for the jugular?"

Everett looked silently up at Morris, not sure if he had been flattered or patronized. He chose flattered. But he did not choose to practice small talk.

"How is it, Morris, that you know the enigmatic young man Buddy Morrow?"

"Good word, *enigmatic*," Morris said. "Your fellow alumnus, Buckley, would be proud to hear you use it. How is it that you *know* that I know him?"

Everett actually smiled, but his gray eyes never flickered. He did not have to say it was his business to know. If he was anything, the small tidy young man in his blue blazer and linen trousers was all business.

"I just met him for the first time over a domestic beer," Morris said. He threw in the adjective *domestic;* it seemed appropriate speaking to a Yale man.

Everett raised one tidy eyebrow. He did not ask Morris how he had managed the meeting, when young Buddy Morrow was carefully avoiding most human contact, including with major league agents bearing checks of seven figures.

Everett said, "He did accept an offer to fly on my plane from Houston to Long Island. When we were airborne, I asked if he preferred the seating arrangement on my Gulfstream jet—or if he would prefer a less formal arrangement on his own jet."

Morris waited.

"He said that he'd 'prefer a little less tonic and a little more gin.' " Everett actually laughed for one abrupt note.

"A few hours in the air alone with golf's new crown prince couldn't be a bad sign for an agent," Morris said, offering nothing else.

"He didn't mention the flight?"

Morris ignored the question, more out of mischief than to protect the sanctity of his conversation with Buddy Morrow.

"So you believe him to be the nearest thing we have to a young Nicklaus?" Morris said.

"I would have expected you to say 'to a young Hogan,' " Everett said.

Morris nodded. "So you've seen him play?"

"Twice."

"From Greensboro to Houston to Long Island—you must have the true fever," Morris said.

Everett did not deny it. "What do you think of him?"

"Can't remember another young man winning his first *two* American tournaments. Crenshaw won in San Antonio, his first time out as a pro. Of course, Mickelson won as an amateur, the first time on the PGA tour since Doug Sanders won the Canadian Open a generation ago. I've only seen Buddy Morrow play on television. You get no sense of the clubhead speed, or of the true flight of the ball, on the small screen. But I was impressed with his balance, his ability to visualize a shot. Who wouldn't be? And watching him practice a few wedge shots, you can see his swing is of a piece. Does that all spell greatness?"

Morris paused to order a scotch and water. The bartender might have been working the Oak Room of the Plaza Hotel, he was that quick and effortless. Morris lifted his glass, offering only a smile and his own silence. Then he said, "Only time and results can prove greatness. Many an early bloomer has faded with the season. But you know that. And you are one agent who can afford to wait." Morris teased him with the last.

Everett rose to the bait. "I didn't get where I am by perfecting the waiting game," he said. "I only represent the one golfer. Golf is such an elusive game. With few exceptions it takes so many years for a golfer to establish himself. And his game can leave him in an instant. You *know* a seven-foot man who can run and jump and throw a basketball *down* into a goal is a prospect. Or a wide receiver who can run forty yards in four point three seconds—and catch the ball thrown lethally over the middle. But a golfer standing over a putt is a precarious bet."

"But suddenly you are willing to put up the money," Morris said.

"Oh, yes."

"Well, you're standing in a long line," Morris said, enjoying the slightest flicker of annoyance in Jason Everett's gray eyes.

"If you were me, would you sign him, Morris?"

Morris did not say, *"If I were you, in your occupation, I'd hang myself."* He did say, "What do you have to lose? You'll be putting up some manufacturer's money. Of course, if Buddy Morrow fails to make the cut here, he'll be yesterday's news."

"And I don't live in the past," Everett said.

"Well, it's good to be at Shinnecock Hills and alive," Morris said, meaning nothing more than that.

Everett set down his drink as if he'd been slapped in the face. "What do you mean by that?" The little man was trembling with anger.

Morris smiled before he could stop himself. Then he realized Everett thought he was making some reference to his dead partner. Well . . . why not? "I meant just what I said. Sorry if you took it as some reference to Ed Jemison. But since you apparently did—why on earth did the young man kill himself?"

Everett swelled up as if he might explode.

Morris waited as if it would be his job to gather up the separate pieces.

"I've never spoken of it," Everett finally said, wincing as if he were in physical pain. "I found him, you know," he said, as if it were a long-coming confession.

"I didn't know."

"I never expect to see a more terrible sight."

Morris nodded.

"We'd dissolved the partnership. *I* had dissolved it, to be correct. I'd prefer not to be quoted on the subject, Morris."

Morris neither spoke nor nodded.

But Jason continued. "We'd been so successful, so soon. Ed couldn't handle it. He fell into some fatal habits, with a couple of our athletes. A terrible indiscretion. We couldn't survive that way. I warned him, over and over. Offered to get him, and the athletes, the best help possible. He denied he had a problem. I finally split us up. The athletes all chose to stick with me, even the two in trouble with drugs. And he couldn't handle that either."

Everett's voice shook with emotion. His thin face showed nothing.

"His widow sued for half the business, and you won the lawsuit, I understand," Morris said.

He only nodded, yes. "I made her a significant settlement. I didn't have to. I have no reason to feel guilty for what I had to do."

Morris kept his silence.

Finally Everett said, "Yes. It bothers me. Sometimes. Maybe I could have persuaded him in some other way. But I did my best." He raised his glass and finished his drink. His guilt disappeared with the scotch.

Morris knew he wouldn't be happy to remember this conversation. "I hope you and Buddy Morrow come to the most advantageous decision for you both." Morris gave no hint as to what he thought that might be.

Everett set his empty glass on the bar and was gone with only a nod.

Morris stepped out onto the east balcony to discover if Ms. Sullivan could be seen worshiping golf's younger generation. No Sullivan.

"Goddamn, Morris." A frog-croak of a voice came from below and behind him. He didn't have to turn to know it belonged to Joe Deitz, *the* nasty sports voice of the semiraunchy *New York Daily Mail*, a tabloid that screamed cheap ads and had a news hole the size of a keyhole.

Joe looked up like he was standing in a stump hole.

Chewing on an ugly unlit cigar. He hadn't changed his mug shot in twenty years above the shower of cheap digs that made up his column. Meanwhile he'd lost most of his hair, his face had exploded with freebie alcohol, and he'd taken aboard fifty pounds, which seemed to lower his five feet three inches nearer to the dirt that he loved to spill in his column.

Joe stood, his abbreviated self, blinking his dark eyes behind his prescription sunglasses, chewing his ruined cigar, looking for all the world like "Good old reliable Nathan Detroit," an image he worked and drank, twenty-four hours each day and night, to project.

Morris had read his opening nasty gambit for the tournament: "*Greg Norman is a golfer. He's got a problem. Tournaments. Naw, not the little harmless ones down in Florida against the* boys *amongst the scrub pines. Hell, no. I mean the* major *tournaments where the real* men *play. This Norman wears white golf shirts in the majors, so anytime it gets tough, he can run up the white flag of surrender.*"

"I read your column this morning, Joe," Morris said. "Norman did, too. Said he was inviting you to go shark fishing with him off the Great Barrier Reef."

"Yeah. That boy could shank a shark. Shit, Morris, when he folds on Sunday, I can use that line." Joe had a laugh nastier than his column.

"Did anybody ever seriously come after you, Joe?"

"You bet. We had a perforated catcher from the Virgin Islands—wounded by his girlfriend's husband—who came after me with a forty-five. Not to worry. The son of a bitch couldn't hit his IQ. Did shoot out the windows of two cars twenty yards behind me." He laughed his nasty laugh. "Which one of these country club dandies are you pickin' to be left standing with his mouth open when the other white-bread boys fold?"

"I'm picking Shinnecock Hills," Morris said. "A tough track. If the wind blows, nobody may survive."

"Yeah, this crowd of dandies would like to play the

goddamn tournament *inside*. No wind, no rain, no sun, no rabbits in the goddamn bushes. I'd like to see their pampered asses at bat in Yankee Stadium with us fifty thousand drunks screaming"—Joe loved the idea of himself as a drunk screaming, and for once he had it right—"and Roger Clemens throwin' one at their god-damned heads at ninety-nine miles an hour." He nearly swallowed his stub of an unlit cigar laughing at the imagined sight.

Of course, Joe ripped the baseball players in their turn, the way he ripped the Jets and the Giants and the Rangers and the Knicks, and any manager or coach un-lucky enough to lose a game of any kind with Joe Deitz in the press box.

Just the way he would rip Godalmighty, I guess, if he came back down to earth, thought Morris, who liked the little bastard anyway. At least he put his name and his twenty-year-old mug shot over what he wrote.

Deitz said, "This Buddy Morrow some kind of fake public relations bullshit." Deitz always *said*. He never *asked* anything.

"He finished first at Greensboro and Houston," Morris said. "Don't think he could fake that. He's your kind of guy, Joe. Grew up tough all over the world, son of a military guy. No country club dude. Taught himself out of a Hogan book. Doesn't run around with some golfing guru telling him how to hold his fork at break-fast. What's not to like?"

"I don't know. I ain't believin' it till I see it," Joe said.

"You're not actually going to step out of the press tent onto the green grass?" Morris said, with feigned amazement.

"No goddamn way. I'll take him—intravenously—by tube in the press tent."

You'd never expect Joe to know a word like intravenously, thought Morris, then said, "If he came in a bottle, you'd believe him."

"Damned right. Put a Jack Daniel's Black Label on the bastard, and I'd give him the goddamned U.S. Open. Come on, Morris, let's go to the hospitality tent. Have a drink on the goddamned USGA."

"Naw"—now Morris was sounding like Joe Deitz— "I'm lookin' for Sullivan."

"Yeah, some dame, that. Better than you deserve." Deitz never once wrote as true a sentence. He stepped off the veranda, sinking ever lower to the ground, his cigar bouncing around in his mouth like a cork in a nasty sea.

Two slim hands reached down from the top step of the balcony and closed around the unsuspecting eyes of John Morris, followed by a damp kiss on the neck.

"Oh, no," Morris said, "that sort of thing is not allowed at Shinnecock Hills."

"Would they allow it if I were chewing on a cigar?"

"A proper cigar."

Julia Sullivan rested her chin on his stout shoulder. It felt good to look down on the world. No wonder John Morris, way up here, never suffered from an absence of confidence. "I've had enough golf. What do you think about a shower, a drink, a grilled fish, and—whatever comes to mind?"

"I think . . . one of each," Morris said, squinting at Peconic Bay shining in the distance like a promise of good things to come.

CHAPTER FIVE

A shower, a drink, and "whatever comes to mind" came before dinner.

"You golf writers are an impetuous lot," Sullivan said, looking for her lost towel.

"You have to take your shots when you can. Never know when you'll miss the cut," Morris said, parting the curtains, looking down on the Atlantic Ocean as it washed on Long Island in the fading sunlight.

"Oh, I think you'll always be playing on the weekend, John Morris. So long as you're playing at all," she said, snickering and ducking into the huge modern bathroom of the beach house she had rented in tony Wickapogue. Lord help her if Morris ever found out how much she was paying.

The "beach house," which could sleep fifteen and feed that many at a sit-down dinner, came equipped with its own twelve-foot California privet hedge. Most of the oceanside mansions in Southampton hid behind enormous hedges, trimmed as severely as military hair-cuts. Driving between them was like disappearing into long green soulless tunnels. The great maze at Hampton Court in England was toy-size compared with these clipped green monstrosities. Morris had been startled the first time he'd seen them.

"Why pay an architect a half-million dollars to design your twenty-room mansion, and then hide it with a bloody half-mile-long hedge?" Now he didn't think it. He said it aloud.

"Do you think it's a hedge against poverty?" Sullivan said, sticking her head through the bathroom door, laughing too heartily at her own pun.

"Damn you, that ought to be my line," Morris said.

"Don't worry, you'll steal it. Just like you steal all your good stuff from me—the way Scott Fitzgerald stole all his best stuff from Zelda."

Morris threw a bed cushion as she ducked back inside the bathroom, sans towel.

"What are you laughing at?" Morris called after her.

"You, Morris."

"I didn't say anything funny."

"No, but you will."

She was too late turning the lock on the bathroom door. But then, who was in a hurry?

Sullivan pushed the Ford through the Southampton traffic, heavy with automobiles as expensive as modest houses, then took Sag Road through the island farmland to Sag Harbor. It pleased them both that serious farmers still plowed the land on the exclusive eastern tip of Long Island to plant their corn and potato fields. It was also somehow reassuring that a clutch of lifetime fishermen out of Amagansett and other villages on the South Fork still risked the sea, as fishermen had risked it from the beginning of time—and with faint appreciation. Peter Matthiessen's great book *Men's Lives* came to mind, with its timeless, beautiful, and cruel black and white images of the fisherman's lot on the South Fork of Long Island, in the old days and into the 1980s.

Ironic, and possibly sinful—if man's fate could be held against him—that golfers, safely in designer shirts and caps and sweaters if the wind blew even moderately, could chase a small ball across the tailored landscape of Long Island in pursuit of world fame and millions of dollars, when a "haul-seining" crew, unknown by a world careless of its true heroes but redeemed by Mat-thiessen, shipped 309 pounds of bluefish—hauled aboard in freezing December waters—and "after payin' the shippin'" were left with "eleven dollars and fifty cents." And a friend of Matthiessen's that very week had "ordered bluefish, paying precisely eleven-fifty for less than a half pound, or more than *seven hundred times* as much as the men who caught it were receiving."

To be fair to the golfers, Morris thought to himself, *a man might risk his entire youth trying and not tee it up once in the U.S. Open. And if he failed to make the cut in a professional golf tournament, he collected nothing—not even eleven dollars and fifty cents. But there's no record of a professional golfer being lost on the links forever, as four Long Island fishermen were lost to the depths in Matthiessen's time. Though I can think of a few sour, monosyllabic golfers I might be willing to surrender to the sea, given the chance.* He couldn't help smiling at the thought.

"One thing I love about you, John Morris, is what a magnificent conversationalist you would be, if you took the opportunity to say a word to a lonely driver." Sullivan looked directly ahead, both hands on the wheel, as if drafted into involuntary servitude to drive them across the landscape of America forever, without a word of thanks or encouragement.

"Oh, my," Morris said. And repeated exactly what he had been thinking.

Now tears were in Sullivan's eyes. "You don't have to

overdo it, Morris," she said, wiping her cheek with a bare finger.

Finding a parking place in Sag Harbor was as easy as catching a taxicab on Manhattan Island at seven o'clock on a rainy Saturday night in the Christmas season.

They started with a scotch on the rocks in the rich wooden bar of the American Hotel. Good thing Morris had made their dinner reservations two months ago and that a publishing friend in East Hampton was buddies with the manager, who agreed to save them a table so far in advance.

Morris checked his watch. Their dinner partners were late. But here they came, winding their way among the customers. Couldn't ask for tablemates more entertaining than NBC announcer Jesse Newnan and *Golf Illustrated* editor Peter Bentley. Newnan, who still kept his boyish California-blond looks, had once lost the U.S. Open in a playoff but salvaged his share of immortality by winning The Masters twice, ten years apart.

"I did a Tom Dooley in the Open," Newnan was wont to say, "only I choked to death with both feet on the ground." He always added, "Tell you what, my friend, if you've never choked, you've never played."

Bentley, short and stout and, Sullivan said, "lovable," himself loved golf as an innocent man might love a heartless mistress, but he couldn't break 90 with a crowbar, which only endeared him to his subscribers.

"Here they are," Sullivan said, standing up to hug them simultaneously, Newnan towering over her head and Bentley tucked under her chin.

"Morris, you can leave now," said Bentley, "we'll look after this child."

"Careful, Bentley, you'll overstock your pasture," Morris said, shaking the hands of the two of them.

"Three beautiful guys—and *me*. That's the way God planned the world to *be*," Sullivan rhymed.

"Oh, yes. Just remember which guy belongs to the *me*," Morris said.

The newcomers had barely lowered their glasses after a toast to the Open, when Jesse Newnan said, "Morris, I followed the youngster, Morrow, yesterday on a practice round. The last time I walked a practice round, I was a boy fifteen, following Hogan himself. It was eerie, I tell you. If this kid wore a white cap, you would swear Hogan had been cloned. You know how Hogan worked the fade, the ball traveling on a low arc, but never quite as low as it seemed, and stopping on slick greens as if by an act of God. I had to shut my eyes and open them again the first time I saw Morrow swing through a golf ball. And I stood close enough to check out his clubs."

"I know. A mixed bag," said Morris, remembering Tom Rowe's upcoming piece in *The Times* of London.

"Oh, hell yes. Clubs from all over the place. Some of the irons I haven't seen on the tour in twenty years. Of course, a couple of them Hogans, the five-iron and the two-iron. The son of a bitch swings a one-iron with the ease of a wedge." Newnan paused with his glass in mid-air. "Of course, I never saw Hogan putt as a young player. I know he didn't win four Opens with the yips that bothered him as an older man. But this kid Morrow can work the blade. And he uses an old blade putter, Morris, like something out of the nineteen thirties. I couldn't tell the make. But mercy, don't you know the original manufacturer would love to reintroduce it."

"If this kid wins the Open," Bentley said, "he'll be the hottest thing since the steel shaft. We'll have to put out a special issue of the magazine. You ready for that, Morris?"

"Off the record?" Morris said to Peter.

"Sure."

"Morrow promised me an extensive interview about his life."

"Godamighty," Bentley said, an eager sweat breaking out under the stout little man's eyes over the editorial possibility of such a story.

"You can't look at a golfer's swing and know what's in his soul," Jesse said. "But this kid has won twice on the tour. Against the best out there. He has it in him to win *everything*. Watching him makes the hair stand up on the back of my neck."

"It's remarkable the way the game reinvents itself every generation," Bentley said. "Old Tom Morris and then his son came along, greater than the old man. Not to forget Willie Park, winning the first British Open in 1860 and then winning it twice again, *twenty-seven* and *twenty-nine* years later. How long do you suppose it's been since anybody on Long Island said the name aloud: *Willie Park*?"

"Oh, the game is apostolic," Morris agreed, raising his glass to theirs.

Bentley might have been reciting for his sixth-grade homeroom teacher: "Vardon and Braid and Taylor. And the great Americans came to the game, Willie Anderson and Quimet, and Hagen and Sarazen and Jones, God bless him, and Nelson and Snead and Hogan, and Palmer and Nicklaus and then Watson—always a man, or men, to take the game to another level of greatness."

"Let's not forget all of the two-time Masters champions sitting at this table," Sullivan said, raising her glass to Jesse Newnan, who had the grace to blush.

Jesse said seriously, "I knew a few afternoons when I held true greatness in my hands." He looked at his open hands as if they had once taken another form. "It was astonishing. It was as if they were capable of anything. I knew for a few hours what Vardon and Hagen and Jones and Hogan and Snead and Palmer and Nicklaus held in their hands all of their competitive lives." He closed his hands and opened them again. "And when it left me, it was gone forever."

Jesse drank from his glass and set it on the table. "To tell you the God's truth, I was happier. Magical power is a frightful thing to hold on to. I can't imagine holding it in my grasp year after terrifying year."

"Jesus," Bentley said. "You just wrote your next editorial for my magazine."

"You're off the hook, Sullivan. Now I know what working editor gets the check," Morris said as he stood, leading the way from the bar to the restaurant to the grilled swordfish, which proved as magical in the hands of the chef as a wedge in the hands of Hogan.

Thursday, June 15
8:00 A.M.

The Scots say, "Nae wind, nae golf." Not to worry. A devilish breeze off the Atlantic Ocean blew across Shinnecock Hills on Thursday morning, rippling the tall grasses in the rolling rough like wheat in a field, only with a more malevolent consequence.

"Could you imagine being anywhere else in the world?" Morris asked Sullivan, as they looked down off the veranda on the first-day spectacle of the 1995 U.S. Open.

"Maybe in Paradise—if it plays to a par 72," Sullivan said.

The young phenom, Buddy Morrow, would not tee off until later in the day.

"We might as well follow along after the number-one player in the world, Nick Price," said Morris.

"And a sweet guy," Sullivan said.

"You concentrate on his golf swing, love."

"Of course I will," she lied.

Nick Price's attraction was compounded by that of his playing partners: defending Open champion Ernie

Els of South Africa, and U.S. Amateur champion Tiger Woods, famous Stanford University freshman.

The 1st hole of 394 yards fell sharply away below the 1st tee with its grand view of the western half of the course, which needed only the Firth of Tay and the North Sea to be Scotland.

Els, a tall powerful young man, chose a driver for his tee shot, defying the narrow fairway and the treacherous fescue in the rough. His easy, almost lazy backswing recalled the age of Bobby Jones, and with perfect balance he completed the great arc of his swing, sending the ball into the air for such a distance as to draw the audible breath from the appreciative crowd around the 1st tee. The driven ball found the narrow fairway a mere wedge from the first green.

Price chose a more prudent three-wood and, with his quick "one-two" swing, lashed a shot into the heart of the fairway—but understandably quite a distance behind Els's huge tee shot.

The slim, six-foot-two, 155-pound Tiger Woods, smiling under his U.S. Open baseball cap, disappointed the fans, alert to his reputed power, by choosing a one-iron for his opening drive. His supple body turned its back entirely to the ball, his hands reached as high as those of the young Nicklaus and unleashed the clubhead with such speed it tore the very air, sending the ball nearly out of sight until it came to rest *within ten yards* of the ball struck by the powerful Els *with a driver*.

The crowd exhaled aloud, Morris and Sullivan with them.

"*There* is the future," Morris said, "if not the present."

"Don't forget our boy Buddy Morrow," Sullivan reminded him.

"No. But the man hasn't been born of woman who can equal that one-iron," Morris said. Then he amended, "Well, perhaps John Daly. But who could say what island it might come down on?"

They were off, Morris poling with his cane and swinging his stiff left leg, and Sullivan smiling and jostling cheerfully through the eager New York crowd.

Els struggled in defense of his championship, his shoes often out of sight in the tall grass as he stood in the rough after a wayward tee shot.

Woods could not dominate the suddenness of the greens—his putts raced hopelessly past the holes. He was so disgusted with his three-putts on the 2nd, 3rd, and 4th holes that after the round he spoke of them as if they had occurred separate from himself. "It wasn't my fault," he told the amused press, referring to his 74. "I didn't make bogeys due to bad ball striking. I just couldn't make my putts."

Morris leaned over to Tom Rowe and said, "Don't worry about the awful story you're writing. It's not you, old man—it's the word processor that's doing it."

"Except for whoever it was putting for ol' Sam Snead on Sundays, he would have won eight U.S. Opens—instead of none," Rowe whispered back.

But they both liked this irrepressible young kid, Tiger Woods. The next day Tiger would take a mighty slash at his ball in the deep rough on the 2nd hole, sprain his left wrist, and be forced to withdraw from the tournament, to the regret of the thousands mesmerized by the unequaled power of his swing.

Price, having recovered from recent burnout and won sixteen tournaments and $7 million since 1992, played carefully within himself this first round. He ignored the flags on the front side, keeping his ball safely on the green and twenty feet below the hole.

On the tee to the 5th hole, which played 535 yards to a relatively benign par of 5, Price boldly chose to hit his driver—only to see Tiger Woods crush his ball three hundred yards, a full forty past his own best drive. Price played a three-wood to the green. Tiger got there with a three-*iron*.

"The guy [Woods] *is* unbelievable," Price told the press, who were as thirsty for his opinion of his young playing partner as they were for their first drink of the young evening. "I can't see where he gets all his power from. But the ball just takes off his club like a rocket. He kept going forty to fifty yards past me. Ernie and I felt sort of powerless out there with this kid."

But golf has never been a singular game of "how far," only of "how many." Nick's three-wood second shot on No. 5 found a green-side bunker. His explosion shot skidded over the green and down an embankment. He coolly chipped the ball thirty feet into the hole for a birdie 4 and went on to turn the front nine in 33 strokes.

Morris and Sullivan followed the threesome to the 10th tee. Tiger Woods again struck his one-iron, which caught the downslope of a hill and came to rest *310 yards* from the tee, *seventy-five yards* past the balls of Price and Els. Morris was sure they had stood witness to an act of golf that would one day change the face of the game.

Morris and Sullivan left the three to their separate fates, catching them later in the press tent. Price described birdieing three of the last five holes to shoot 66, one shot off the course record and good for the first-day lead over former Open champion Scott Simpson, who scored 67, and Phil Mickelson and Greg Norman, who scored 68. Jeff Maggert, Fuzzy Zoeller, Bill Glasson, young Steve Lowery, Bob Tway, and Jumbo Ozaki each scored 69. These were the only players to break par 70 over the deadly beauty of Shinnecock Hills.

Ernie Els suffered through a 75 and faced the possibility of missing the cut as defending champion.

Working back toward the front nine, Morris and Sullivan stopped to see Greg Norman drain a five-foot putt for par on the treacherous 12th hole on the way to a 68, the best first round in all the U.S. Opens he had played.

"Perhaps this will be his year," Morris said.

"I don't know. He's so beautiful. I think the gods are jealous," Sullivan said. And maybe she was right.

Another young lion, Mickelson, who would be twenty-five the following day, was scorching the course, 5 under after fourteen holes. But on the par-5 15th, of 544 yards, he left his drive so deep in the grass that a sand wedge could barely lift it back into the fairway. His third shot was short of the green, his chip was a rare catastrophe, and he three-putted for an unholy 7.

Afterward, Mickelson said philosophically and accurately, "It's not going to be my last double-bogey on this course." But his 68 had the left-hander where he wanted to be—high on the leader board.

Sullivan led the way back to the 1st green. As was her habit, she shanghaied Morris's binoculars from around his neck and focused them on Buddy Morrow, high above them, addressing his first tee shot in the U.S. Open.

She followed the ball bending in the air to the heart of the fairway.

"Bold stuff, risking a driver," Morris said, seeing the ball come to rest within 120 yards of the green.

Morrow was playing with an older Englishman, well past his prime, and a young American amateur, obviously over his head in the pressure of the event. The two bogeyed the 1st hole and never got it together, neither managing to break 80.

Morris admired the soft lash of Morrow's wedge, and the low Hogan-like parabola of the ball, which bounced twice on the green and stopped in its dimples three feet from the hole.

Morrow, despite Sullivan's alarm at his exposure to the sun, wore no hat, and his dark thick hair swirled about his forehead to the four directions. His lean, powerful torso was captured in a simple white shirt, and his long legs in plain khaki trousers. Even his brown bag, absent of all advertising, rode anonymously on the back of the skinny teenager carrying it. They made a quiet daguerreotype from the 1920s; you expected to see Walter Hagen or Bobby Jones mark his ball on the green.

"Oh, my," Sullivan said.

"No hyperventilating, the boy has to putt," Morris said.

Morrow proved a wrist putter in the rare tradition of Casper and Palmer and the unmatchable Bobby Locke of South Africa. Morrow had obviously honed his putting on the Bermuda grass greens of Africa and Asia with their rivers of grain, provoking a solid *rap*, if the putt was to stay on line. Only young brave nerves could dominate the wrists in the putting stroke when the pressures became unbearable. Most all of the professionals on the American tour relied on the large, less-sensitive muscles of the arms and shoulders to drag their putters through the ball.

Buddy rapped his ball in the first hole as if it had been wound into being for only that purpose. He was off with a birdie 3.

The 2nd hole of 226 yards was the most dangerous par 3 on the course, playing to a raised green surrounded by six sand bunkers. Morrow drew the two-iron from his bag and, with a brief waggle and no practice swing, caught the ball dead in the face of the club, sending it carefully twenty feet left of the pin, avoiding the deep grass and deeper bunkers on the right of the green.

"Our boy has a plan beyond his years," Morris said.

Sullivan wormed her way tight against the ropes at the 3rd tee. The green on the par-4 hole rose up 453 yards in the distance.

Morrow's drive leaked just off the fairway into the deep second-cut of the rough.

"Poor baby," Sullivan said into the silence.

Morrow turned and smiled and actually gave her a thumbs-up.

Sullivan returned a balled fist of encouragement, to the smiling delight of a rather tall athletic woman pressed against her, her strong face burned and somewhat worn by the sun but her hazel eyes matching her sudden laughter.

"Isn't he beautiful?" Sullivan said.

"He'll do in a pinch," the tall woman replied, her voice sounding of Texas or the Southwest.

"But he needs to wear a hat in this sun," Sullivan whispered, as the older Englishman hooked his tee shot over the trees and out of bounds.

"Doesn't look like a man who would listen," the woman replied, her own short reddish-brown hair her only protection against the bright sunshine.

"He doesn't sound like one either."

"You've met him?" The woman seemed impressed.

"For a beer. Yesterday. John Morris and I." Sullivan turned and pointed to Morris, who lifted one finger to his lips—"Shhhh . . ."—as the Englishman, now quite unnerved, pushed his 2nd tee shot deep into the right rough.

"Is he terribly conceited?" the woman asked Sullivan, as they followed Morrow and his threesome down the fairway.

"Not a bit. He grew up a military brat. Quite lonesome, I bet, as a little boy, without a mother. Taught himself to play golf, when he was *ten*, out of Hogan's book. He's well spoken."

"Not the golf bum you'd imagine?" the woman said, raising a sun-bleached eyebrow. Her hazel eyes were truly beautiful, and she walked with a long, purposeful stride.

"No. But he does know the value of being a mystery man. I mean, look at the two of us. Following him, instead of the proven great players of the world. You'd like him, I promise."

"I believe it," the woman said, touching Sullivan's arm as if they were old friends.

"My name is Sullivan. Julia Sullivan."

The woman's hand and grip were as strong and athletic as her stride. "I'm Jerry Martin."

"Are you from Texas?"

"I used to be. Does it show?"

"I'm from Colorado. But I also love Texas."

"My binoculars," Morris said, behind her.

"My master's voice," Sullivan said, turning reluctantly to hand over Morris's binoculars.

"Do meet Jerry Martin," she said.

"Yes, indeed." Morris tipped his wide straw hat, not missing her athletic form, her friendly smile.

"She's from Texas," Sullivan said. "We were just worshiping young Mr. Morrow."

"You could do worse," Morris said.

Jerry Martin nodded her agreement, easing away into the restless crowd, still smiling to herself.

Morrow obviously had drawn a better lie in the deep rough than he could have expected. He chose what appeared to be a four-iron and with a steep descending blow sent the ball burning up the fairway on a low trajectory. Morris knew that the raised No. 3 green was not fronted by a sand bunker. Morrow's ball ran along the fairway and up the slope into the middle of the green, setting up two-putts for a par of 4 on the fifth-toughest hole on the course.

On the 4th hole Morrow did not challenge the cup cut perilously close to the front bunker, accepting par 4 as a sensible result. Morris, looking through the trees, could see the No. 10 hole of the National Golf Links designed by Charles B. MacDonald himself in 1911.

Morris wondered if, like Hogan, Morrow carried an extra twenty-five yards in his bag, which could be brought out on reachable par-5 holes. He was not disappointed.

Morrow, with the same absolute balance and controlled swing, made an even greater shoulder turn, resulting in a fiery drive that split the trees on the right and the knee-high fescue on the left, fading into the fairway at least 280 yards from the tee. Not Tiger Woods length, but making the green reachable in two perfect shots. His three-wood carried all the way onto the second tier of the green, leaving him a slick fifteen-foot putt for eagle.

Again, a bare flick of the wrist, and the putt dived in the hole, putting him 3 under par for the day.

But this is Thursday, thought Morris. *Many are the first-round leaders of the Open who vanish into anonymity. Come Sunday, all the oxygen will have gone out of the air over Long Island. And good men's hopes will die of asphyxiation.*

Now came the second most difficult hole on the course: 471 yards downhill and across the only water hazard at Shinnecock Hills—ironic, as it lay between two great saltwater bays.

Again, Morrow's tee shot faded less than a yard too far into the right-hand rough.

Morris and Sullivan, positioned down the fairway, saw the ball disappear as if it had escaped civilization.

Morrow winced at the lie. The pain might have been physical. Should he wedge the ball into the fairway and risk a wayward long iron and a possible double-bogey 6? Or should he try and gouge the ball out of the deep rough over the seductively near pond, leaving an easy wedge to the green? He took bare seconds to pull out his wedge and hack the ball back into the fairway.

And now he stood over a three-iron, the tension of

final-round Sunday afternoon already in his face, and drifted the ball over the bunker into the dead center of the green, accepting bogey 5 as a fair penalty for his near-miss with his drive.

At the abbreviated par-3 7th hole, Morris felt he was surely in Scotland, standing on the historic 15th at North Berwick, as designer William Flynn intended he should feel, having duplicated the hole. The narrow elevated green 183 yards away might have been a watercolor swatch in a sea of sand.

Morrow eschewed the right-to-left midiron that the hole called for and risked his low fade over the deep left-hand bunkers, safely into the middle of the green. He took his par 3 with a bow to the fans, heavily peopled by giggling girls and smiling young women. Sullivan smiled and giggled, not to avoid either lustful camp.

Buddy ignored the continuous catastrophes of his playing partners to strike an iron off the tee at the short 8th hole and just miss a ten-foot putt for birdie, his hands dropping his putter and burying themselves in his dark hair as every young thing around the green ached to do.

The 9th was the one hole on the course that Nick Price had declared to be of poor design. Morris thought, *It should have suited Nick's draw to a "tee."* In fact, it was the toughest tee shot on the course, bending sharply to the left, with a fairway that undulated as if to a Latin beat, presenting an almost certain unlevel lie for the second shot. The green itself rose some thirty-five feet above the fairway, swirling fearfully below the clubhouse veranda. An exhausted player might want to take the five steps up to the bar and drown his bogeys in good scotch whiskey.

Morrow abandoned his fade and put a resolute draw on his tee shot, which turned the corner as if it had changed identities. The ball came to rest eighteen inches above his feet. Morrow choked up on a midiron and lifted the ball high onto the elevated green.

John Morris had seen enough for one day. The kid might not be the Second Coming of Hogan, but he was the real deal. Morris figured his aching left knee could just make it up the incline to the clubhouse where they might watch young Mr. Morrow address his twenty-five-foot putt from the bar.

"Don't you know you're trampling on the code, leaving the press tent for the—do I dare say it aloud—bloody actual golf course?" Speaking was Tom Rowe, waiting on the veranda just outside the bar, holding two grand scotch and waters to a twosome dying of sobriety.

"God save the Queen," said Sullivan, tilting her glass against first Rowe's and then Morris's.

"Down with the Declaration of Independence," Morris added. "We'll concede the colonies back to Mother England."

"I saw you coming up the incline, old chaps. Now tell me everything. Do you believe the lad can play the game?"

At that moment Buddy Morrow drained the putt for a birdie 3 to turn the western nine in 33 strokes, hot on the pace of leader Nick Price.

"Oh, he can play the game," Morris said, "on *Thursday*. We'll have to see if he can breathe in oxygen and breathe out carbon dioxide come Sunday. And there is still the back nine to be covered today."

"I've got a bill or two in my handbag, boys, that says he can cover it under par," Sullivan said.

"*Oh, no,*" the two of them said together.

"England yet suffers a balance of payments from your last winnings at St. Andrews," Rowe said.

"Let's do this again"—Morris held up his empty

glass—"and then join the ink-stained wretches in the press tent."

"Done," said Rowe.

Buddy Morrow, sitting with his long right leg crossed over his left knee, sipping on a bottle of mineral water, was more at home in front of the press than the royal family of England had ever been. *And more talented,* thought Morris.

"Yes, I hit a terrible nine-iron to the 16th green—into the front-left bunker, actually," Morrow said. "If he were still alive, I could hear Henry Longhurst saying, 'Dreadful shot, that.'"

The laughter was remarkable from a tentful of cynics.

"This lad's presence will dominate the game," Rowe whispered to Morris, who was pleasantly surprised the kid would have seen or remembered the great Henry Longhurst as a television commentator.

"He's got my vote," said Sullivan, an illicit crasher of the press tent. "And you guys are buying dinner. You saved big bucks not betting against him on the back nine."

Morrow had birdied the treacherous 18th hole with a killer putt of fifty feet to turn the back nine holes in 34, tying Scott Simpson at 67, one stroke behind first-day leader Nick Price.

"No I don't have an advertisement"—Morrow used the English pronounciation of the word—"on my bag. Perhaps your newspaper would like to buy the space?"

More laughter.

"Let me say it's a wonderful golf course." Morrow set his other foot on the floor, as if the course deserved all dignity and respect. "It's wonderful that it's lain here so many years, so well cared for. It will take every amount of courage a man can summon to hold out against its intelligence, its unrelenting variety and diffi-

culty, and win the Open. I can only hope I'm up to it."
He stood as if standing gave him greater strength of
character.

The silence was as near applause as Morris had ever
heard in the press tent.

"Who the fuck *are* you?" came the unmistakable
voice of the outrageous Joe Deitz.

An awkward silence.

Then Buddy Morrow bent over laughing, and the
entire tent fell into laughter.

"It's wonderful to be back in polite America," Morrow said.

Another quantity of laughter.

"Me? I'm a Texas boy. An army brat. A kinda home-
made golfer. Apologies to Mr. Hogan. A guy who's
beaten balls on five of the seven continents. Here I
stand one shot off the Open lead. And maybe I'll be as
forgotten as the Yank Lee Mackey, who shot a 64 in the
Open once and disappeared forever. Maybe that's even
a better life, the anonymous life. I knew it, for a long
time." Morrow paused, deepening the silence in the
tent. "But I mean to hang as tough as an old top sergeant. And let the blood flow where it will, including
my own. Thank you." He ducked his head and raised
his bottle of mineral water.

Sullivan blew him a kiss. He didn't miss it either. He
gave her his now-familiar thumbs-up.

Morris wondered how on earth James "Buddy" Morrow had ever heard of Birmingham, Alabama's, Lee
Mackey. Not since Ben Crenshaw had so young a man
been so devout a student of the game's past. The kid's
appeal, ironically, suddenly, brought out the reluctant
cynic in John Morris, aging journalist, who'd learned
always to doubt the improbably genuine. But then he
was disgusted with himself. The kid was obviously who

he seemed to be. And a damned fine golfer. With luck, the best in the Open.

"Write fast, Rowe. There are those of us who hunger and thirst," Morris said, delighted to no longer be lashed to somebody's bloody deadline.

CHAPTER SIX

Someone was singing where there was not supposed to be song in Buckley's Irish Pub in posh downtown Southampton.

"Oh, no, Morris. They don't need a failed baritone," Sullivan said.

"Not to worry." Morris settled back, reluctantly, in his seat. "I'm too far starved to carry a tune."

"The lad must have been suffering malnutrition all of his singing life, not that you could tell it by the size of him," Sullivan said to Tom Rowe, who egged Morris on.

"The swells won't mind, Morris. You know your Irish tunes."

"Tom Rowe, you're supposed to be a gentleman. You're worse than Morris."

"Yes, but I could never be accused of standing up among grown men and singing songs cold sober."

"Be thankful for small mercies," Sullivan said, "and here comes the lad with our food."

Just in time. The meat, rare enough to recover and walk the pasture, sizzled on the plates. The cold beers wept in the frozen mugs. God was in his heaven, and all was right at the table by the window.

At that moment came the pulpy, squashy, splattery sound of glass against flesh.

"Ah, the Irish at play with one another," said London's Tom Rowe, ungallantly.

Morris stood at the *thud* of a large body striking a bare floor, as screams went up among the diamond earrings and designer frocks.

"God bless Southampton. A beer-bottle fight," Morris said, moving into the bar to catch the action. The "action" was laid out on the floor like "Big Bad LeRoy Brown," with a crossword puzzle of fresh blood running down his split forehead into his closed eyes.

Standing over the huge unmoving carcass of Jack "Speed" Wallace was the new beer-bottle champion of Buckley's Irish Pub.

"Let's hear it for the unbeaten, untied J.C. Stroud from Nashville, Tennessee," Morris said, lifting the large right arm of the red-haired country-boy-grown-old, whose hand still gripped the intact bottom of a shattered Bud Lite bottle.

Morris heard the word *outrageous* from a shocked older lady at ringside, but not so shocked that she was not standing out of her chair on her pricey high heels to get a better view of the victim.

Morris checked the pulse of the temporarily extinguished Speed Wallace. It beat like a hammer in a shoe factory.

"Hoss, you might find another county to drink in before this ex–New York Giant gorilla wakes up," Morris said.

"Had the sumbitch back in Nashville, he'd wake up in a boxcar headed for Nuevo Laredo, Mexico."

"Damned NFL needs to sign you fat old agents and forget those slick college boys who puke at the sight of blood, especially their own. You fellows wouldn't be fighting over young Buddy Morrow?" said Morris.

"I done taught him not to be lying about me to that boy," J.C. said.

"Lying ought to be all right, J.C. Think how awkward it would be if he told him the truth about you." Morris couldn't help laughing, even with the blood still running into Speed Wallace's eye sockets and him lying there as peaceful as in the day of his Last Rites.

J.C. turned his nastiest glare on Morris and lifted the jagged rim of bottle in his right fist. Morris kept a firm grip on his wood and steel cane, about three feet longer than the broken beer bottle. J.C. didn't miss the sight of it, and gradually a smile, real or faked, crept across the freckles of his own wide face.

"Shit, if he'd a-told the truth on me, I'da had to kill the sumbitch."

That was when the two large cops grabbed J.C. Stroud by each arm, lifting him, big and fat as he was, in the air and hustling him toward the door, only one of his big feet hitting the floor every third step they took. A younger policewoman knelt beside the prone form of Speed Wallace, lying on the floor like a beached rowboat.

"A friend of yours?" she said to Morris.

"I know him when he's awake."

The policewoman smiled in spite of herself. "What was it all about?"

"Oh, nothing much. Maybe a hundred million dollars. Mainly they don't like the sight of one another."

"Well, this one's looks won't be improved. Who is he?"

"Jack 'Speed' Wallace."

"Should I know him?" she asked.

"You're too young. He was a down-and-dirty tight end for the Giants, in the old days."

"The Giants could use a tight end. What does he do now?"

"He's got a dirtier job: trading on the names of athletes—some of them nice enough guys, some of them nastier than he is—to push his overpriced sporting goods line on a gullible public. Only in America," Morris said with a genuine smile.

"John Morris," Sullivan said behind him, "your steak is getting cold."

"Not as cold as Speed Wallace," Morris said.

The Irish know the secret of a good steak—and, heaven knows, of a good beer. Between swallows, sometimes with tears in his laughter, Morris told them what had happened in the bar.

"What 'lie' did Wallace tell on J.C.?" Rowe asked.

Morris said, "I can't imagine anything that could hurt J.C.'s reputation—for sneaky, greedy, lying, low-down, double-dealing, double-crossing, arm-twisting, testicle-busting business tactics, in the best American tradition."

Morris thought a bit. "What surprises me is that Wallace had a chance to speak to Buddy Morrow at all, much less lie to him. Wallace and J.C. both were complaining to me yesterday that Buddy wouldn't give them three minutes of his time."

"Maybe today's 67 put our boy in a more favorable frame of mind to make a deal," Sullivan said. "You know golf. Tomorrow, or Saturday, or Sunday could bring a rain of double-bogeys."

"And the boy wonder could become yesterday's headlines. You may have something there," Morris said. "Let's ask Buddy tomorrow what's up with his business doings, if we can catch his eye before he gets to the practice tee."

"I'll catch his eye," Sullivan said.

"Don't go and overdo it. But then, you've never been one to underdo a thing."

"Morris, excuse me for interrupting." The polite voice, born of Princeton, could only belong to tall, thin Edgar Spencer IV, who stood quite erect, quite at ease, like the owner-chef of a five-star restaurant come to accept a worshipful obeisance from around the table.

"Not to worry, we've eaten everything but the designs on the plates," Morris said. "What's up?"

"My son saw and overheard a bit of what happened in the bar. Unfortunate, that." He said it as if it were a regrettable quarrel among lesser beings.

Hard to argue with the philosophy, thought Morris, who waited without answering.

"It seems the dispute was over young Buddy Morrow?" Spencer said it as a question.

Still Morris waited to make him say what he wanted to know.

"Was my son correct? Was young Morrow the subject of the disagreement?" It pained Spencer to phrase a direct question.

"If upside the head with a beer bottle is a *disagreement*—yes. The fight was over young Buddy Morrow." Morris waited sadistically to provoke another direct question.

"May I ask what the—violence—was about?"

"J.C. apparently accused Speed Wallace of 'lying about him to Morrow.' He did admit the truth would have been even more painful. To him. Not to ol' Speed, lying there bleeding into his eye sockets, out like a burned-out bulb." Morris laughed all over again. "Don't ask me what lie Wallace told, if a lie is possible about J.C. I have no idea."

Morris did not say he was only surprised Morrow

had agreed to talk to either of them, or to any of the robber-baron merchant-princes, one of which stood erectly, now nervously beside him.

"Morris, do you think Mr. Morrow would now entertain a business conversation with me?" There was a rare plaintiveness in the manner of his speech.

"I don't know, Edgar." Morris enjoyed saying his first name. "It couldn't hurt to give him a go. If he's negotiating with either of those two bozos . . . though I have to say I have a weakness for J.C. Not every man can take crudeness to an art form."

Spencer nodded his head once, as if Morris had given him an official license to call on American golf's new phenomenon.

"Edgar, you look pretty snappy in that suit. I don't think it came off the rack at Macy's," said Sullivan, to remind him to watch his Princeton manners and acknowledge the other two persons seated at the table.

Spencer cleared his throat and touched his pricey lapels in embarrassment: "Thank you, and good evening, Sullivan." He bowed slightly and raised one long thin hand to Tom Rowe, who lifted only a finger in return; it takes a lifetime Londoner to approximate the absolute disdain of royalty to a commoner.

"I think our boy Spencer smells blood on the barroom floor," Morris said, as Spencer found his way to his own table.

"Do you think Buddy is now taking commercial offers?" Sullivan asked, somehow disappointed in him if that were true.

"Perhaps it occurred to him he might have a disastrous second round and not make the cut for the weekend," Rowe said.

"He'll make the cut," Morris said. "But one bad round, and he could fall out of contention. After seeing him play only the nine holes, maybe I have more confidence in him than he has in himself. But I doubt the hell out of that. The boy knows he can play the game."

"But it's a fickle game, golf, old souls," Rowe reminded them both. "Name one great player it has not brought to his knees."

"Of course, you're right. *The Times* is always right," Morris admitted. "God bless the kid. I hope he bleeds the bastards dry and wins the tournament for himself. I can see it now, a television movie starring Mark Harmon, with computerized golf swings by Steven Jobs."

"Let it be done, Morris." Sullivan lifted the last of the wine in her glass, and they touched their own glasses against hers.

"I hope that's a good California cabernet." Speaking was the California golden boy himself, Jason Everett.

"Ah, 'the squeaky-clean, buttoned-down agent for the thinking athlete,' " Sullivan quoted *Sports Illustrated.* She did tilt upward to accept a buss on the cheek. Nobody could say he wasn't beautiful, she thought.

"The 'thinking athlete'? Isn't that an oxymoron?" said Everett.

"Careful, Berkeley boy. Slinging around words of four syllables—you'll lose the confidence of your clientele," Morris said.

"So long as they think capitalistic thought—even if they can't spell it—I'll have my share of athletes," said Everett, careful to shake hands with Rowe and Morris, saying, "Gentlemen," to the both of them.

"I know," Morris said, "you're curious about the brawl in the bar?"

"Forgive Morris. The man is a master of the obvious," said Sullivan.

"If J.C. hit him with his beer bottle, it must have been empty," Jason said, laughing too soon at his own good line.

"I'll quote you, young man, in *The Times*," Rowe said. "It'll go big in the London pubs."

"Whoever reads the good, gray *Times* in a bloody pub?" Morris asked, throwing up his napkin in mock surrender.

"Out with it, Morris," Everett said.

Morris told all he knew of what had happened. "You never saw Speed Wallace looking more content, laid out on the barroom floor."

"I hope J.C. is back in Nashville when he wakes up," Jason said. "Morris, I'll be frank with you."

"My God, man. Don't you know the agent's code? Candor could cost you your license."

"Agents, *like journalists*, don't require licenses."

"Touché," Morris said. "Go ahead and stun me with your candor."

"I want to make Buddy Morrow an offer. *One* offer. Is this the time? Will he listen?"

"Old sport, I have no idea," Morris said. "I drank a beer with the kid once in my life and watched him play nine holes of golf. He manages both very well, I might say. But I'm not his social secretary, despite what the nouveau riche visitors to Long Island may think."

"I'm not 'newly rich,' Morris. I've had my own private jet for three years." Everett laughed disarmingly at himself. "But Morrow *talked* with you, old man," he insisted. "Don't tell me you didn't get instantly close to him. I saw you. I *know*. It's my business to know."

Morris didn't deny it. "In truth. If he's listening to Speed Wallace *lie* about J.C. Stroud, maybe it's time to get your licks in. Hell, I don't know. You're the guy who flew him from Texas to Long Island." Morris hesitated and added, "I don't pretend to know the young man. I like him. I only hope you guys don't screw him up."

"Are you kidding?" Everett said. "He plays us like a one-foot, uphill putt. But he can't con a con man. Do you know where he's staying, Morris?"

"No."

"Some journalist. Perhaps I do. Never underestimate

the nouveau riche." He leaned down and kissed Sullivan lightly on the lips.

"God save the poor," she said to his trim retreating form.

"Why is the entire golf world gathered tonight in Buckley's Irish Pub?" asked Rowe.

"Good question," Morris said. "Coincidence always makes me put one hand on my wallet. News flies at any Open. Word must have gotten out that J.C. Stroud had cornered Morrow after his 67. Maybe in the parking lot. You know J.C.—he'd crash a one-man Port-o-Let."

"And the others followed him here?" Sullivan said.

"You can bet Speed Wallace did. And now the boys have split a beer, not to mention ol' Speed's scalp."

"Hard to picture Edgar Spencer the Fourth dogging J.C. Stroud," Sullivan said.

"For tens of millions of dollars? He'd chase Charles Manson. In fact, I shouldn't be surprised, any day, to see a 'C. Manson' golf shirt, with the logo: 'Stick It to Your Opponent.' "

"Morris, that's awful," Sullivan said.

"Yes, maybe: 'Bad Guys Finish First.' "

Sullivan rolled her eyes and made the sign of the cross.

The sun was barely pulling itself up out of the Atlantic Ocean. Morris watched the eternal feat from the floor-to-ceiling bedroom window of the beach house. *Some beach house,* he thought. *Sullivan must be paying five thousand dollars for this baby for one week.* He could not imagine she was paying *five times* five thousand dollars.

Sullivan, as she did every morning, was meeting the new day with her head carefully under the pillow, eyes shut, dead asleep. The woman could sleep through an avalanche and probably had up in Colorado. Just the thought of the snowbound state increased the ache in Morris's newly mended leg. Why had the world invented snow skiing when it already had Russian roulette?

Morris did his magical thing with the instant-coffee pot, even whipped up two orders of toast and fried eggs. He was in luck—orange marmalade came with the beach house, not to mention orange juice, probably at a cost of no more than a few hundred dollars.

He looked out the front door, just by habit, and there were the Friday newspapers lying in tight rolls on the lawn, all the calamity in a helpless world waiting to be let out in a silent scream.

"What's this?" Sullivan sat up.

Morris had found a tray, and here was her breakfast carefully deposited on her lap.

"No, John Morris. Whatever it is you are going to deny, I don't believe you." Sullivan's sleepy eyes were all suspicion, and then, looking down at the eggs, they were ravenous.

"Me? The soul of innocence?" he said. "Here I've been up at dawn, cracking eggs, manning a hot stove, torturing off the lid of the marmalade jar, what thanks do I get?"

She blew him a kiss. "MMMmmmmm. I forgive all of the things you might have done and didn't get around to. But *none* of the things you are *thinking* of doing," she said, narrowing her blue eyes.

Morris unrolled *The New York Times*, which he took with his own eggs. It was fun to read Dave Anderson aloud: "Golfers swing in silence, raise their arms or droop their shoulders in silence. . . . So quiet the occasional whistle of a Long Island Rail Road train howls across the British-type links like a metallic Hound of the Baskervilles."

"That's good, Morris," Sullivan said around a mouthful of toast. "I'll watch for when you'll be stealing it."

Morris took a bite out of a piece of her toast and was threatened with the silver tines of a fork.

He enjoyed quoting to her notes of the first day's round: Fuzzy Zoeller hitting seventeen greens but putting his way to only a one-under 69. Fuzzy saying it was the only Open course with twelve par 5s.

"That's Fuzzy," Sullivan said, laughing. "He whistles on his backswing."

David Duval making five sand saves in saving a 70. John Daly making one of three eagles, chipping in on No. 5, having come 535 yards in two blows. Big John managing a 71, despite finding his ball, from time to time, in knee-deep rough.

"I worry about John," Sullivan said quietly. "Sometimes the sorrow of the world is in his eyes."

The other two first-day eagles: Corey Pavin holing a wedge from a hundred yards, and John Connelly holing a seven-iron from 160 yards.

"Corey reminds me of pictures of a young Charlie Chaplin, in that square little mustache," Sullivan said. "He has the funniest practice swing. I think he wouldn't give up if you dropped him alone in the middle of the Atlantic Ocean."

Loren Roberts injuring his back, bending over to mark his ball on the 8th green, but wrapping himself in an Ace bandage, hanging in there for a 73. Mark McCumber tearing a calf muscle marking *his* own ball on the 10th green and hanging in to shoot even-par, but he might have to pull out of the tournament.

"And the brutes in the National Football League think they have it tough," Sullivan said. "All those three-hundred-pound Neanderthals have to do is try and tear each other's heads off in those colorful helmets. Suppose they had to bend down and put a coin where the football ought to be? Why, there wouldn't be a survivor in the game."

Morris looked at her over his reading glasses.

"You're not challenging the manhood of our golf professionals?"

"I didn't know it was allowed. You get jealous, Morris, if I kiss one on the cheek."

"Good thinking. We wouldn't want one of the boys fainting on national television. Now, love, that you've fed the inner beast, jump in the shower and let's catch fate's next chapter at Shinnecock Hills."

CHAPTER SEVEN

The blue coats and striped ties were sprinkled over the landscape of Shinnecock Hills like formal summer flowers, as USGA officials tried to keep their heads above the overflow of golf fans come to Long Island for Friday's second round of the Open.

Buddy Morrow had teed it up in the afternoon on Thursday. He was scheduled to go off today in the morning. But he had not yet taken to the practice tee.

Sullivan, in her walking shorts, kept watch on the locker-room door, while Morris hunted up the teenager caddying for Morrow. He found him waiting just inside the ropes on the practice tee, leaning on Buddy's bag.

Morris introduced himself. The kid nodded and shook hands, seeming to remember Morris's face, or bulk, from the day before. His hand was thin, as thin as the rest of him, but strong.

"And what's your name?" Morris asked.

"Pitts. Jimmy Pitts."

"You caddy here before?"

"No."

Morris looked at him more carefully. His working jeans might not have come off the rack.

"You grew up playing the course?"

The kid smiled. He had a good smile below his brown eyes and narrow face and thatch of brown hair.

"You any good?" Morris asked.

He nodded, yes. "I'm the junior champion. Going up to Yale this fall."

"Can you make the golf team?"

"Sure." He said it matter-of-factly, no way bragging.

"How did you hook up with Buddy Morrow?"

"Just an accident," said Pitts. "He came up one day early in the spring, to get in a practice round. I had no idea who he was. I was on the practice tee. He watched me hit a few balls. Asked if I was going to play, if I had a game. I said yes, and no I didn't have a game. He asked if he could join me. I said sure."

"Had you seen him hit any balls?" Morris asked.

"No."

"How did you know he wasn't a hacker?"

The kid thought a minute. "The way he stood, with the club resting in his hand. It seemed to belong there."

"I believe you have a future up at Yale," Morris said. "What did you think when you saw him swing?"

Pitts nodded his narrow head. "I believe you know golf, Mr. Morris. You can guess what I thought. Jesus, I was playing with a young Hogan. My dad has a film of Hogan. I've seen it dozens of times. I wish I could say it has influenced me. But I play square to square and with a draw."

"What did he shoot?" Morris asked.

"He hit a couple of balls on each hole. But he was around par, or under it, all day. He *dropped* balls in the rough to test it. He rarely hit them there off the tee."

"Did he give you any advice about your own game?" Morris asked.

"One thing. He told me my elbows were flying 'a bit apart on the backswing.' He was right, too. I've worked on it. My game's improved."

"What kind of fellow is he?"

Pitts thought. "Serious about golf. But curious— about the club, about me, what I'm going to take at Yale. When I said liberal arts, he said, 'Good choice.' My dad is dying to get me into the school of business."

"Maybe your business will be the same as Buddy's: tournament golf," Morris said.

"No," the kid said immediately. "My putting is plain as dirt. Not terrible, good enough among amateurs. But Buddy hooks his putts so true, so tight to the green, you think every putt is going down. I was amazed. I grew up on these greens. He saw breaks it took me years to understand."

"Did he ask you to caddy for him?"

"Not exactly. He asked if I knew a good caddy he could pick up." Pitts grinned. "I told him, 'Yes. A guy who knows every blade of grass out here. Who's played it since he was barely higher than the rough—me.' Oh, he took me up on it, right there."

"We followed you two the first nine holes yesterday," Morris said.

"I know. Buddy said you were a writer. I remember you and the handsome woman." The kid was not yet so much of a Yale man that he couldn't blush.

Sullivan will love that: "the handsome woman," Morris thought. "Did he play as well on the back nine?"

"Better. We could have turned it in 31. He hit his only fat shot on 16. Dumped it in the front bunker, got an impossible lie."

"What's he like under pressure?"

"I swear he doesn't feel it. I'm standing out on the 18th fairway, unable to breathe. And he says, 'Jimmy, my man, what would you take from here?' I opened my mouth to say three-iron and couldn't speak. He held up three fingers. I nodded. He pulled a five-iron. All day when we played, he used two clubs less than I did. He remembered and handicapped *me and him*. He put the five-iron on the back of the green and got down in two putts from fifty feet, as coolly as if it was a practice round. I still couldn't breathe."

"He told the press he didn't know how he would stack up as a golfer when the four days were over, but he had the best caddy of the lot, who just might be playing in the Open himself one day," Morris said, as accurately as he could remember.

"He said that?"

"Yep."

"I wish you hadn't told me. Now I'm tighter than ever."

"If he plays like yesterday, he'll loosen you up. What kind of guy is he? I don't mean golfer."

Pitts thought. "He's smart. He'd read up on Shinnecock Hills. Knew a lot more about the history of the club than I did. And about the Shinnecock Indians. He compared various holes here to holes he'd played in Scotland and Asia and Africa and all over the world. Not bragging, I don't mean that, just analyzing the holes. He even knew that Hogan had played here and what he said about the course. He seemed to have memorized Raymond Floyd's four rounds when he won the Open here in 1986."

Pitts looked past Morris toward the clubhouse, but Morrow was not yet in sight. "But he wasn't just interested in golf. He'd read Peter Matthiessen's book on the fishermen of the South Fork. I was embarrassed: Living here all my life and going up to Yale, and I hadn't read it. I've read it since. I even went out on a commercial boat three weekends and did grub work. For minimum wage. I told Buddy about it this week.

He'll only let me call him 'Buddy.' No 'Mr. Morrow.' When I first called him that, he called me 'Mr. Pitts.' He was really pleased I had read Matthiessen's book and gone out on the fishing boat. He said so twice. He made me tell him all about the fishermen I went out with. I told him I would never eat another fish and not think of those guys pulling in those handlines and nets."

Pitts lifted the bag as if to test its worthiness. "I like the guy. I hope he wins the tournament. I hope to God I don't make some terrible mistake and cost him the chance to win it."

"Not to sweat," Morris said, convinced it was true. "Anything else about him, anything that surprised you, not necessarily about his golf?"

Pitts's mouth flew open to say, "One thing I'm sure about. I've read all the stuff the papers are writing. And he's—" Pitts lifted his hand, obviously in a salute.

Morris turned. There was Buddy Morrow with his arm around Julia Sullivan's shoulder, walking toward the practice tee. Only *his* feet were touching the ground.

"Hello, Jimmy. Hello, Morris. Meet my girlfriend, Julia Sullivan. From Colorado. I knew it was a beautiful state. I just didn't know how beautiful the people were."

He put his hand in Morris's big one.

"Watch her for me, Morris. Jimmy and I are going for a walkabout here at Shinnecock Hills. Can you find a wedge in that bag, my man?"

They were off to the practice tee. Applause broke out among the youthful aficionados. Buddy tipped his white Scottish cap and lifted an old Spalding wedge.

"I'll never wash this shirt," Sullivan said, kissing Morris on the chin.

"You may get a bit gamy in there," he said, "but who'll notice in Colorado? They'll all be busy freezing to death. What did he say, Sullivan? Is he open to business offers?"

"Oh, yes. He said he'd 'been around the world learning the game. Now it was time for the world to come to him.' He was so pleased with himself. I got the sense he's already cut at least one big deal. He said, 'First cabin, Sullivan. It's the only way to travel.' "

"I wonder who he chose and who the big losers are?" Morris said. "Maybe that's what the beer-bottle fight was really about last night. A dangerous bunch, the big-time losers of the world, be it in business or politics."

Sullivan lifted a hand to catch the eye of the athletic woman with the short reddish-brown hair. What was her name? Martin. Jerry Martin. She still wore no hat, careless of the damage the sun did against her face, which was strong and appealing but definitely sun-worn.

"Are you game to follow our boy for another round today?" asked Sullivan.

"Sure."

"He looks fit," Sullivan said.

"Yes."

"Morris's stiff knee is acting up. We're going to catch him on the back nine. You keep him between the hedges on the front."

"That would be nice," Martin said, her hazel eyes smiling.

"I understand he may be richer today than he was yesterday," Sullivan couldn't resist saying.

"Oh?"

"I believe he's signed a serious contract with somebody."

"They're lucky to get him," Jerry said.

"See you at the turn." Sullivan gave the victory sign.

Morris led the way to the press tent, where they camped out under one of several television sets. You could hear the wind whistle through the microphones.

The Shark was quickly loose between the twin Peconic and Shinnecock Bays. Greg Norman eased a twelve-foot putt down a slippery incline into the hole for a birdie on No. 2, and he nailed an iron shot to within one foot of the flag on the 453-yard No. 3.

Being the ever-erratic Norman, he bogeyed Nos. 8 and 10. But he ran in putts of eighteen and fifteen feet on the back side and putted home a "bellied-wedge" from another eighteen feet on the 450-yard finishing hole.

His 67–135 put him 5 under par, and that would stand up in the wind all day for a share of the Open lead at the halfway point of the tournament. Jumbo Ozaki did not go away in the wind, launching his huge drives and putting the slick greens for a 68–137, good for second place, one stroke ahead of left-hander Phil Mickelson and Bob Tway.

"Let's hope Mickelson doesn't prove to be one of the great players who never wins one of the great tournaments," Sullivan said.

"He's so talented," said Morris, "has such genius in his hands, the game comes to him so easily. Maybe he has to bleed a bit. And hurt a bit to gain the toughness, the ruthlessness it takes to drown the other great players in the world in their own sweat."

"Careful, Morris. You haven't had your first beer of the day, and you're sounding like a philosopher."

Later in the day, having found that first beer and wandering down to the 18th green to wait for Greg Norman to hole out and take the second-day lead, Morris said, "Norman's been there and done that. Exactly nine years ago, here at Shinnecock Hills, he led the Open going into the final round."

Sullivan said, "Wasn't that the year he led The Masters, the U.S. Open, the PGA, *and* the British Open after the Saturday round?"

"Oh, yes. The infamous 'Saturday Slam.' He did come away with the claret jug that goes with the British Open title, and now he's won it twice, and that ain't shabby. Just the oldest golf tournament in the world. But the other three majors have always eluded him."

Norman seemed totally in control of this year's tournament and of himself as he lifted his hat to salute the crowd around the 18th green. He smiled his cattle-rustler smile at his ball, resting against the first cut of the fringe surrounding the green. He drew his wedge like a sword, lowered the edge until it rested opposite the equator of the ball, and then stroked it in the belly as you would strike a putt, sending the ball across the green and directly into the hole.

After the explosion of noise from the crowd had subsided, Sullivan said, "How can so powerful a man have so delicate a touch?"

"And how can it leave him so quickly?" said Morris.

At that moment Thomas Boswell of *The Washington Post* was writing in the press tent, "The knock on Norman's whole career has been that, in the heat of battle, he never knows when to step on the gas and when to hit the brakes. He just puts the pedal to the metal until, in The Masters, U.S. Open, and PGA, he hits a wall."

After the Friday round Norman sat in front of the writers and cameras, inviolate from all pressure. He said, "I love the golf course. I think it's one of the greatest courses in the world—probably the best U.S. Open course I've ever played. . . . I'm happiest with the way I'm controlling myself. When I bogeyed the 10th hole, I said to myself, 'Hey, just come right back with a birdie,' and I did."

Nick Price did not enjoy the same control of his own game. He had trouble with the slick greens and high grass, and only his remarkable patience held the damage to a 72–139, four strokes off the pace.

Nick told the press, "I never felt comfortable. But overall I'm still happy. Today's round could have been a 76 or a 77 very easily. I just hung in there. I hope it's just my one bad round."

The other Nick, Faldo, playing his long irons with absolute mastery, scored a 68–140 to tie Davis Love III and Curt Byrum and Mark Roe, five shots back.

Faldo, with his British Open and Masters championships safely in his past, hungered after his first U.S. Open title. "Five shots back is not a bad position to come from," he said. Then he fled to the practice tee, where he continued his confrontation with perfection, likely more at home silently striking balls than at any other time and place in his life.

Buddy Morrow did not disappoint. Despite the gathering wind and the pressure, he turned the front nine in even-par 35. He birdied the 1st hole and bogeyed the treacherous 9th, leaving his tee shot in the high fescue.

Morris and Sullivan waited at the 10th tee, opposite the clubhouse and on the same height, looking out over the eastern half of the course. The landing area far below was nowhere to be seen from the tee.

Morrow stepped through the crowd gathered around the tee box and held up two fingers to Jimmy Pitts, who pulled the aged Hogan two-iron from the bag. Jimmy's hands did not shake, but there was little color in his thin face.

Buddy Morrow tossed a pinch of grass in the air and shook his head to see it swirl to the four directions.

He said, "Jimmy, my man, I think the Fates can't make up their minds in whose direction they want the wind to blow." He smiled, as if he were in collusion with the gods.

Sullivan caught his eye with her own, and he pointed a finger accusingly at her, as if she, and not he or the Fates, might be responsible for the fickle winds.

Sullivan flashed a smile and the victory sign.

Buddy played a slight fade that Morris was sure had found the fairway far below them, but not so far as to leave a blind pitch shot from directly below the green.

In 1986 Nicklaus had suffered the only lost ball of his

career in a major tournament and taken a six on the 409-yard par-4 hole, one of three double-bogeys he suffered on the back nine that windblown day.

Sullivan caught up with her new acquaintance, Jerry Martin, who patted her shoulder as if she were rejoining her old regiment in a foreign war.

"He's played very steadily," Jerry said, brushing her short reddish-brown hair out of her eyes. "Not much luck on the greens, which have gone deadly fast. Twice he had true putts spin out of the hole."

"He looks confident," Sullivan said.

"He does," Jerry said, looking at him as if for the first time that day, or maybe in her life.

Morris poled his way after the two women setting the pace with their long legs down the steep slope of the fairway.

Buddy, as deliberate as a bird on her nest, settled over the ball and lifted a wedge gently onto the green, ten feet below the flag.

Sullivan and Martin released their breaths as one as the ball ceased spinning backward and came to rest. One foot farther below the hole, and it would have rolled off the green and thirty yards down the steep slope of the fairway, as balls did randomly the entire tournament.

Buddy drilled the putt home in one flick of his wrist. At that moment he was one shot off Norman's Open lead at 4 under par.

And now Morrow entered a loop of holes that the Shinnecock members loved and feared, beginning with No. 11 and ending with No. 14, called Thom's Elbow, after storied Shinnecock pro Charlie Thom, who lived for years in a cottage near the 14th tee. It was reminiscent of holes No. 11 through 13 at Augusta National, long revered and feared as Amen Corner.

Morrow again tossed a pinch of grass and again shook his head at the wind swirling in all directions.

The 11th, known as Hill Head, seemed a simple matter of 158 yards to a par of 3. But in front of the tiny, sharply elevated green were steep bunkers that sloped away dangerously to the back. A man might toss as easily a penny onto a radiator cap as land a seven-iron on the small slanting green.

Buddy played his iron long over the bunkers and safely on the green, accepting a two-putt and a par and moving to No. 12.

Named Tuckahoe, the 12th is the longest par 4 on the course, at 472 yards. The prevailing wind is normally from the southwest and with the golfer, but today it swirled madly about. Buddy reached back for an extra thirty yards and pulled his tee shot ever so slightly, leaving it in the deep rough on the left.

Morris could not see the ball, could not see the tops of Buddy's shoes.

It never occurred to Morrow to do anything but lay up in the fairway with a wedge. Now even a bogey was no sure thing. He needed a strong midiron to the green high above him. The USGA had shaved the grass below all the steeply elevated greens, so that any ball, short or long, would spill all the way to level ground, requiring the most delicate and dangerous of blind flop shots. Some players chose to chip or even putt up the brutal slopes, but rare was the player who got down in two strokes with any method.

Buddy seemed oblivious to the peril above him and played the shot to the green without hesitation.

Morris remembered it was here on the 12th, in 1986, that Raymond Floyd had holed a desperate twenty-foot putt for par, keeping him within reach of Payne Stewart, who birdied the hole for a two-stroke lead on the final day, with only six holes to play, to win his second U.S. Open. It was not to be.

Buddy lagged his own first putt and took his 5 this

day and himself fell two strokes behind Greg Norman for the second-round lead.

The 13th, a relatively simple 377-yard, dogleg-right par 4, had proved the undoing of Payne Stewart nine years ago. Morris could still see his iron shot from the tee missing the fairway, while Floyd's found it. Stewart's approach shot had not held the green; his chip back had lipped the cup, and he missed the four-foot putt for a bogey 5. Floyd's resolute six-iron had found the green within four feet of the hole; he drained the putt for a birdie and left the 13th green tied for the lead, not to be denied in the '86 Open.

Buddy Morrow knew every shot the two of them had struck that day on the 13th hole, and he tossed grass twice, three times, to test the erratic wind. His own two-iron split the fairway. His six-iron found the green. But his putt lipped the hole and died on the edge. Buddy never flinched, as if he and gravity were in agreement with the result.

The 14th hole played the seventh most difficult on the course, 447 yards down the hill and up again to a par of 4.

Morrow pulled his driver, then hesitated for the first time on the back nine. He swapped it to Jimmy Pitts for the three-wood. It was the correct choice. His tee shot came within one foot of running through the left-to-right bend in the fairway.

It was here that Floyd had taken the lead from Stewart for the 1986 Open. Both players had missed the green with midirons. Both had chipped within five feet. Stewart had missed his putt. Floyd had stared the ball into submission and stroked it with his long-shafted putter into the center of the hole.

Buddy left himself ten feet below the hole. Hogan himself would have approved of the four-iron that leaped twice and died in its dimples. His putted ball crossed the cup on pure air, leaving Buddy with his head between his legs in disbelief. But par is never a futile score on a hole setup for the U.S. Open.

Morris did not remember the tee box on the 15th hole. No wonder, he realized: it had been moved back since 1986, stretching the downhill par-4 hole to 415 yards. But it was still a rare chance for a birdie on the back nine.

Buddy cut the two-iron into the heart of the fairway. Morris poled his way down the slope, his ruined knee complaining of the up-and-down march of the linkslike course. He could see that the pin was cut to the right, where the green fell alarmingly away to a collection area, offering another blind lob result for the tentative approach shot.

Buddy nipped his short iron, and the roar of the modest crowd around the green announced that the ball had stopped within a hairbreadth of the hole. He tapped it home, now one stroke behind Mr. Norman.

Sullivan felt a powerful grip on her bare arm. Jerry Martin, her strong face burning with the sun and wind and possibility of the moment, shouted, "Go, Punter Boy!"

Buddy actually looked their way and gave a grin, Sullivan was sure, to her personally among the mob. She gave the victory sign and looked to be sure Morris had seen the grin and the sign, but he was poling his way up the slope.

Sullivan couldn't stop smiling. She said to Martin, "Not a Texas word, *punter*. I think you've done your time in England."

"Oh, I've lost a pound or two with the bookies," she admitted.

"And you've risked your money on our boy Buddy Morrow?"

"Oh, yes."

"Stick with me," Sullivan said. "I never lose a bet." She smiled dangerously. But she did not exaggerate.

John Morris said he would rather bet against time than Julia Sullivan. Many had been the openmouthed, empty-pocketed bookie who would have agreed.

The par-5 16th hole had played the second easiest on the course to the Open field of 1986. It was here that Floyd, who had not carried a nine-iron that last round, had choked down on an eight-iron and struck the ball within birdie range of the hole, giving him a two-stroke cushion coming into the long and deadly 18th hole. "I was sure I'd won the damned Open at last when I hit that eight-iron," he'd told Morris a couple of years later. His 66 had lifted him from fifth to first place that last fateful day.

The 16th tee presented the classic view, high above, of Stanford White's Shinnecock Hills clubhouse. The undulating fairway of 544 yards made the green reachable only for the longest hitters.

Morrow never considered trying for the green in two shots and an eagle 3. He laid up with an iron off the tee, as Hogan would have surely done—and laid up again in the heart of the fairway. And he sent a short iron snugly to the raised green. With no evidence of panic in his face, he pushed the twelve-foot putt, never threatening the hole. The par cost him half a shot to the field on the one easy birdie hole on the back side.

Jerry Martin's strong hand flew to her mouth as if to prevent a cry of alarm.

Morris leaned between her and Sullivan, all the time looking into Buddy Morrow's green eyes, looking for a hint of fear but seeing nothing but a deeper green.

"Jimmy, my man," Morrow said, "that was a horse-shit putt."

Jimmy Pitts, who was as pale as the Shinnecock Hills columns, looked shocked to hear himself laugh.

The 181-yard par-3 17th was no hole on which to risk a quick recovery. The tee had been lengthened since 1986, but any ball hit over the green was still dead in the tall, thick, unyielding fescue. Buddy played a five-iron safely to the middle of the green, ignoring the flag on the back. He two-putted for his par 3.

The 18th tee looked squarely up at the clubhouse, 450 frightful yards to the green. It played to a par of 4, and had been the most difficult hole on the course during the 1986 Open.

Buddy took the driver out of his bag without a thought to the three-wood. His left-to-right fade was born for the bend of the fairway, which had to be found for any second shot to reach the green. Nine years ago Floyd had played a four-iron thirty-five feet below the hole, lagged his putt to the cup, and tapped in for the Open title that had eluded him for a generation.

Morrow needed a three-iron, and a strong one. He did not play safely to the middle of the green but carried the ball to the flag, mounted fearfully near the green's far edge. A rolling thunder of noise, as if from a football stadium, crashed down the fairway as the ball came to rest three feet from the hole.

"Oh, Punter Boy!" Jerry shouted, unheard into the noise.

The crowd stood in a loud New York welcome, as if for one of the old legendary names—a Palmer, a Hogan, or a Nicklaus—as young Buddy Morrow walked up the slope, raising his hand to his thick dark hair in a friendly salute. A simple putt, and Buddy was in with a 69–135 for a share of the lead on the second day of the Open.

Sullivan turned to hug Jerry Martin, but she was gone, vanished in the crowd.

Many golfers were still on the course. A most unlikely one, an Englishman, Jeffrey Burns, who had come across the ocean to qualify, finished the day birdie, eagle, birdie, par for a 66–135, to tie Norman and Morrow for the second-round lead. The television cameras and much of the crowd had gone home for the day when Burns, a stout man well past forty, holed out his remarkable round.

Morris and Sullivan and Tom Rowe got the news in the Shinnecock Hills bar.

"Lord bless old man Burns," Rowe said, looking at his watch. "I'll have to rewrite my bloody story. Worse, I'll have to listen to him replay the round into the next century."

"We'll see you tonight at the party in Westhampton Beach," Sullivan said.

"I wouldn't miss it, love," Rowe said, downing his drink and sprinting for the press tent.

Rowe lied. He never made the party. Lucky him.

Morris finally hid in the kitchen that night from the overdressed, overprivileged, underwhelming hosts and guests at the house the size of a small hotel in Westhampton Beach.

Certainly the party hadn't lived up to its ocean address in swank Westhampton Beach. The mansion behind the gigantic privet hedge was large, the ocean was close, and the booze was vintage, but the people were too goddamned polite. Maybe it came with too much money, this affliction of correctness. Women standing in long dresses and men in neckties drinking very carefully, as if the United States Golf Association—whose officers were much in evidence at the party—extracted a grievous human penalty for an unpopular opinion. Nobody ignored Greg Norman's two British Open titles to suggest he was a "gutless wonder." Nobody passed out. Nobody threw a punch. Nobody threw up once on anything. Obviously Morris was the only oversize ex-sportswriter on the carefully mown acres-wide premises. The tall, elegant hostess, whom Sullivan knew because the two of them flew twin private jets from the same manufacturer, spoke of the Open as "a terribly sweet match for the Shinnecock Hills Club but isn't the traffic for the weekend unbearable."

The Unbearable Lightness of Being *was born at this party*, Morris said to himself, before escaping to the kitchen.

Sullivan found him drinking with the cooks, who'd pooled their money and placed it on Greg Norman to finally win the U.S. Open.

"Oh, hell, it's not too late to lay off your bet," Sullivan said, leaning on a butcher block, twisting open a fresh Budweiser. She wrote a name in her day calendar, tore out the page, folded it over several times, and handed it to the chief cook, an old man who secreted it into the pocket of his apron as if it were a recipe for Caneton Tour d'Argent, stolen from Claude Terrail himself of Paris, France. Morris could not imagine what name she had printed but would not have bet against it even on the advice of Old Tom Morris, were this still his century and he alive.

Each time the kitchen door opened, it let in the loud sounds of an overrated rock band unable to enliven a crashingly dull party.

"Your pal Tom Rowe didn't make it," Sullivan accused Morris.

"*My* pal? Well, he's from London. He knows his way around parties. He must have gotten a look at the guest list. We could be drinking and bashing each other with beer bottles in Buckley's Irish Pub."

"I'm game to sneak out—our hostess not only has sold my plane's twin, she's retired with a headache," Sullivan said, checking her watch. It was 11:20 P.M.

"Not too late for a nightcap at Mr. Buckley's pub," Morris said. "If we catch the eternal bachelor Rowe with some Long Island babe, he gets to pick up the check."

The old cook showed them out the back way, bowing to Sullivan as if in the presence of punting immortality—as he very well might be, thought Morris.

Sullivan, like the good pilot she was, found her way

through the fog to Highway 80 at a modest twenty miles an hour.

Morris leaned back to look up into the mist that enveloped the sky, which reached out over the Atlantic and around the world with the cold, hidden indifference of a billion stars.

Friday, June 16
11:50 P.M.

CHAPTER EIGHT

Highway 80 fell from under them in anticipation of the Shinnecock Canal. Headlights of the rental Ford dissolved into the fog, which poured over the road as if the Atlantic Ocean had breathed across the narrow width of Long Island.

Julia Sullivan squinted into the gathering mist.

"We're lost, like the sinners we are," Morris said.

"Oh, no," Sullivan said, "we're going along fine. It's the island that's disappeared."

"That'll push the U.S. Open off the front pages," Morris said. "I can see *The New York Times:* 'Long Island Lost at Sea.' What the hell? Bobby Vann lost his saloon years ago. What else would anybody miss?"

"All the writers, Morris. They have *real* writers on Long Island."

"You mean that know vowels and consonants and all the hard parts?"

"Writers that make *real money,* Morris. You know, the

kind that spends with Gucci and Tiffany." She did not have to say her birthday was coming up in another week.

"Don't be tacky. We literary types never talk of money."

"Especially when the check comes at Buckley's Irish Pub," Sullivan said, ducking a bit as if she could see under the fog.

"Where'd all the Friday-night traffic go?" Morris said, aware of the dark, now-empty highway and wishing to change the subject from money, which Julia Sullivan had mountains of in her native Denver and which ex–Associated Press writers made in mounds like ant-hills.

A low mist from the canal mingled with the fog over the road, which was still strangely empty.

"The island must be drunk with golf and sleeping it off," Morris said.

"Or under arrest," Sullivan said, slowing to a stop at the light spinning on the roof of a patrol car parked at a dangerous angle on the bridge.

A young, startlingly handsome patrolman, his eyes alive with alarm or excitement, approached their Ford with a twelve-cell flashlight and waited until Sullivan rolled down her window.

"Sorry. Can't stop here. You'll have to turn it around. Catch Highway 27 across the canal. There's been an accident."

Morris already had his outdated Associated Press card in his wide hand.

"The AP," he said. "What's up?" He had never kicked the habit of calling in spot news to the local AP. It was like an addiction to nicotine.

"Damnedest thing. A car went off the bridge. A young woman got out alive. Actually, my partner pulled her out of the canal. She's about crazy. Can't say I blame her." He turned his sunburst of a flashlight on Sullivan, who squeezed both eyes shut.

"Sorry," the deputy switched off the light, then bent closer. "Miss, you might be able to help me with the girl. She's hysterical. Don't know what's holding up the ambulance."

"Sure, I'll help," Sullivan said, pulling the keys, opening her door. "Any officer who calls me 'miss' has got my cooperation. Come along, Morris."

Morris was already propping himself out of the car with his cane. A nearly drowned girl. A hero deputy. It sounded like a story that might have legs all the way to Manhattan.

The deputy needed the comfort of his own voice: "I can't leave. I've got to stop the traffic on this end. My partner—he jumped off the damned bridge and dragged the girl out of the canal, over to the far bank. He's stopping traffic on that end. Soaking wet." He checked his watch. "Goddamn our backup."

The deputy suddenly remembered his manners, touching the bill of his cap. "I'm Sheriff's Deputy Perry Angle."

Sullivan identified herself and John Morris, who shook hands with the deputy.

The mist off the Shinnecock Canal gave an unworldly look to the yellow light spinning without sanity on top of the patrol car. Sullivan made out the wet wisp of a girl wrapped in the deputy's coat, weeping against the top of the car.

When Sullivan stepped within reach of the girl, she knew her instantly, despite the blond hair plastered over her forehead. There was no hiding the legs under the deputy's coat. The girl shivered, standing light-years from the rich young socialite she had been while stepping out of the limousine in front of the Plymouth Theater. Sullivan took real estate heir Tenney Bidwell in her arms, careless of the water running onto her blouse.

She turned her face from the weeping girl and whispered her name to Morris.

Here we come, Manhattan . . . with this story, thought Morris, his mouth open with astonishment. Now he remembered the young socialite, sticking her long legs out of the limousine on Broadway, and the older guy, looking like Al Capone, stepping out behind her. The bored expression was likely to have left his face if he was sitting down there in the car at the bottom of the canal.

Morris walked over and took hold of the top railing of the bridge, just a step from the tortured gap in all three railings. Looking down through the shifting mist, he had to force his breath in and out. He could imagine too well the automobile bolting weightless into the night. The canal water ran thirty feet below, blacker than the sky and impossible to see. How in God's name did the girl get out of the car? Only near the east bank could Morris make out the surface of the dark water, dancing under the lights of a marina. A clutch of curious voyeurs was making its way from the marina up to the bridge, where Deputy Angle turned them back, along with any approaching cars.

On the west bank Morris could make out three old, abandoned, unlit buildings, more like failed houses than marine structures. A hint of a road seemed to lead behind them.

Morris followed the path of the doomed automobile, from the gap in the railings back toward the east bank. There was no sign of a skid mark. *Jesus, the driver never hit the brakes*, Morris thought, as he bent near to the surface of the bridge in the headlights from the deputy's patrol car.

Damn. Sideways scuff marks twice as wide as his hand. Morris was careful not to step on them. A huge force had slammed against the car, sending it into the railing. Could only have been another car. Or a truck. He bent even closer, balancing himself with his cane. A small trail of debris . . . dirt . . . rust . . . maybe even flecks of paint . . . smashed from the colliding vehicles. Morris was careful to step around it. *Hit-and-run. Had to be*, he thought. *And the girl is rich and a looker. This story has legs to run from coast to coast.*

Twin sirens from opposite directions tortured the night as if wailing for their own kind.

The patrol car hit the bridge from the west bank at the same time as the ambulance screamed down from the east bank.

A big man, almost as wide as Morris, stepped out of the passenger seat of the patrol car, careless of the door left swinging behind him. Before he opened his mouth to identify himself as the sheriff of Suffolk County, Morris knew who he was and what county he was born in. Morris and Sullivan might have been standing on a bridge to times past.

Morris knew better than to call him by his hated boyhood nickname, "Snakeeyes," but could not resist saying: "Willie says the umpire was right. He was as safe at home as in his mother's arms. You never laid a mitt on him."

The sheriff stopped dead in his shoes.

"Who the hell are you?" The sheriff leaned forward to see Morris's face.

"You'd know me in Bobby Vann's old saloon."

It all came back to Sheriff Otis Haggard in an instant. "Willie Morris knows who turned his shit green," he said, his voice suddenly dripping of Yazoo County and the Mississippi Delta, where he'd grown up one of nine boys. It was not an accent he would run on for sheriff of Suffolk County, Long Island. Oh, no. He was now the man who graduated college in the Empire State, who married the daughter of a Long Island potato farmer become a real estate mogul. Those old July-hot days on hardscrabble infields, playing brass-knucks baseball—Otis Haggard's Yazoo County country boys against Willie Morris's Yazoo City city slickers—were long past, but fiercely in the mind.

John Morris, no kin to Willie, had umpired arguments in Bobby Vann's long-vanished saloon between Willie and Otis, with Willie's cronies ragging him mercilessly: James Jones, rattling his shoulder purse of pocket knives; John Knowles; Peter Matthiessen; Wilfrid Sheed, maybe Styron, and on one occasion Capote himself, who didn't know how many bases were on an infield, all of them taking first one side of any baseball argument and then the other, and Willie's dog, Pete, the mayor of Bridgehampton, sitting at the door as the saloon's official greeter.

"By God, I know you, you're John Morris," said Sheriff Haggard. "What do you hear from Willie?"

"He's lucky in marriage. Writing well. His Ole Miss Rebels beat LSU. I think he may be elected governor of Mississippi for life."

"I hate to say it, but we miss him. Not as much as we miss his dog," said the sheriff.

"Pete died years ago. But he lived the good life."

"What the hell's goin' on on this bridge?" Haggard said.

"A car went off it," Morris said, pointing toward the dark gap in the three rails. "A girl escaped, if you can believe it. One of your deputies jumped off the bridge and pulled her to the far bank."

"Was she drunk?"

"I hope so. Who could have made it out sober? Julia Sullivan—you remember Sullivan?"

"We haven't got so many beautiful women on Long Island we're likely to forget one."

"No wonder you politicians get reelected," Morris said. "Your deputy Perry Angle asked her to help calm the young woman. Until the ambulance came."

"They were working another wreck," Otis said. "So was I. A bad one. Four people killed on old Highway 27. Damned fools can't drink or drive."

"Some night," Morris said. "You better take a deep

breath. The young woman who went off the bridge was Tenney Bidwell."

"Mother of God, no!" the sheriff said.

"I figured you'd recognize the name."

"I know her old man. The island knows her old man, since he owns most of it. Thank God my deputy saved her ass. We've saved it more than once, believe me, stoppin' her on these roads a long way from sober."

"If this night doesn't sober her up, nothing ever will," Morris said. "But it might be worse than you think. Take a look over here. There don't seem to be any skid marks. The girl, if she was driving, never hit the brakes. But there are *scuff* marks, like her tires were knocked sideways by a collision."

The sheriff squatted and turned his flashlight on the spot Morris pointed to with his cane.

"Oh, shit!" he said. "Nobody stopped to help?"

"I don't believe so," Morris said.

"That's all I need tonight. Four people killed in a two-car collision. And a hit-and-run nearly drownin' Jack Bidwell's daughter on the Shinnecock Bridge. Any poor bastard still down there in the canal?"

"I don't know," Morris said. "I don't think the girl has enough wits about her to say. Hard to blame her for that."

The sheriff, holding on to the last foot of intact railing before the twisted gap, leaned precariously over the canal.

"Can't see a goddamned thing," he said. "Plenty of current under this bridge. She got out of there alive, she needs to get her money down on the lottery."

Sullivan had been unable to talk Tenney Bidwell into the backseat of the patrol car. She became more terrified when Sullivan opened the door, as if the car itself would leap into the air and off the bridge.

"Were you driving?" Sullivan asked her when her

moaning had slowed. Her distress quickly deepened as she buried her head in Sullivan's bosom, as if they had been lifelong companions.

When the ambulance pulled up, the girl clung more tightly. Sullivan never considered letting her go in the ambulance alone. She waved to Morris, but he was with another large man in uniform, looking off the bridge, and didn't see her as the ambulance doors closed behind them.

Deputy Angle told the sheriff how they had driven onto the bridge, and seen the gap torn in the railings, and how Deputy Mark Donovan "heard the girl cry out and jumped off the goddamned bridge to help her. He pulled her out over on the east bank. She was too hysterical to say if she was alone in the car. Mark dived back in, but no hope of reaching the car. Not in that current."

"Where'd Sullivan go?" Morris asked, not having seen the ambulance leave.

"She left in the ambulance. The girl wouldn't let go of her."

"A hit-and-run. There'll be hell to pay on this," the sheriff said, as if it had all happened to complicate his life.

"Where will the ambulance take them?" Morris asked.

"To Southampton Hospital."

"You didn't see a car or a truck leaving the scene?" the sheriff asked his deputy.

"No. Nobody was on the bridge when we got here," said Angle.

"Those people from the marina, on the east bank. They would have heard a crash," Morris said, pointing to the clutch of curious onlookers gathered opposite that end of the bridge.

"Ask 'em, Perry," the sheriff said. "I want this bridge

shut down until forensics can do their job. No stepping *here*." He shined his light on the scuff marks on the concrete.

A new roar came up behind them onto the bridge, a man on a motorcycle in a black wet suit and crash helmet, looking like the son of the Creature from the Black Lagoon, with an oxygen tank strapped on his back.

"Other end of the bridge," said the sheriff, blocking the scuff marks with his own person. "A wrecker is on the way. There's an old road down to the canal behind those empty buildings." He pointed to the east bank.

The motorcycle rider roared off without speaking.

Other deputies arrived to help secure the bridge. The sheriff got on the radio to put a sense of urgency in the forensics team.

Morris made his way to the east end of the bridge. *What the hell*, he thought, and poled and slid his way down the grassy embankment to the abandoned east side of the canal.

He introduced himself to Deputy Donovan, who straightened his soaking-wet shirt collar as if prepared to pose for a photograph for the Associated Press. There would be photographers aplenty soon enough, thought Morris.

The motorcycle rider had lost his way but finally roared up on the road behind the boarded-up buildings. He kicked down the stand on the motorcycle and stepped off, swinging the oxygen tank around as if it were weightless. Then he pulled off his crash helmet, and soft, dark hair fell around his ears—except the he was a she. And from her profile and trim figure in the black wet suit, she might have been a *Vogue* model.

Deputy Donovan obviously knew her, thought nothing of her sex or occupation, didn't bother to introduce her to Morris, began talking and pointing to the spot in the canal where he'd jumped in to help the young woman.

The diver glanced up at the gap in the bridge railings, which looked as if some great beast had broken out. Without a word, she fooled with the dials on the oxygen tank, swung it onto her back as if it were casual wear for evening cocktails, spit in her clear mask, pulled it over her face, switched on a waterproof flashlight, and fell over backward into the canal, disappearing in a froth of bubbles.

Morris caught himself holding his breath as she went under. *Just routine duty*, he thought, if diving into a strange, ink-black, saltwater canal with a dangerous current, in the dead of night, looking for a submerged automobile and possibly a drowned human being, was as routine as preaching on Sunday morning. And maybe it was.

She was under water forever, it seemed to Morris. But really only twenty minutes, and when she broke the surface so near to the bank, Morris almost lost his balance. She swam nearer and raised one hand, and Morris lifted her out of the canal; it was not easy, the dark water seemed to suck her back to the depths. She held a thin fishing line in her free hand.

"You found the car," Deputy Donovan said.

"Yes." She blew on her mask and fiddled with the dial on her oxygen tank. "Lucky it's upright on its wheels."

The deputy waited. And so did Morris; he could not imagine any other luck could be left down there in the dark after the young woman's escape.

The diver looked at each of them with her dark eyes. "There's a man down there. A young man. Behind the wheel." She said it softly, as a terrible fact that could not be fixed.

"Oh, shit," said the deputy.

The girl, now silent, stood awkwardly on the land. She'd seemed more at home falling backward into the dark water.

An old wrecker whined its way down the neglected road, then backed up to the canal.

Morris worried about the weight of its cable and its great hook for so slim a girl, but she took it into the water and under it like a fish taking a live bait. The cable played out easily on its huge spool until finally it stopped.

Morris tried not to imagine the scene at the bottom of the canal. The minutes seemed again to take forever. Then the diver broke through the water in a silent explosion of bubbles and was holding to the bulkhead. Morris offered his hand, but she shook her head.

"Ready!" shouted the aging man from the wrecker, who had dragged up remains of the mortal world from every conceivable disaster. The young woman answered with a small shout, and the big winch on the truck began to turn.

Morris dreaded and hungered after the sight of the car and the young man in it. He felt the old visceral stirring for deadly news, the curse of the working reporter at any tragedy.

A bulge appeared in the dark water, as if a great fish were about to surface.

"Hold it!" the diver shouted in a small voice that might have been calling "Out!" on a tennis ball hit beyond the baseline.

The controller of the winch knew what was expected and began to play out a second cable. The diver disappeared with it under the place where the bulge had receded in the water.

She surfaced and now reached up with her hand, and Morris took it, lifting her again, like the catcher in the canal, onto the bank. She smiled a thank-you, which was plenty enough.

"Okay!" the driver called out. "Here we go!"

The bulge rose again in the black water, and then the hood and windshield appeared and the great bulk of the car, exhaling water like some prehistoric creature emptying its gills. The metal frame scraped on the wooden bulkhead, and then the car sat tamely on its wheels, as if very little had happened to it except for the water bleeding at every orifice.

Sheriff Otis Haggard was suddenly standing beside Morris, who had been unaware of his presence. Morris, the sheriff, the deputy, the young woman diver, the old driver of the wrecker, all of them moved reluctantly toward the driver's side of the car.

The diver's flashlight suddenly exploded into the dead face of James "Buddy" Morrow. His eyes had rolled back horrifically into his head, as if to escape the cold depth of the Shinnecock Canal. Only his dark hair seemed strangely alive as the water receded from it, plastering it softly over his forehead.

"Godamighty," Morris said softly.

"You know him?" said Sheriff Haggard.

"The world knows him," Morris said. "Buddy Morrow. He's tied for the second-round lead of the U.S. Open."

"Jesus Christ." The sheriff called on the Deity one more time. There was no answer. "Now we're sittin' on a case of first-degree murder," the sheriff said to himself.

Morris had a great urge to beat his cane against the side of the drowned and innocent automobile. Tears of rage filled his eyes—the tears of regret would come soon enough. Sullivan would be inconsolable. No need to fear tomorrow's sun on Buddy Morrow's face. She wouldn't be giving him a plantation hat for his birthday. Morris was confident the kid hadn't driven to his death from drunkenness or carelessness. He'd been forced off the bridge. The sonofabitch who did it would find no refuge—not on Long Island, not on the mainland, not in this life or the next one. Morris knew, at the moment he thought these things, that they were all melodrama.

Some drunken rich kid probably lost it on the bridge and fled in panic. And the family law firm would get him off without so much as a loss of his driver's license. Still, Morris remembered the scuff marks on the bridge, and the absence of any skid marks. Morrow had never had a chance to hit his brakes. This "chronicle of a death foretold" was no accident. Rage rose up in him again. Let the bastard who did it go to ground wherever he would, however rich his hidey-hole. He would answer for it in the light of day.

Morris had failed to answer Sheriff Haggard, who repeated, "How the hell did he get hooked up with Bidwell's daughter? It would have been hell to pay if she'd drowned, too."

"It'll be hell to pay all over the world, with her alive," Morris said. "I don't know, Otis." It seemed natural to call him by his first name, as a man might instantly identify with a seatmate when fire breaks out in the engine of an airliner. "But young women who didn't know a golf ball from a hailstone fell all over him. He was young, suddenly famous, handsome, seemed to have his head on straight, and about to be plenty rich."

"That'll do it," the sheriff said. "From what they say about Miss Bidwell, it'll be tomorrow before we can get any sense out of her. How did this Morrow expect to win the Open, out chasin' and drinkin' until after midnight?"

"I doubt the drinking, serious drinking," Morris said. "The medical examiner will know soon enough. Morrow wasn't scheduled to tee off today until after one P.M., with the two other leaders. He had twelve hours to get his sleep in. I don't know his habits. Maybe he was a night person. He was by reputation."

"What do you mean?"

"I mean, the popular press saw him as a good-time guy," Morris said. "And he seemed to be. Often in the company of some sweet young thing. But he was no hard-drinking playboy, I'll bet you that. You don't beat the best golfers in America the first two times you tee it up against them, if you're a party drunk. The Open meant millions to Buddy Morrow. I don't think he would have deliberately thrown it all away on the Shinnecock Canal bridge. But the young woman—that's another matter."

"Do you think she's drunk? Or just in shock?"

"Very likely both."

"She's damned lucky to be alive," the sheriff said, looking behind him at the dark water of the canal and up at the height of the bridge with its severed rails.

"It's amazing she got out of the car, in her condition," Morris agreed. He made himself turn and step closer to the automobile that was still hemorrhaging water. He looked carefully through the window.

"Oh, shit," Morris said, overwhelmed by the obvious. "Buddy Morrow was more man than anybody ever imagined."

"What?" The sheriff was distracted by the thought of media madness, which he could already hear, despite the silence of the canal.

"We damned sure know how she got out of the car."

Haggard looked at the streaming automobile as if he expected it to speak.

"Nobody else was down there with her but the kid," Morris said. "Both doors shut and locked. And the passenger window raised. The air conditioner is *still* turned to on. Only *his* window is lowered. She could only have gotten out over him."

Morris shut his eyes against the image of the kid, startled by the sideswiping of his car and the crash into the bridge, free-falling, smashing into the canal, stunned out of all reason, water rising up over the car plunging, sinking to the bottom, terrifyingly aware, tearing his own muscles and fingers to free himself without hope, the girl conscious, sober enough to scream, flailing the shrinking air in the car, the kid un-snapping her seat belt, deciding in an instant, rolling down his window to the dark, cold, unbreathable chill of the water, dragging the girl, pushing her over him out the window, himself down there left alone forever, trapped in the dead silence.

The sheriff knew his thoughts as if he'd said them aloud.

"Poor bastard."

"I'm thinking he was as far as you can get from a bastard," Morris said. The irony of the word would come back and haunt him before the week was over.

No effort was made to free Morrow's body until the county photographer, now on the scene, finished and until the medical examiner and forensic team got there and completed their own dark work.

"I've got to get to a telephone," Morris said, ever the old ex-AP warhorse.

"Get the goddamned story as straight as you can," Sheriff Haggard said, sounding very much down-home-Mississippi. "I don't know golf or golfers, except that the ones on this island are richer than sin and think they run the world."

"I'm going to say there are scuff marks on the bridge, and I think there might have been a collision," Morris said.

"Yeah"—Haggard shook his head—"and the god-damned reporters and cameras will eat me alive until I find out who was driving the other car—*if* there was another car."

Morris touched his hand to his forehead, looking past the sheriff to the car and to the kid still bent over the wheel, as if he'd been taken down from the cross.

CHAPTER NINE

L ucky for Morris and the Associated Press, one old hand was on the overnight sports desk in Manhattan. He knew him well enough to believe him and could clean up dictation while he took it.

"Oh, shit!" he kept saying while Morris dictated. Morris insisted the story go out under the byline of the AP golf writer Pete Ward, whose telephone number in Southampton he now had. Morris called Ward as soon as he hung up to New York. Damn if Ward wasn't already asleep. What was with the new breed, sleeping in the single-digit hours of the night? During Open week? Morris could hear him putting on his clothes with one hand.

"Thanks, Morris." Ward dropped the phone on the floor, putting on his shoes.

"Yeah," Morris said, the one-time heat of a huge story as cold as death in his gut. He dialed Tom Rowe's rented apartment. Of course, he was not in it asleep. He left a tight narrative of what had happened on an answering machine that he hoped Rowe would not be too hung over to check when he stumbled in.·

There were enough cameras and television lights under the bridge to film a movie for Metro Goldwyn Mayer. But Sheriff Haggard was holding his own, giving all possible credit to Deputy Perry Angle for taking charge of the scene and preventing further tragedy on the bridge—and especially to Deputy Mark Donovan, still there, soaking wet and not unhappy with his sudden celebrity, for having jumped off the bridge and pulled the young woman, Tenney Bidwell, out of the canal.

The sheriff didn't have to identify Tenney Bidwell to the Long Island and Manhattan press. Her society profile only added to the media feeding frenzy.

If Morris found himself on Long Island for the next election, the sheriff would get his vote. (But, oh, how impressions could change.) Most sheriffs he had known would have sent the deputies packing and taken all the credit they could suck up toward the next election.

The old man from the wrecker was still prying the body of Buddy Morrow out of the raised automobile. It was taking so long because the medical examiner—a tall, spare, balding, humorless man who had the silent aspect of an undertaker—insisted they not traumatize the body until he had the chance to lay it open from brain to pelvis. The TV cameramen jostled among themselves and with the deputies to catch the grimmest possible profile of the drowned young man still trapped behind the wheel. Finally a medical team was lifting him out and placing him on a stretcher, his damp hair now dangling, still eerily alive.

"Drunk was he, Sheriff?" yelled a young reporter Morris did not recognize. In fact, he saw only a couple of golf writers whose faces were familiar, and he didn't know either of their names.

"I doubt it," the sheriff said over the clatter of questions. "One of your own writers, John Morris, saw the open window on the driver's side of the car, and understood immediately that this boy Morrow had to have rolled down his window and pushed the young woman out before he drowned. I don't imagine he was drunk when he made the effort."

His words shocked even the feeding news sharks. Still, the blood was in the water, and they quickly covered him up with nasty questions. What was a world-class golfer doing out partying in the middle of the night? To hell with whiskey, were they both on drugs? This socialite Tenney Bidwell—was she also dead? Maybe of an overdose? If not, where was she? What did she say happened? Where were her rich parents? What did they have to say?

There was a pause in the madness, then a quiet question: "If the golfer did save her life—what did he say, if anything, with his dying breath?"

Morris felt the hair rise on the back of his neck.

Then someone shouted, "Was it a one-car accident?"

"No," Sheriff Haggard said without hesitation, which was like throwing bloody meat among circling sharks. The sheriff said he'd seen enough scuff marks on the bridge—and streaks of red paint on the driver's side of the blue car just pulled out of the canal—to know there'd been a collision with a second car on the bridge. As soon as his forensics team finished its work, by tomorrow, he'd know what kind of second vehicle they were looking for. He said the second driver had better come forward on his own. Or her own, he amended. He said his office meant to get to the facts of what happened and who was involved. He said perhaps the young woman, Tenney Bidwell, could be of help when she was over the shock of the accident.

Then came a blizzard of unanswerable questions.

Morris eased over to the old wrecker operator, waiting to tow the car away when forensics was finished with its initial examination.

"Will they take the kid's body to Southampton Hospital?" Morris asked.

"Yep," the old man said.

"That would be where they took the girl, too?"

"Yep." He was not a man of many words.

Morris struggled back up the embankment. The eastbound lanes of the bridge were still closed to traffic. He walked across the bridge, cranked up the rental Ford, and joined the traffic being herded over to Highway 27. Sullivan, for sure, had gone with the terrified girl in the ambulance.

Morris found a parking place off Meeting House Lane, near Southampton Hospital. He knew better than to present himself as one of the media, none of whom had yet descended on the hospital. He convinced the head duty nurse to make an in-house phone call to confirm that his *wife*, Julia Sullivan, was with the patient, Tenney Bidwell. Finally he was escorted to a VIP suite. A sheriff's deputy whom Morris did not recognize sat outside the suite. The good sheriff was taking no chances that Tenney Bidwell would be disturbed or, God forbid, threatened before he had a chance to question her.

Sullivan sprang out of her chair and put both arms around Morris's neck, as if his own life had been at risk.

"How's the girl?" Morris asked.

"Out like a dead pipe," Sullivan said. "The doctor put her under. She was so afraid, Morris, she wouldn't let go of me. Even when they took her out of the ambulance and put her in the bed here, she wouldn't let go of my arm, as if I were her only link to the living world."

"Do you think she'll remember what happened?"

Sullivan shook her head. "I'd be amazed. She was incoherent. She kept fighting the air over her face with her hands, as if it were water and couldn't be breathed. I don't know if she'll ever be able to face what happened down there, trapped at the bottom of the canal."

"Who could blame her? Did she say the name of the guy trapped down there with her?" asked Morris.

"No. She made no sense at all," said Sullivan.

"Hang on, pal. It was Buddy Morrow."

"Oh, no, Morris." She held to him as if his strength could change fate.

"Our boy must have been something down there." Morris described the closed door of the car, the one open window on the driver's side. The kid caught under the wheel so terribly, it took experts an hour to get him out. The effort he must have made to save the terrified girl.

Sullivan ignored the tears running down her face. When she could talk, she said, "I knew I liked him. Everything about him. I even knew I loved him, Morris. Young as he was, he would have been one of the old gang. Golf would have loved him. You would have written about him to the last."

"He was for real," Morris said, drying her tears against his jacket, "down there in the dark. Winning the Open would have been a simple matter for him. Too simple to bear thinking about."

After Sullivan recovered her composure, he described the scuff marks on the bridge and the streaks of red paint on the driver's side of the drowned car. "It was no one-car accident. The sheriff said so to the press. He found the streaks of red paint, not me. The other driver'd better come forward. I wouldn't want Sheriff Otis Haggard after my ass on the eastern end of Long Island. Just two bridges across the Shinnecock Canal and the ferry boat off the eastern tip. I don't like the driver's chances of getting his wrecked red vehicle off the island. God help the body shop that repairs it for him."

"Do you think it could have been an accident?" Sullivan's eyes took on more anger than sorrow.

"No. Somebody sideswiped the car and drove it off the bridge. No way the kid was drunk and lost it. I'd bet downtown Denver on that. The medical examiner will know soon enough. Somebody slammed his own vehicle into the kid's, knocking it off the bridge."

"Why?"

"That marvelous, timeless, human verity that will never let you down," Morris said. "Greed, greed, and greed. The kid stood to make millions for himself and more millions for others. I think we better stir among the *others*."

"He best hope the sheriff finds him before I find him," Sullivan said quietly, lethally.

"Was the girl, Bidwell, drunk?" Morris asked.

"Sure. She reeked of scotch. And hashish. I shouldn't be surprised what they find in her purse, if they find her purse. But the boy was no drunk. No druggie. His hands were as steady as a young Hogan's. What was he doing with the likes of her, Morris?"

"A sexy lady," Morris said, "an occupational hazard for professional golfers, like suicide for poets. But something about his being with her so late seems . . . oddly out of joint with his purpose for being here, having come from the ends of the earth, from total anonymity, for this moment." Morris shook his head. "Kingdoms have been lost for a pair of legs."

Sullivan almost smiled, despite the anger and sorrow in her face. "I wonder where Buddy and the girl had been?"

"Good question. Surely she'll remember that."

"And who else was there with them?"

"In a red vehicle?"

"Maybe a jealous lover?" Sullivan said.

"The older man who climbed out of the limousine on Broadway, maybe he wasn't so bored after all. Or maybe an angry young woman from South Africa or Jakarta? Could be."

"I hadn't thought of a young woman," Sullivan said.

"I'll stick with my old favorite motive rampant among advanced civilizations: overwhelming, everlasting, most-human *greed*."

"On that cheerful note, I promised I would spend the night on this sofa," Sullivan said. "Nobody can reach the girl's parents. Will you bring me some clean things to wear in the morning?"

"I think you look pretty swift in that black cocktail dress." He stepped nearer.

"Oh, no, Morris. Not here. It isn't done in hospitals."

Morris gave her his best palm-out British salute and turned on his cane and left. Waiting for the elevator, he couldn't put it out of his mind what the medical examiner was doing in the hospital morgue at that moment with the kid. Life—and death—could be a kick in the ass.

Sullivan struggled for her breath, called out Morris's name, beat the air with her hands until they found his. Now she was almost awake in the near dark. The hands were comforting, but not John Morris's.

"Hold me . . . Julia . . . Sullivan," said the voice—a woman's voice, a woman whose face and even the fringes of her hair were smeared with tears.

Sullivan pushed herself upright, still in a sleep-drunk daze, and took the strange woman in her arms without speaking, as she had done, it seemed years ago, on the bridge. Sullivan held her for a long time until she was startled to recognize the reddish-brown sheen of hair, shining in the dim lamplight, to be that of her new-found fairway pal Jerry Martin.

Her weeping slowed, but not into sleep.

"How . . ." Sullivan began, holding the strong but trembling hands in her own.

"They . . . interrupted . . . the . . . television," Jerry was able to say in separate words, as if they explained everything. She wept again for a long time.

Sullivan was now absolutely awake. She looked at her watch. It was 3 A.M. She feared for the woman who had seemed to her so athletic, and so strong, and so ironically amused about the two of them, women of a certain age, following a beautiful kid golfer in the U.S. Open. What terrible infatuation had brought her here in such a state? How had she got by the head nurse? She risked the question: "Did you . . . actually know him?"

Jerry Martin swallowed her tears. She said into Sullivan's shoulder, with a voice suddenly as firm as the new strength in her hands: "He was my husband."

"Oh, God." The holy powers had rarely been called on so often in one tragic night on Long Island. Sullivan squeezed her to hold back the pain. Her own mind raced after the improbable idea of young Buddy Morrow married to this somewhat older, seemingly independent woman, Jerry Martin—and the young girl socialite asleep in the next room, who had been with him in the automobile when he drowned. Sullivan knew only enough to keep silent.

Jerry knew exactly what she was thinking and looked back to the closed door of the bedroom. "The girl? She meant nothing. She was a last dash of color in the packaging."

Sullivan had not a clue as to what she meant.

Jerry laid her head back against Sullivan's shoulder. In the near dark of the silent room, she might have been Sullivan's younger sister the night their father died.

"I pushed Buddy out the door myself," said Jerry, unable to keep the words inside her, "I promised him she was the last bimbo window dressing he would have to be seen with. The myth of the 'bachelor wunderkind' of golf had exhausted its usefulness. We would sign one last contract, and he could come out of the closet as a married man." A glimmer of a smile crossed her tear-stained face.

"Buddy called me from the party," she said. "He always did, when he could. He said Tenney Bidwell could barely walk, with what she had been smoking and drinking. If only he hadn't driven her home. He'd never have crossed the canal. Our rooms are on the western side of the canal, in West Tiana. I only wish I had been the one with him when they killed him. I'd have never left him down there alone. And I'd never have to miss him, ever again." She was unable to cry. She had no tears left. Now she did smile. "The game was all but over. We'd won already."

Sullivan could understand only half of what she was saying. What "they" had killed him? She wished for daylight so that Morris would come—and bring the sheriff. What "game" was "all but over"? The Open was only half over. There was still the terror of Saturday and Sunday to come. But it was a faint terror compared with a young man drowning in the dark.

Jerry Martin was weeping again. Sullivan soothed her with sounds and not words.

"They . . . wouldn't let me see him," Jerry said.

"There's plenty of time," Sullivan said, understanding that the wife, when known, would have to identify the body.

And then Jerry began again to talk, this time about the past.

Morris awoke facedown in his clothes, his feet swollen in his shoes. The silence of the room trapped the memory of the silence, the horror, of the canal. He hadn't smoked in twenty years, but he would have sacrificed a small automobile for a cigarette. The need passed in the shower.

He carefully packed a blouse and skirt and underthings and flat, practical shoes, and all of Sullivan's morning makeup kit, with its mysterious vials and tubes and jars and brushes.

The sun was just rising over the Atlantic, bringing a new day to the eastern edge of the continent, which could damned well use a new day after last night.

He parked Sullivan's fresh clothes with the hospital reception desk. He didn't want to face her until after he'd visited the dark work in the morgue, if he could talk his way down there.

Sheriff Otis Haggard, hat in hand, came through the hospital door, leaving a small gaggle of early-morning news media croaking out unanswered questions.

Morris could see that the sheriff was wearing the same uniform as the night before; his unslept face looked like an unmade bed.

"Mind if I go down with you to the morgue?" Morris asked.

"If your stomach can stand it," Haggard said. "All we're gonna learn is the boy drowned."

"You'll know eventually if he was drunk or on drugs," Morris said.

"He was sober enough before it was over," the sheriff said, nodding for Morris to follow him. "Keep your mouth shut. I'll ask the questions. This pathologist, a nasty bastard already, has been working all night. My orders. He won't be happy."

Morris nodded.

Morgues of the world share the same chemical smell, the same well-damp cold, the same rolling steel furniture, the same harsh fluorescent lighting, as if death could be kept in its place with an absence of human warmth.

The medical examiner, as tall and spare and bald and humorless as the room, sat with his long legs crossed, smoking a cigarette, as if he'd never cut into hundreds of diseased lungs. He stuffed the last of the cigarette into a half-empty Coca-Cola bottle and stood up, a couple of inches taller than the sheriff or Morris.

Haggard did not bother to introduce them.

"Drowned. No doubt about that," the pathologist said.

"Alcohol, drugs?" the sheriff said.

The doctor just barely shook his thin head. "Had the lab run tests in the night. Like you ordered," he accused the sheriff. "Not a beer's worth of alcohol in his blood. No cocaine. None of the ordinary addictive shit we see. Just some salad makings in his stomach, the lettuce all but digested." The doctor lit another cigarette as if to show his own contempt for mortality.

"Healthy otherwise?" Haggard said.

"Oh, yeah. In excellent shape." The tubercular-thin doctor paused for effect: "For a forty-one-year-old man."

"Say what?" The sheriff's hat rose in his hand as if it, too, had heard incorrectly.

"Some *kid* golfer," the doctor said, laughing, choking on his cigarette. "The dead son of a bitch was as old as I am."

Morris closed his eyes as if to improve his own hearing. He stepped past the thin doctor, who was still choking or chortling and coughing up phlegm, which he spit in a waste barrel.

Morris looked down on the dead face of James "Buddy" Morrow. It was so pale, so bloodless, so without any human expression that he might have been any age or dead for a hundred years.

"How do you know his age, so absolutely?" Morris said, violating his promise of silence.

"A dozen ways," the doctor said, having cleared his throat. "You can see the tucks under his chin and under his eyes." He pointed to thin scars with a scalpel, as if lecturing to a couple of medical interns. He pried open the mouth. "All the teeth are capped. Damned good job. No jackleg dentist." He ran his fingers, somehow obscenely, through the seemingly alive hair at Morrow's temples. "A touch of dye here. But the rest of his hair is unusually thick and still naturally dark. He was born with the hair and the thick skin that took a tan in the sun."

The doctor lifted up one of his hands. "Even under the tan, you can see the veins working in the back of the hand." The doctor chortled again, as if it were great sport to catch time in its disguise.

"Still, young men have tucks, and cap their teeth, and dye their temples. How can you say he was forty-one years old with any precision?" Morris asked skeptically.

The doctor lit another cigarette; he might have been firing up his imagination. He threw a towel off the genitalia of the corpse, revealing a great gash in his groin. He had cut through the strong cartilage of a disk that joined the separate halves of the pelvis. He turned and reached into a plastic bag and pulled out a small section of bone. He scraped the one-inch-long, rather flat piece of bone even finer with his scalpel.

Now he held it up. "You are looking at the right pubic symphysis." He himself looked at it as though it were a rare jewel of Mediterranean antiquity, and he an Egyptologist.

"There is no more *absolute*"—the doctor used Morris's own defining word—"measure of a human's age than this symphyseal surface, where the two halves of the pelvis come together. It becomes more fine-grained, more deeply pitted, from first adolescence to late middle age. It does this in recognizable stages. No one can say why."

The doctor enjoyed holding a simple magnifying glass over the surface of the bone. Morris and the sheriff could easily see the fine grain and the pitted nature of the bone. But they could only look at each other with expressions of mutual ignorance.

"Any informed pathologist will tell you this is the right pubic symphysis of a forty-one-year-old man, give or take no more than a year, possibly two. I say forty-one. I stand by it."

John Morris leaned on his cane in the winter chill of the light-blasted room. He looked at the scalpel-ravaged corpse and thought, *Who are you there, lying on the gurney, Buddy Morrow? Who knew you to kill you? And why?*

CHAPTER TEN

Jerry Martin told her story of Buddy Morrow, her head resting on Sullivan's shoulder until Sullivan's left arm fell entirely asleep. She told the story as if she'd read it in a book and committed it to memory. Sullivan did not move and tried not to interrupt, no matter how surprised, even amazed, she was, for fear of breaking the spell of the narrative:

I met Buddy in Acapulco, Mexico. In August, four years ago, in a small bar off the lobby of the Princess Hotel. He was the bartender. He didn't go by the nickname Buddy, or even the name Jim Morrow. But I'll try not to get ahead of myself.

I was an account executive with the Dallas advertising firm Tracey Locke, but before that I had been an English teacher at a junior college in Oklahoma City. I also coached the women's golf team, if you like coincidence. I loved the

*kids. No money in it, of course. And no long-range challenge.
But it did keep me fit.*

*I was in my twenties when I met a guy with a big food
company, traveling out of Oklahoma City. We hit it off for a
while, until I learned he was married. That kind of guy.*

*But he was a big noise with the company at an early age. I
learned a lot about the world of supermarkets and especially of
packaged goods. It seemed fun to me, outrageously inventive,
the idea of taking something as simple, as universal, as rice—
and packaging it in such a way as to sell it as an original
product. We broke up, the guy and myself. When I learned he
was married, I dumped him.*

*But by then, I'd met an advertising executive, a bright
man with Tracey Locke, who worked this same Oklahoma
City food account. He was an older man, well educated. We
read some of the same books—laughed at the same things.
Sometimes when he was in town, he called me for dinner.
Never closer than just friends. He had grandchildren. He
would show their pictures to waiters and strangers and company presidents.*

*I woke up one morning and called him. Asked him how
did you apply for a job with Tracey Locke? He said to send
him a letter and put in it my interest in and knowledge of
supermarkets and packaged goods. He returned my first letter
with edits and suggestions. After the second letter I got an
interview with the agency. I even got the job.*

*Not so surprisingly, I started out a rookie copywriter on
the Oklahoma City food account. Time passed. The older man
retired, and with his blessing I replaced him as account executive on the Oklahoma City account. The guy I'd known had
long since left the company, still married, still lying about it, I
suppose.*

*We had some good years at Tracey Locke. I worked on
many accounts but always seemed to specialize in packaged
goods.*

*Four years ago we held a planning session for account
executives in Acapulco. In truth it was a boondoggle reward*

for having a good year. We planned for an hour in the morning what we were going to do for fun in the afternoon. Oh, we did some work. They're a good outfit, Tracey Locke.

I was thirty-six years old—a spinster by Texas standards. I'd known my share of guys. Not so many in the last few years. Sex didn't seem to be my best thing. Maybe I knew too much about packaging. I think I was waiting for the real goods inside the package. Maybe I flatter myself. Nobody was throwing rings and bouquets my way.

I came back to the hotel from a swim in the Pacific early one afternoon. I looked a mess, my hair wet, an old robe over my still-wet swimsuit, dripping water on the barstool. This guy was behind the bar, his back to me. Lean build, dark hair, just a bit gray over the temples. I'm alone, feeling maybe a little sorry for myself though I'd just been given a nice raise, and he turns and puts both hands on the bar and looks at me as if I'm the most favored customer in the house—which I was—it was early, as I said, and I was the only customer in the bar. He smiled. I could see his teeth were going bad, even in the dim light. It didn't bother me. It was still a nice smile.

"My favorite customer," he said, "my first one. The drink's on the house. What would please you?"

He had a warm voice. I couldn't pick up the accent. It wasn't exactly American. It wasn't English. It wasn't Australian. It wasn't South African. I'd run into a lot of accents in the world of packaged goods, which circles the globe. His voice might have been American aged in English oak. I don't know. You've heard him speak. It was the same voice.

I'll try to remember just what we said to one another over the years. I've kept it in my mind like a diary. In fact, I've kept a diary.

I said, "I think a Bombay gin and tonic with a touch of lime."

"Done," he said, mixing the drink with easy skill, an economy of motion. Very much the way he swung a golf club. But again, I'm getting ahead of myself.

He watched to see if I wanted to be alone. I didn't. He said, "You're from Texas." It was not a question.

"Did my wet, scraggly hair and burned complexion give me away?"

"The easy roll of your words." He looked at me as if he could see into my past. "I'm guessing the Hill Country."

I raised my glass. "Outside New Braunfels. I grew up on a sheep ranch. If this was television, you'd be winning a set of living room furniture. How on earth do you know that?"

"I can see you, a red-haired little girl, swimming at Landa Park in the San Pedro River."

"You know the Hill Country."

"I was born in San Antonio." His voice took on the vowels of the Texas ranch country outside that old bilingual city. Tears jumped in my eyes, shocking me. He reached over with his clean dish towel and caught the tears as naturally, as unintrusively, as if he'd known me all my life.

We became friends from that instant. Even after we became lovers, even after we were married, we were still friends.

He could have taken me to bed that first day. I think he knew it. But he didn't. We talked at the bar for half an hour before another customer came in. I told him what it was like growing up on a sheep ranch, with a father who read everything and a mother who rebuilt diesel engines on tractors. I told him what I did in the advertising world. What I'd done before I joined Tracey Locke. Among other things, that I'd coached the women's golf team at an Oklahoma City junior college.

He slung his dish towel over one shoulder as an act of disbelief. "You must be kidding me," he said. He reached behind the bar and handed me—of all things—a pitching wedge.

It cracked me up, a bartender with a pitching wedge. "What do you do with this in the bar—conk drunks over the head?"

"No bad drunks in the Princess Hotel. They just fall asleep and have to be helped to their rooms. Let's see your swing."

It was an ancient Wilson Staff wedge, a Walter Hagen model. "I haven't played in a year," I said. He just folded his arms with his dish towel over one shoulder and waited for me to take my stance.

I put the club behind my back, each end tucked under an elbow, and torqued my upper body gently from left to right, loosening up as if I were really about to tee off in the bar. I stood up to the imaginary ball. The club was wonderfully old but had a new grip. It was a men's model but felt good in my hands. I've always had strong hands, growing up working on a ranch. I put a rather clean swing on the club, just nipping the carpet, shifting my weight, keeping my balance.

He applauded. Then he slapped both hands on top of the bar in appreciation.

"Well done! Very well done!" He stepped around the bar and gave me a spontaneous hug, despite my wet suit.

He took the club and duplicated my stance, the dish towel still draped over one shoulder. "You carry your hands a bit low," he said, soling the club, to show me. "But that's not all bad, and your swing, your balance—you're a player. Tomorrow afternoon. I'm off. We'll play. Let me see your feet."

I lifted up one foot, pleased that my legs were my one swell asset. But he ignored the leg.

"Size ten. A real foot. No fake, dainty thing. Good. I'll bring some shoes and clubs and pick you up outside the lobby. How about one P.M.?"

"I don't know your name."

"A bartender by any other name," he said.

"Is a golfer." My mind made itself up. I didn't even think. I said, "I'll play. I'll play badly, but I'll play. My name is Jerry Martin."

He took my hand in his own, which was surprisingly wide and strong. He said rather formally, "My name is Clarence Noland."

He stepped back behind the bar.

"That's it? Your name? You've got my entire life story."

"That's what bartenders are for, documenting life stories. My own? My life would bore the tonic out of the bottles. We'll play golf. Then I'll take you to dinner at a place tourists never go and tell you the grim little narrative of my life. You can package it in your memory like a box of grits for sale on the shelf."

He was there the next day at 1 P.M. He pushed open the passenger door on the most disreputable old Plymouth, rusting on its four tires. I had to laugh. But I got in.

"Don't laugh at my Plymouth," he said. "It's almost one of a kind."

"I believe it. Did you dig it out of a junkyard in Mexico City?"

"Almost," he said, hitting the accelerator and spinning us away from the hotel. The interior was surprisingly clean, and the engine had a gutsy kick to it.

"Like your mother, the farmer, I've rebuilt a few engines in my time," he said. I was to learn he had done one of almost everything in his time. He was easy to be with. Didn't try to impress me with how well he knew Acapulco. But I had a hard time saying his name: Clarence. He didn't look like a Clarence.

I assured him I was free for the rest of the day.

He drove as fast as the road would allow, into the town of Tlalpán, about fifty miles south of Mexico City. He pulled up to the bag drop at the Club de Golf Mexico. I was surprised. It was so obviously a rich man's club. The caddy picking up the bags couldn't have been happier to see him. They slung a bit of Spanish, and both laughed at something.

"I'm welcome here," he said. "From time to time I give lessons when the pro is out of town or playing himself." He told me the course had been built in 1951. Designed by Percy Clifford, who won the championship of Mexico six times, and an American architect, Laurence Hughes.

"It's seven thousand feet high," Buddy said. "The ball

travels twenty percent farther than at sea level. But it is a world championship course to test your nerves and your ability."

The shoes fit. That he brought me.

"I'd keep the legs, too," he said. I was wearing walking shorts. If you have red hair, you blush easily, even if you aren't embarrassed. I wasn't embarrassed.

The caddy, a young Mexican boy, had propped our bags up on the practice range. The range was lush and would have fed a hundred sheep.

Buddy handed me a glove from his bag. Well, his name wasn't yet Buddy. But the glove also fit. "Don't tell me," I said, "you once sold women's clothes."

"I don't deny it."

I was eager to hit a golf ball. I'd missed it. I teed a range ball up just above the grass. I made a few practice swings, addressed the ball, and clipped it off the tee with a slight draw.

"Oh, yes," he said. "Now I know where you got the swing. You had to be one of Mr. Penick's protégées. Lucky he was just up the road from New Braunfels, in Austin. A great teacher, Harvey Penick. Always begin your practice 'clipping the ball off the tee.' Even with a short iron. Your father was wise to send you to him."

"My mother," I said, amazed that he could look at my swing and know who'd taught me.

"Your mother of the diesel engines. I should have guessed. But I never favored the draw," he said, as if to himself.

Now I crossed my arms and stared at him as he twisted his torso a bit and bent forward . . . he could place his open palms on the grass, easily. Then he stood over the ball with a wedge, his stance a bit open, his grip weaker than most amateurs could dominate, his left thumb directly on top of the shaft.

He took the club back with his left hand and arm, his left arm quite straight, his elbows so close, they might have been lashed together, the right elbow folding at the top of the backswing, his chin hitting against the top of his left shoulder. Then, with his hips leading his arms, his hands, his legs driving forward, the club lashed through the ball in one blinding explosion that only a sophisticated camera could catch, the ball rising off the face of the wedge, climbing, drifting, then fading ever so slightly, dying on the grass.

His clubhead left a divot as thin as a dollar bill and half as long. All that pent-up fury controlled and released to nip the ball off the earth.

Ball after ball climbed into the air, the trajectory changing only with the angle of the clubface as he moved through his entire bag of clubs. His stance widened more than you might expect of an expert when he swung the driver. His hips began the downswing an instant before the backswing was completed, putting an enormous flex in the shaft and tremendous velocity in the clubhead that detonated the ball off the tee. Always with the same quiet fade running through the shot, the ball dying into the middle of the practice range.

There's never been but one Hogan. And I've only seen his swing on film. But it was eerie. Watching Buddy strike balls was like being drawn back into time, only the driver head was metal and not persimmon. But his swing seemed natural and not mechanical, as if he'd invented it himself. As you know, Julia, he did create it from age ten, from Hogan's book.

We played. When he swung, he was sealed inside himself. Not aware of me or our caddy or the beauty of the course, which had been carved out of a grove of cedar, pine, cypress, and eucalyptus trees. As soon as his ball was on the ground, he was fun to be with. I hit a few good shots. He loved them, as if he'd hit them himself. When I skulled a wedge or hooked a drive, he was not impatient. He only offered a tip when I asked him. After a few holes he understood my swing far better than I ever had.

His own game was so deceptively predictable. He faded his drive into the fairway, cut his iron onto the green, and putted his ball to the hole. His putts died at the hole. Not one to charge past it. He quoted Bobby Jones: "One hundred percent of the putts that go past the hole did not go in." I loved it how he knew the literature of golf.

His fades seemed . . . what's the word . . . inevitable. When the draw was the only reasonable shot off the tee or to the flag, he had to work harder, became a bit more mechanical. But most often he executed the draw to the target. A few shots failed to draw at all. And now and then, setting up for his regular fade, he would come over the top of the ball: the awful "double-cross," a disastrous hook when you are playing for a fade. His expression never changed. But he made practice swings each time until he was satisfied with his correction.

The course, from the championship tee, played to a full 7,250 yards. The shortest par 4 was 425 yards. The longest, 470 yards. But at that altitude Buddy's ball seemed to stay in the air forever. He reached the par-4 greens easily.

We didn't keep a scorecard, but I kept his score in my head. He was 5 under par on the narrow, tough, treelined course, which had hosted the 1966 World Amateur Team Championships. And that's with three bogeys. He made an eagle on the damned tough par-5 2nd hole of 563 yards. His three-wood second shot threaded the trees into the narrow opening to the green. He dropped a fifteen-foot putt. The man could play.

I put my glove back in the long pocket of his golf bag, which had seen better days. There was a book in the pocket, a paperback that had also seen better days. I could see the title: The Good Soldier, by Ford Madox Ford. That great dance of the English language was a rare thing for a one-time English teacher to find in the bag of a bartender-golfer down in Mexico. And I already had a weakness for him. Isn't that what Gertrude Stein said—she "had a weakness for Hemingway"? When he was twenty-four. Clarence Noland, like myself, was a long way past twenty-four.

We had a beer in the mixed grill. I said, "Why aren't you playing golf for a living?"

He quoted Hogan, of course. The exact quote escapes me.

But Hogan knew that tournament golf was a lifetime away from social golf. The terrible pressure of a tournament.

I said, "Of course, the terrible pressure was what Hogan lived for." I asked him—I found it impossible to call him Clarence—I asked him, "Who are you?"

Sullivan's left arm was now dead asleep, but she didn't dare change position or shift Jerry Martin's head from her shoulder. Buddy's life might have been her own, Jerry knew it so intimately. She told his story carefully, as if as long as she was telling it, he was still among the living . . . in the near-dark of the hospital suite.

Buddy cranked up the Plymouth. He said, "You game for some real Mexican food?"

"Always."

"Good. We'll go to my place." I didn't know what he had in mind. I didn't care. He drove back to Acapulco, past the high-rent tourist district. Turned down to a beach I couldn't find with a road map. Stopped right at the Pacific Ocean beside a strange little hut called Abron's. The restaurant was just that, a hut. Run by a man and his wife and a bunch of their kids. The kids climbed all over Buddy. Out on the beach were hammocks under open tin roofs. That's where Buddy lived, on the beach, in one of the hammocks. He had bathing privileges in the hut, unlike the others, mostly college kids, who had found the place. The food was wonderful. I'd never tasted such enchiladas in my life. Served in old, traditional granite bowls. They wouldn't let Buddy pay. Because of me, I'm sure. Because I was with him. They made a big fuss over me. It was more fun than the Princess Hotel.

Buddy said, "Come outside. We can watch the greatest sunset God left behind Him." We propped up, side by side, in hammocks. The sun went down into the sea like a sexual experience. Or maybe it was just the way I was feeling. Nobody else was around. The college kids were off to chase the

Mexican night. Buddy lay back in the growing dark and began to tell me who he was:

"I'm thirty-seven. On the downhill road to thirty-eight."

I didn't mean to interrupt him. I couldn't help it. I said, "I didn't know this was confess-your-age time. I'm thirty-six. On the uphill road to thirty-seven. My face is older. I'm sorry. I love the sun."

"Your face, as you well know, is strong and damned appealing."

I didn't interrupt again for a long time.

"I told you I was born in San Antonio. I don't know where. My mother's name was Mary Noland. I never knew my father, or even his name. They never married. My mother met Master Sergeant James Morrow in a San Antonio bar. He was stationed at Fort Sam Houston. They got married the same week. I was not yet three years old. I can barely remember my mother's face. Her short yellow hair. She took up with another man within six months. We never saw her again. I don't know where she came from or where she went to.

"Sergeant Morrow, my old man, was all right. Not so big, but wiry. A plenty tough guy. Did two tours in Vietnam. Won a box of medals he only wore on parades. He was Old Army—a man, off duty, to drink until he was drunk. He was not a mean drunk. He raised me. He never hit me once. He raised me with a long line of maids and nannies, speaking many languages. Took me all over the world like a set of luggage with legs. Never said my mother's name. Never said anything against her. When I was older I asked him who she was, what happened to her. He told me straight. He didn't know where she came from, who her people were. He didn't know what happened to her. She just called and said she was leaving—with another man. She never came back. As far as he knew, my old man and my mother were still married. He had no idea who my real father was. But he made it plain: I belonged to him. It was enough for me.

"Fort Sam Houston had a championship golf course. They

played the Texas Open on it back in the nineteen fifties, when Jimmy Demaret and Tommy Bolt and those guys were still around. Wish I'd been old enough to see them play. My old man never picked up a club. I found one somewhere when I was about seven. I hit rocks in the yard. Never hit a golf ball with it. Never had one.

"The sergeant was posted to Panama. I remember it green, like a garden. I didn't run with the other army brats so much. Never did. But I explored the whole base. Found the golf course. Hung around it. They had a clinic for kids older than me. I watched. I didn't try it, but I hung around. Got to know the pro, a staff sergeant. Did some odd jobs for him. Cleaned shoes in the pro shop. He let me hit a few balls. They were easier to hit than rocks. He didn't offer to teach me. Afterward I knew I was lucky he hadn't.

"I was ten. I liked books. My old man, when he was sober, read. Read magazines. Never finished high school but liked to read Time magazine. Talked aloud about what he was reading. Some words he couldn't pronounce. He'd look 'em up in the dictionary. Taught me how to do it. He was big for President Kennedy, even if he'd been a navy swab. He'd been in the Big War.

"The sergeant always treated me like I was already grown. Never wanted me to go Army. But he had plenty of Army manuals around, whatever place we lived in. I figured if you could learn Army in a book, you could learn golf. I went to the Panama base PX. They had a few instructional books: how to catch cheats at poker, improve your vocabulary, how to talk to God, that sort of thing. They had this one copy of Hogan's book with Mr. Wind. And the great drawings by Anthony Ravielli. I'd never heard of Hogan, of course. The drawings were like they were alive.

"The copy was marked down to four dollars. I had two dollars saved. My birthday was coming up. The sergeant couldn't believe I wanted a book. At age ten. It pleased him. He went down to the PX with me and bought it. On my birthday, sitting by my bed, was a set of junior clubs. Used.

Sort of rusty. Slick, worn grips. But I loved 'em. I still have 'em.

"I looked at the drawings. I read Hogan's book every day. Kept it in my bed at night. I looked up a lot of words: 'supinate the left wrist.' Supinate is a tough word to understand. Half the pros on the tour couldn't tell you what it means. But it's critical to understanding Hogan's swing. The drawings, not the dictionary, helped me know what he was talking about. But it took several years.

"Now I hit balls every day. The pro let me, if I picked up two hours' worth of balls off the driving range. I didn't try to play. Sometimes during the week nobody would be on the course. But it didn't make sense to me, at age ten. To try to play before I knew how to hit the ball. I hit balls for a year. I was eleven the first time I played nine holes. I used the members' tees, not the championship tees. I shot 41. I could replay every shot of that first round. I skied my drive on the first tee, I was so pumped. But I recovered with a fairway wood to the front of the green. My chip shot was too long, and I two-putted for a bogey. My short game was not good. My chips were erratic. I'd been working on my grip, my stance, my backswing, the plane of my swing, the downswing. Not on getting the ball in the hole. But I did make a birdie on a par 5.

"I couldn't stop talking about it to my old man, the sergeant. He didn't know what a 41 meant. But he believed it was good. He encouraged me. If I was on the golf course, he didn't have to worry about me. Especially as I got older. Army kids can find a lot of ways to get in trouble, especially in somebody else's country. Me, I just found a golf course.

"To this day I don't know exactly what the sergeant's job was. He never talked about it. He was good at it, or the Army wouldn't have put up with his drinking. Not that he was drunk during the working day. But the Army works on weekends, too. Some weekends he didn't sober up until Monday morning. I don't know what he was trying to drown. He was not a man to talk. I don't believe he missed my mother.

He never spoke of her. I do believe he had a dangerous, cut-ting-edge job, training guys to go behind enemy lines, or to go where they might not come back alive. He often came home in the daylight hours, his face smudged black as soot. A big knife on his hip. Hungry. Especially thirsty.

"Wherever the sergeant was stationed, I found golf courses. Wonderful, lush ones in England, of course. Even got to play in Scotland. Took the train up by myself. I was four-teen. Played Carnoustie, the hardest damned course I ever teed it up on—in a forty-mile-an-hour wind. Couldn't afford a caddy. Carried my own bag. Didn't break 80 where Hogan set the Carnoustie record, winning the only British Open he ever played in. I found golf courses in places you couldn't imagine. I played on sand greens in North Africa. They packed the sand down and oiled it. Scotland was a still day compared to the winds that blew in the Falkland Islands. The ocean there doesn't have the highest waves in the world by accident. I was sixteen and strong. I hit a ball four hundred yards downwind. I played in Thailand. You didn't go after your ball in the rough—cobras. In France, in Normandy, the 1920 courses kept the grass so long in the fairways, every shot was a flyer; the grass was cut closer in the American cemetery on the landing grounds.

"My old man, the sergeant, never saw me hit a golf ball. Always asked how I did. First time I broke 70 from the championship tees, even he understood that was a watershed score. Broke out the wine bottle and poured me a glass. Of course, he poured himself three glasses. That was all right with me. He was not a mean drunk. I like a drink myself. Never had to have one, thank God.

"When he was stationed in Vietnam, and other countries where I couldn't go, I stayed in San Antonio, at Fort Sam Houston. I learned the game there on a serious golf course. In the wind. The same wind that shaped Hogan and Nelson and Demaret and Trevino and those guys. If you can work the ball with and against and across the wind, you can play golf.

"The sergeant would be gone, maybe a month, maybe six

months. I never heard from him, or he from me. In my teens I had housekeepers. They came and went. None of them would remember me. It's true, I came from everywhere and nowhere. I liked it. Being on my own, signing my own report cards. When I was lonesome, I read. I liked the girls well enough. Didn't hustle them. Didn't have to, to tell the truth. But mostly when I wasn't on the golf course, I read. I liked fiction, I liked travel books, I even liked Churchill's History of the English-Speaking People. *I just read. Mystery novels. Spy novels. I liked John le Carré,* The Spy Who Came in from the Cold. *I didn't try to remember or even understand everything I read. I just checked out a book in the base library. Let it roll through me. Didn't care much for school, except for the reading. That got me by. I did okay. I knew Hogan turned professional when he was nineteen. I meant to do the same.*

"Never played in an amateur golf tournament. Didn't interest me. Most countries I was in didn't have 'em. I loved to play for money. Hotshot kids in Texas learned the hand in their pockets was mine. They avoided me like a cobra in the rough. Here they were trying to win some high school tournament in San Antonio and get a scholarship up to UT, but carrying their bag on an everyday round in the afternoon, they didn't want any of my ass by the time I was fifteen. Not to brag—just the way it was. Older guys took me on. A few of them cleaned my plow. But not by the time I was seventeen.

"The draft was still on. I didn't want to get drafted. I joined the Army the day I was eighteen. The sergeant came home shocked to see me about to report for basic training. The only time in our lives we got drunk together. Every Army instructor I ever had knew my old man or knew who he was. They didn't let up on me. I know they told him how I did. I did okay. I could Army. Where did I spend my two years? At Fort Sam Houston. The general loved golf. Knew my old man, too. But it was the golf. I played seven days a week. The general got away every chance he could. He and I never lost a match. I took care of the ex-college boys, and the regular Army guys weren't about to beat the general.

"I was discharged. Never served in Vietnam. Never felt guilty about it. Like Muhammad Ali, I 'never had nothin' against no Vietcong.' My old man, the sergeant, kept his silence. But I never felt he wanted me to volunteer for Vietnam. He'd done war duty enough for us both.

"After the Army I was going to try for my PGA playing card. Didn't know exactly how to go about it. I was staying in the sergeant's apartment at Fort Sam Houston. Got a knock on the door. Two guys in dress uniforms. With a telegram from the Army. I knew goddamned well the sergeant was dead. They couldn't tell me anything. I went to the general at Fort Sam Houston. He knew already. He told me it was hush-hush stuff, all of it over his head. He lied. His aide, a major who had served with my old man, did tell me he had been lost with his outfit in a winter storm, on a hush-hush deal at the Arctic pole. He couldn't say what they were doing. Said even the general didn't know. I never believed him. They never found the bodies.

"I got a ten-thousand-dollar check from the Army. His insurance. The old man didn't leave anything else but the clothes in his closet. And his sidearms. No diary. No letters. No family photographs, not even of his wedding day with my mother. No nothing. I never knew who his people were. Only that he came from Kentucky. I doubt he ever wrote a letter in his life. I was surprised how much I hated the old man being dead. I'd seen so little of him. But it was like we'd been equals. I can't explain it. He never talked to me like I was a kid.

"I had the ten thousand dollars. That September, 1972. Got my application to apply for the next PGA qualifying school. It was coming up that winter in California. I had all fall to get ready, and I was playing well. It was a Thursday, in the morning. All I did was pick up the old man's trunk to take his clothes to the Goodwill. And I ruptured a disk in my lower back. A pain ran down my left leg like an electrical *wire. I thought I'd torn a muscle. Not so lucky. I went to the doctors at Fort Sam Houston. They saw me, even though I was out of the Army. The operation for a ruptured disk in 1974 was a bitch. It still is. The scar tissue it leaves often strangles the sciatic nerve even tighter and heightens the pain down your leg. The doctors advised against an operation. They prescribed rest, and then the classic Williams back exercises.*

"*I couldn't rest for the pain. The back exercises made it worse. I couldn't lean over to putt, much less strike a golf ball. Then the pain would diminish. The exercises would help. I would be back on the practice tee, hitting golf balls. The pain would come back down my leg until it drove me a little crazy. Finally I sold my golf clubs. For fifty dollars. To hell with it.*

"*I still had the ten thousand. I started on a trip around the world I had known following the old man. This time without the golf. I bribed a merchant marine license in Panama. Caught a dirty, leaky ship sailing for North Africa. I couldn't do any heavy lifting. But I was a self-taught mechanic. Always had an old piece of a car I kept running after I was sixteen. Every old, sorry merchant ship needs every mechanic it can get ahold of. Caught a Greek ship up to Rotterdam. Saw six-foot-tall Dutch women unload a cargo of lumber on the Mohawk River. It hurt my back to watch 'em.*

"*Worked my way to South Africa. Learned how to cadge—or bribe—a work permit in damned near every language. Never spent my ten-thousand-dollar nest egg. Tended bar in Johannesburg. Hard to believe there could be so much hatred in so beautiful a country. Most dangerous job I had was working the small boats out of Scotland that supplied the oil rigs in the North Sea. Terrible storms, high seas. Good whiskey. My old man would have loved it. We lost two men, fell off an icy ladder. Good men. Gone forever. Sometimes on shore I'd be laid up for a month with my back.*

"*One Christmas I sold ladies' coats and sweaters at Harrods. I swear. I was quite the dandy then. My teeth hadn't gone bad. It was a good Christmas.*"

* * *

I couldn't help interrupting. I said, "I don't think I want to hear about that particular Christmas." I made no secret, the second day I knew him, that I had a weakness for him, lying in those twin hammocks looking at the now-dark Pacific Ocean.

Buddy said: "I caught on with a huge oil tanker all the way to Japan. Most modern ship I was ever on. Jesus, you could have hit a full driver on the deck. Everything automated. But that automation shit breaks down, too. By then I'd seen every nut and bolt and gauge and wrench there was, I could have worked on a rocket to the moon or a Model-T Ford. Even got to the Falklands long after the war and to Thailand. And in all that time, I made a point never to look at a golf course, not even driving by one.

"My back started to get worse. Laying up in a bunk didn't help anymore. Not even good whiskey helped. I was on another boat out of Panama sailing to New Orleans when the pain drove me out of my head. They had to lash me to my bunk. Put me out of my misery with morphine. I woke up in Charity Hospital in New Orleans. I looked like death and felt worse. Lucky I had my American passport, and they could admit me. Better luck than that—my doctor was a young intern in neurosurgery from Tulane. A cowboy, really, from Fort Worth. Needed to cut into some damned body for his confidence. I didn't care anymore. He could cut me open with a rusty bayonet.

"He turned out to be hell with a scalpel. Buck Watson was his name. Dr. Buck Watson, now with a big hospital in Houston. He'd taken to this new technique for back surgery, not so bloody, so invasive. So he said. I didn't give a damn. If I didn't make it, they could dump the body off the docks in the Mississippi River. I woke up. I thought I was paralyzed. I didn't hurt anymore. Not down my leg. Not in my back. Nowhere. The first time in seventeen years. I haven't hurt since, and that was 1989, two years ago.

"I was scared to death to pick up a golf club. I walked out on a practice range back in San Antonio. Said, 'What the hell.' Started hitting some balls. First time in the seventeen years. No pain. Couldn't hit the ball for shit, but no pain. It took a year to get my flexibility back, my tempo, my rhythm, my strength. I still do stretching exercises and work with light weights. Finally I can hit the ball again—how I want to and where I want to. It seems I'm whole again. Except—my life passed me by. No big deal. The world always needs a good bartender."

Sullivan called the night desk and had them send up coffee. She didn't expect to go to sleep before the sun came up, if then. She wanted to keep Jerry Martin talking until Buddy Morrow's entire story had been told. Perhaps it might offer some insight into who killed him.

He drove me to the Princess Hotel. I didn't let him go back alone to that hammock. He still loved to read, but he never had to be alone again. Not even when he took his golf game around the world. There I go, getting ahead of myself.

We woke up in Acapulco. It was like we had been together for years. I don't mean it wasn't exciting. We were like kids. We couldn't get enough of each other. Our lives had been sidetracked in opposite ways. He'd been physically damaged all those years, working as a roustabout. Golf was lost to him. I'd been chasing advertising clients—keeping them happy, selling their packaged goods. Just drifting in my own life. Suddenly we woke up in the same bed. We were alive again. I even woke up laughing. He could always make me laugh, even in my sleep.

I didn't make another Tracey Locke meeting. I left a message for my boss—I'd see him in Dallas. I didn't say when. In truth I never saw him again.

"You've been around the world, I haven't," I said to Buddy. "All I've done for years is make money for supermarkets. And a bit for myself. Haven't bothered to spend much of

it. *I want to see the world. I want to see you play golf. I want
to see how good you can be. I used to know a golfer when I saw
one. If you can't play, I'll hand in my scouting merit badge.*"

Buddy said, "*Too late, kid. I'm thirty-seven. I missed all
those years. The world of golf has passed me by.*"

"*Bullshit,*" I said. "*Hogan was his greatest after forty.
You missed all that wear and tear on your nerves for seven-
teen years. You have your strength back. Your flexibility.
Don't say another word. Show me.*"

"*I'll show you the world,*" he said, not batting an eye.
"*I've seen it twice. I want to see it again without the pain. I
can't promise a damned thing on the golf course. I still have
my original ten thousand dollars. I never touched it. It's
worth five times that now. But traveling the world, it will
melt away quickly, believe me.*"

I told him I had twice that much in my savings and in my
401(K). "*All I ask is show me.*"

Buddy said he had known his share of women but had
never awakened in a bed with a woman before in his life. He
had never been close to another person, as a boy or as a grown
man. In school, on the golf course, even in the rotten holds of
Panama merchant ships, he'd kept to himself.

Buddy drove me back to Texas in his Plymouth. It looked
posthumous but never missed a beat. He was a good driver.
He loved to talk about books. He'd read his way around the
world. He'd read everything. He didn't pretend to be a
scholar. But he understood much of what he had read. It was
fun listening to him. He made me describe every nuance of
the advertising business. Which set me thinking. But I wasn't
ready to discuss my thoughts. Not yet.

We went to the practice range every day at Fort Sam
Houston. The sergeant running the course knew Buddy.
Knew him as Clarence, which was, of course, his given name.
I had to quit hitting balls myself. Buddy would spend too
much time watching me. And helping me. I read while he
practiced. He gave me books. His favorite, to my surprise, was
Samuel Johnson, *by W. Jackson Bate. He said he would

never live anywhere, even in a hammock, that didn't have a copy of that book. I think Buddy spent so many years on the "Grub Streets" of the world that he identified with Dr. Johnson. I think, also, without ever admitting it to himself, that he knew he had a certain genius for golf, no matter how impossibly far removed from the game he found himself. Maybe I'm inventing that. I don't think so.

He practiced in the mornings and played in the afternoons. There were several lieutenants at Fort Sam Houston who had been college golfers. He could give the best of them two shots a side. Of course, they no longer were able to practice and play every day, as they had in college. Still, they couldn't touch Buddy, who most often broke par.

Hitting from the top continued to be a problem for him. Once or twice a side, he would yank a ball to the left of the target. He tried everything. I called Mr. Penick. He had just come out with his wonderful Little Red Book, his Lessons and Teachings from a Lifetime in Golf. I was amazed. He remembered me. And my mom. He had been retired for some time. He agreed to watch Buddy hit some balls.

Buddy couldn't believe I had called him. He was flattered Mr. Penick would help him. He'd already bought and read the Little Red Book.

Mr. Penick rode up to the practice tee in a golf cart at the Austin Country Club. He used a wheelchair when he wasn't riding. He was crippled up with arthritis. But wonderfully alert. He prided himself on using simple words to teach the game. He'd taught Tom Kite and Ben Crenshaw as kids, on into their professional careers. He'd taught Mickey Wright and Betsy Rawls and Kathy Whitworth, all Hall of Fame players. And many others.

I know he was surprised at Buddy's ability to strike the ball. I could see it in his face.

Buddy hit balls until he inadvertently came over the top and pulled a couple. To "hit from the top" means the player begins his downswing with his hands, rather than his legs and hips and arms. "Casting," the British call it.

Mr. Penick said, "You have a pure swing. I'm surprised I never saw it on television."

I explained he had injured his back very young and been unable to play for some years. I didn't say how many.

"I can see you've read Hogan's book," Mr. Penick said. "I think maybe you've memorized it. Of course, you prefer your left thumb straight down the top of the shaft. I never taught that. Certainly it worked for Hogan. The weak grip is necessary for the fade, but it can provoke hitting from the top. The fade is the most consistent shot if played by an expert. But if the club gets to the outside in the backswing, it can lead you to hit from the top. You make a nice correction with your practice swings after it happens. I'd recommend you make the same practice swing in very, very, very slow motion. Barely take the club back. And barely bring it down. Teach your muscles to remember how to set the club at the top and how to start it down."

Mr. Penick was curious as to Buddy's plans.

"I'm hoping to get my game under control and try it in Asia," Buddy said. I had to clap my hands in surprise. We hadn't spoken of which continent we would try first. He'd told me stories of the Far East. I hurt to see it.

Mr. Penick said, "To score in golf is another thing altogether. I doubt you'll run into many better-grounded swings in Asia than your own."

He asked who Buddy had studied under. He told him only Hogan; he'd read his book since he was ten.

Mr. Penick had a wonderful chuckle. "If everyone had read it so thoroughly, I would have been out of a job."

Mr. Penick would take no pay. I sent him a large basket of fruit. He sent a thank-you note in a spidery hand: "Good luck in Asia."

When we got back to our small apartment in San Antonio, I got my nerve up and said, "Clarence Noland. I have a suggestion. A string of suggestions, to be truthful."

He stopped his very-very-very-slow-motion swing in the

living room–bedroom. "You want me to move my thumb off the top of the shaft."

"Oh, no. Your swing has its identity. All it needs is to be tempered under fire. I want to repackage you."

"A bit late to teach me proper manners," he said, laughing.

"Your manners are impeccable. Your voice, your accent is memorable. I want to change your name. I want to dye the touch of gray—I love very much—out of your temples. I want to fix your teeth. I want to finance a small tuck under your chin, and a tiny tightening under your eyes. I want to repackage you. I want to introduce you to the golf world as twenty-five-year-old James 'Buddy' Morrow."

Buddy was too stunned to answer. He put one hand under his chin as if he could feel the years.

"Why?" he said finally.

"The advertising world worships youth," I said. "I have no doubt you will win at professional golf. As a guy who made it late in life—after being injured all those years—you would be a twenty-four-hour-virus of a news story. A curiosity. Maybe a throwaway ad campaign for Advil. You win. And I can sell you as the next golfing phenom for millions. And when we reveal your true age, I can sell that for more millions. Trust me."

Buddy's response surprised me. "What about you and me? You are younger than I am, but you want to sell me as some kid? Are you going the cosmetic surgery route?"

"No," I said. "We'll sell you as the bachelor phenom. It's sexier. You'll stay yourself inside. I'll stay myself outside and inside. I can't stop the sun and wind on my face. But I can keep the old bod in good shape. We'll be a secret twosome as long as it suits us."

"Some 'old bod,' " he said, catching me in the small room. Believe me, he was a sexy guy.

Funny. Buddy never wanted me to change. Maybe he liked the idea of time in my face. I don't suggest an Oedipus *complex. Maybe so, having lost his mother so young. Anyhow, he liked me—he loved me—as I was.*

At first, he thought my reinvention of himself was a screwball idea. But he agreed to think about it. He did. For several days. One day on the practice range, he came over to where I was reading Dr. Johnson and said, "Okay. I'll do it. If you will marry me this week."

I dropped Dr. Johnson on the grass. I said, "You don't know me. I can be pretty moody. I may have promised more than I can deliver. I might let you down."

He didn't say a word. Just kept looking at me.

I didn't think. I just took a deep breath. "Okay, Buddy." I said his nickname, which seemed absolutely right to me, and to him, from that moment on. Of course, his father's name had been James Morrow. It was a simple thing to legally change his own name to his father's. Ultimately we got him a new driver's license, cheating on the age. Luckily a Social Security card doesn't carry your age.

We found the best dentist and the best cosmetic surgeon in Houston. It put a hole in our savings. The result—well, you saw the result. The caps on his teeth were the biggest change. Damn if he didn't look twenty-five.

I stood back from him after he'd healed up. "What will people say? I'm robbing the cradle."

"Wait'll the girls in Asia see this face," he said to his reflection.

I knew it was true. I thought I might lose him one day. I thought I might've anyway, if he became famous. The famous don't often stay married. I never doubted he would be known in the world of golf. I was wrong only about losing him. It wasn't to another woman. It was to the Shinnecock Canal.

Tears came to her eyes, but she only paused in her narrative.

We left for Asia. Just like that.

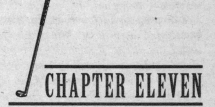

CHAPTER ELEVEN

Sullivan had never been so consecutively quiet in her adult life. Jerry Martin continued her narrative, the sound of her own memories denying the long solitude to come.

There was a dark side to Buddy. I don't mean evil. I don't even mean hostile. I mean dark as in silent. He had lived alone all his life; he often disappeared inside himself. Then he would look up, surprised to find himself on an airplane bound for Malaysia, and a stranger in the next seat.

His silences never bothered me. Away from the job of advertising, with its continuous clatter, I had spent most of my own time alone. I could be as silent as the Texas sky.

Then we would both find ourselves talking at the same instant, as if we'd just met after long years apart.

We were married at the Bear County courthouse. Just the two of us in the party. My parents are dead. An enlisted man, there to get a Texas car tag, stood up for us. I've never felt so sure of a decision in my life. Buddy kept looking at me as if he thought I might disappear—I suppose like his mother.

The last plane we caught landed in Kuala Lumpur. A beautiful name. And the people fit the name. Malaysians. Chinese. Indians. Still many English. Also Pakistanis, Arabs. Most Malaysians are Islamic. But in the capital city as many religions as languages. The narrow streets paved with talk. I loved it. Small people. Very warm, like the climate. Tropical.

We were born lucky. Both of us. Cast-iron stomachs. So many Americans, Europeans fell sick all over Asia. Sometimes too sick to play golf. It was our secret weapon. We ate wherever we sat. A miniature Malay restaurant. Two tables. No English spoken. No menu. The tiniest little woman motioned me to the tiniest little kitchen. Not big enough to sneeze in. A wood-burning stove. She held up a fin. A shark fin. A smile as big as the kitchen. I watched her make shark kabobs. The shark was soaking in milk. She added butter. Two large shallots she minced in a tiny fury. Juice out of a fresh orange. Wide cuts of zucchini. Pearl onions. Two oranges quartered. Peanut oil. Crumbled dried thyme. I've made shark kabobs many times since from memory. It's never tasted so good as cooked in another language on that wood-burning stove in that lean-to restaurant. On other streets the Indian curries. The Chinese with their spicy chicken. And rice, always rice. Across Asia.

It was the cruelest stop, Kuala Lumpur. Our first tournament: the Asian Qualifying School. Survive or go home. And we were twelve thousand miles from home.

Buddy loved the course: Royal Selangor. It made all the difference. It's the second-oldest club in Malaysia. Founded in 1893. Hard to believe that. The course was built in 1920. Some of it over an ancient graveyard. They are proud of the local rule, which says, You cannot ground your club or move anything, however loose or dead it may be, when you find yourself in a grave. *Buddy loved to quote that.*

* * *

She paused at the word *grave*, then closed her eyes to block this final reality out of her mind.

The grass on the greens was called serangoon, a hybrid Bermuda. A bit slow but not so grainy as the old-time Asian greens, some of which still exist.

Rain was forecast every day. Peninsula Malaysia gets 160 inches a year. But the course had a bumu. He burned sticks and chanted in his hut off the first tee. All day and night he chanted. I never saw him sleep or eat. He didn't weigh eighty pounds. All chant and spell. Don't smile, Julia. It didn't rain all week.

It seemed natural, the two of them suddenly laughing together, as if death did not lie silently below them. Jerry was eager to remember so natural an event as a round of golf, the telling of it somehow keeping the night's terror at bay in the room. She picked up her story in midstream.

The first hole at Royal Selangor is a tough par 4 of 428 yards. Buddy pulled his tee shot into the cypress trees. Unplayable. He took a drop. Was short on his approach. And three-putted. A triple-bogey 7. So much for his iron-plated nerves.

I couldn't spit. He never changed expressions. He reached the par-5 3rd hole in two shots and made birdie. So did much of the field. But he nailed a two-iron to the flag on the par-4 10th hole, which plays 467 yards, the only man to birdie it the entire tournament. He birdied the 579-yard 15th hole, a par 5. And finished the first round even-par. Well in the middle of the pack.

I can still see him, sitting on the end of his golf bag as it lay on the ground, totaling up his score that final day, then looking up at me with a big smile, making a victory circle with his finger and thumb.

He had one terrible hole each day. He never threatened T. Kono's course record of 64. But he qualified for the Asian tour. He even got his name printed—in one line of six-point type—in the local English newspaper. We celebrated, just the two of us, all night in a Chinese club. I can still hear Texan-soldier-golfer-world-traveler-untrained tenor-Buddy Morrow with his clear American voice joining in on a Chinese singalong.

Most of that week we kept to ourselves. It was our habit for the next three years. Only a handful of Americans were trying to qualify for the Asian Tour. None with their wives or girlfriends along. A few English, a few Scots, several Australians entered. Some had beaten their way around the world for years, living harder than they played. I kept a low profile. No one paid a drop of attention to me.

Buddy put his clubs away and showed me things he loved about Malaysia. Mostly the everywhere-friendly people. I enjoyed the elaborate kites they flew in Kelantan on the east coast. I still have a beautiful batik scarf he bought me. The artists work without even a pattern. They lay down wax where they don't want color. Then they dye the rest of the fabric and boil away the wax. It leaves a miracle. We went sailing in a fisherman's junk on the South China Sea. It was quite a honeymoon, despite the terror of qualifying. Hard to believe it all happened in one week. That week seems more alive in my memory than any other year of my life.

Three years later we went back to Kuala Lumpur. Buddy scored in the 60s all four days and won the Malaysian Open. His name was in headlines in the local papers in four languages. He had his photograph taken with an Asian movie queen. It made the American papers. No mystery how they got the shot. I set it up. I learned the actress was on location in the city. Never been an actress who didn't worship publicity. With his still-new teeth and tuck, Buddy looked cuter and younger than the actress. The players had accepted him as a kid and a rookie pro three years before.

Now the Malaysian champ, professional golf's bachelor phenom, Buddy Morrow, was officially launched on the international scene.

But that was three years after we started. That first year we rode the train down the peninsula to the Singapore Open. We rode third-class with the people. Infants, grandmothers, live chickens. It was wonderful. Little boys were amazed to be given golf balls. They invented games with them on the crowded car in a minute.

You cross the Strait of Johore and step off the train among three million people on one tiny island. Mostly Chinese. None of them ever sleep, Julia. They are up all night, walking the streets, chasing the Singapore dollar. Their People's Action Party makes us Americans look like socialists.

One thing they don't chase: the drug dollar. Not in Singapore. The day we got off the train, they hanged two English kids from Bath. Caught smuggling cocaine into the city. They were caught ten days before they were hanged. I cried. I could only think of their mothers. Not a place to go around the world to, to commit a crime.

But the Singapore people love their golf. A great gaggle of young girls took up following Buddy. That proved to be true all over the world the next three years. They didn't care that he missed the cut, which he did. The greens at the Bukit Course of the Singapore Island Club had a grain like a river at flood stage. The grain baffled Buddy. It's the same course where Lee Trevino and Orville Moody won the World Cup in the sixties. The grain didn't bother them. I was careful not to say that. Three years later, Buddy figured it out and finished second.

We spent more money sightseeing than we did golfing that first tour of Asia. We almost went broke. Buddy wouldn't skip any of the places he wanted me to see. Our money was running low when we got to Hong Kong. It costs a lot there to breathe in and out.

We spent the week with an old married couple Buddy had known years before, when his father was assigned to the British guard on the island. They lived on a boat. Made their living selling food and dry goods to the other boat people. They *had a small dog and a cat, neither of which had ever set foot on dry land.*

Buddy tried to explain golf to them. The old man lifted his clubs as if they were dueling swords. Even said a special prayer over them. It must have helped. Buddy won his first serious money in Asia.

You look up from the Royal Hong Kong Club and see great mountains. It's as if China is looking down on your life. As well it is. Three courses have been squeezed onto the land, much of it stolen from floodplains. Again, old graves lie under the courses, and once a year they have Ancestor Worship Day. People come from miles to honor their dead.

Jerry raised up and looked directly at Sullivan, eyes suddenly dry. She said, "I will take Buddy's ashes and scatter them over courses around the world that he played and loved. It's a promise." She resumed her story in midthought.

The young girls came to the Royal Hong Kong Club to worship James "Buddy" Morrow. He didn't disappoint them. The tournament combined 18 holes made up from the New and Eden courses. All the greens are raised so they can drain in the monsoon season. We wouldn't know about that back in Texas. Buddy finished in the top fifteen and won ten thousand Hong Kong dollars. The boat family wouldn't take a dime for room and board, but he had a new outboard motor delivered to them they couldn't send back.

Buddy passed a number of golfers with an eagle on the 72nd hole. It's a par 4. It plays 417 yards up a narrow fairway between deep bunkers and mature trees. A lake and more bunkers guard the raised two-level green. Two players that week scored a 10 on the 18th. Buddy holed a three-iron with his last shot of the tournament for the eagle 2. The young girls didn't know what he'd done, but they thought it was sexy. It was. I can still see him, standing in a sea of young girls, all of them tiny, barely coming up to his waist, grinning at me like a prophet of a new religion.

The Japanese tournaments were rich. A good many of the best American players were under contract with their sponsors to play in Japan. The Japanese players were also excellent. The competition was tough. Buddy missed the cut that first year at both Kasumigaseki, the famous Tokyo course, and at the newer Fujioka course just north of Nagoya, well known for the huge Toyota company. I accused him of being distracted by his caddies, comely young women. Three years later he finished in the money at both tournaments.

Despite the huge hole in our bank account that first year, Buddy could not turn down the chance to play an exhibition round at the first great course built in Japan, Hirono, near the port of Kobe.

Buddy thought it was the greatest course in Asia. It was designed in 1930 by the Englishman Charles Alison, who also designed Kasumigaseki. That's a fun word to say—Kasumigaseki.

Hirono rolls among trees and ponds and what we Texans call arroyos, or ravines. The smattering of Japanese fans were as polite as house plants. Buddy took a 7 on the beautiful par-5, 15th hole, which crosses two ravines—one of which Buddy didn't make it over. The Japanese spectators gave him a quiet sympathetic round of applause as if he'd had an illness in the family.

Buddy said the Japanese followed Alison's plans so well and made so great a course because Alison was a superb illustrator and rendered ink sketches of how each hole should be built. The artful Japanese have loved the sketches as much as they have long loved the finished course.

When we came back to Japan, Buddy tied the young American Steve Lowery in a formal exhibition at Hirono for serious appearance money we enjoyed but didn't really need.

The only sad reality about golf in Japan is that you must be a very rich man to belong to a club near any of the great *cities. Your initiation fee might be as much as a million dollars.*

We lost ourselves in Tokyo, among shrines and nightclubs and formal gardens. It was impossible to believe it was once a bombed-out city ruin. Or that the friendly population had been at war with our own. The world is a strange and amazing place, Julia.

Jerry Martin accepted a glass of water. One of the few swallows she had taken of anything except sorrow since learning of Buddy's death. She couldn't bear to leave her narrative, as if holding on to her past life.

Buddy had a special love for South Africa. He won his first professional tournament at the formidable Royal Johannesburg East Course, designed in the 1930s by R. G. Grimsdell. Buddy said the course rivaled the great Scottish courses. The East Course is more than a mile high and 7,300 yards long. But the ball, at that height, flies as if it had wings.

Buddy's experience putting on the grainy greens of Asia helped him master the heavy nap on the greens in Johannesburg. It was in Sun City, South Africa, that he met Gary Player, who first warned the English-speaking golf world that this young man could play the game. The huge first-place check he received seemed at odds with the poverty surrounding the rich skyscrapers of Johannesburg.

With survival no longer in doubt, it seemed easier for Buddy to finish in the money. He actually won only once in Europe, though he finished in the top ten several times. His win came at Chantilly, France, about twenty-five miles north of Paris. It was the same course over which Argentine Roberto de Vicenzo and Englishman Peter Oosterhuis won French Open titles in separate decades.

Buddy's score of 272 created a sensation in Europe. I managed to have his photograph taken surrounded by spectacular models at the fashion house Saint-Laurent, at 5 Avenue

Marceau in Paris. Buddy seemed to be drowning in elegant necks and arms and legs and the fashions of the moment.

The photograph took on a life of its own, appearing in Golf Digest *and even in* Women's Wear Daily. *Golf equipment companies were making low-ball offers for Buddy's long-term endorsement, gambling that he might become a significant personality in the game. I made sure he encouraged—and declined—all offers.*

Buddy played well in Spain, paired in one round with Seve Ballesteros on his home course Pedrena, near the town of Santander. Seve's game was in shambles. Dogged by the press, some of whom were circling in helicopters, Seve missed 12 fairways and finished nine shots behind Buddy.

It surprised Buddy to find a true links course, in the Scottish manner, on the southernmost tip of Sweden—right where the Baltic Sea and the sound come together at Falsterbo. Migrant geese filled the sky. The players needed wings to fight the winds. Denmark could be seen across the sound. Buddy survived among the top ten finishers.

He missed the cut at the Ugolino Club in the Chianti hills of Italy, because neither he nor I could take our eyes off the city of Florence, clearly visible in the distance. We couldn't wait each day to get back to the city of Michelangelo and Da Vinci. We were not roughing it at the Savoy Hotel, where the towels were as thick as mattresses.

We avoided Ireland, Scotland, and England to keep the life and golf of Buddy Morrow a mystery, especially back home in America. After three years of hand-to-hand combat, he was ready to make his mark in the game and among the world's hungriest advertisers—in good old America. I was careful to keep feeding snippets about Buddy to a couple of friends in the press, one with the Reuters wire service whose brother had worked with me at Tracey Locke. Buddy's photographs appeared on the social pages of Europe as often as the sports pages, often with some famous young thing on his arm.

This was my American plan: Gary Player had many friends in the States, including North Carolina. He'd seen

Buddy play and so had his son, and he agreed to put in a solid word for him. The Greensboro Classic came through with a sponsor's exemption. Buddy hoped to make a good showing, perhaps get a couple more sponsor's exemptions on the American tour before attacking the PGA qualifying school. He was more shocked than any golf fan in America when he won the Greensboro Classic—and followed it by winning the Houston Open. He loved the slick American greens with their total absence of grain. He holed putts from distances he hadn't imagined.

And then we came here to the U.S. Open.

Jerry's eyes suddenly ran with tears, but she struggled on to the end of her story.

Sports Illustrated posed Buddy on its cover, dressed as Hamlet, opposite the play's Ophelia, under the lights of the Belasco Theatre on Forty-fourth Street. As you know, he was the talk of New York, of the Open, beyond anything we could have hoped for. And he played so beautifully in the first two rounds. But Buddy's luck, like Prince Hamlet's, had run out. And so had my own.

At that moment, John Morris, his face shattered with sleeplessness and regret, opened the door of the Southampton Hospital suite.

CHAPTER TWELVE

S ullivan's fresh clothes hung over Morris's arm. He
was carrying only pain in his eyes.

Jerry Martin stood shakily and buried her face in his
large shoulder, as if her own agony could be absorbed
only by all who had entered her life, however briefly.

Morris stood speechless, the clothes draped over one
arm and the woman he barely recognized crying against
the other shoulder.

"Morris"—Sullivan took the clothes and patted his
now-free arm—"this is Jerry Martin, Mrs. Buddy Morrow."

"The hell you say?" Morris was as amazed as if he'd
been told that Jacqueline Onassis was weeping against
him.

Jerry moved her buried head up and down to confirm
the impossible.

"Morris, they've been married for three years. You
won't believe who Buddy truly was," Sullivan said.

"Try me" was all Morris could say.

Sullivan sat him down and collapsed Jerry Martin's biography of Buddy Morrow into a letter-length narrative. "I'll tell you the rest later. It's locked in my memory."

Jerry dried her eyes on a tissue Sullivan handed her.

Morris was too confused to make good sense of what he'd heard. "So that explains his true age," he managed.

"Yes," Sullivan said, understanding his confusion.

"Well, Sheriff Otis Haggard is on the way up here to check on the girl." Morris stopped at the awkward idea of the young socialite and the older wife in the same suite.

"It's all right, Morris," Sullivan said. "Jerry knows that Tenney Bidwell and Buddy left the party together; he was driving her home, nothing more."

Morris kept the doubt out of his blank face. "You'll have to tell the sheriff everything you know," he said to Martin.

"Yes." Her voice was surprisingly firm. "He has to find the person who ran Buddy off the bridge. And killed him."

"Maybe it was an accident," Morris suggested, believing otherwise.

"No. Buddy was too expert a driver. He'd driven all over the world. In every sort of vehicle. Under every sort of condition. Someone meant to run him off the bridge." There were no tears in her eyes, only iron resolution.

But her eyes clouded when she said, "You've seen him?"

"Yes," Morris said.

"The medical examiner wouldn't let me into the morgue. I came up here and found Julia."

"He's finished with the autopsy," Morris said; there was no way to soften that reality. "When the sheriff hears you were Buddy's wife, he'll ask you to identify him."

She nodded, twisting her lips in distress. She was finally able to ask, "How did he die?"

"He drowned. Saving the girl," Morris said. "He was trapped under the steering wheel. He lowered his window and pushed her out. She must have been sober enough to swim to the surface of the canal. As Sullivan must have told you, a young deputy pulled her out of the water. She was still hysterical when we came on the scene. She couldn't have gotten out of the car by herself. She was too terrified. He had to be a stand-up guy, Buddy Morrow."

Jerry Martin wept from some inexhaustible source of sorrow.

Sheriff Otis Haggard picked that moment to come through the door.

Morris introduced them.

Haggard, his big hat in his two hands, was stunned to learn that Buddy Morrow had had a wife but was properly sympathetic with the new widow. He looked into the next room to see that Tenney Bidwell was still asleep with a nurse sitting beside her. No one had been able to contact her parents. They were apparently out of the country.

The sheriff closed the door on the sleeping patient and got straight to the point. "Why weren't you with him in the car?" he asked Jerry Martin.

"It would be easier if I started at the beginning," she said.

The sheriff sat. They all sat. Jerry told of meeting Buddy Morrow in Mexico. She collapsed the strange narrative of his own life. And the story of their life together, touring the world's golf tournaments these last three years. She told of her background in advertising, of persuading Buddy to change his name and have cosmetic surgery, of her intentions to package him—his personality as a young bachelor phenom as well as an accomplished golfer. And that it had all worked, the strategy. Buddy signed a major contract yesterday. Even if he had not won the U.S. Open, all his hard work and her careful promotion would have paid off. Of course, his good looks, without his remarkable skill, would have come to nothing. After all, he'd beaten the best golfers in the world two weeks running before the Open.

"I should have left him tending bar in Mexico," Martin said, "and God knows, for his sake, I wish I had." She could not cry. Her eyes were dry as stones.

"So why were you not in the car when it went off the bridge?" asked the sheriff again, having taken careful notes during her narrative.

"Buddy was the guest last night of Edgar Spencer, of Spencer Sporting Goods," Martin said. "Co-host of the party was Buddy's new agent, Paul Mitchell, a young man from New York. He came over and saw Buddy play in South Africa, when he was just getting started as an agent. Buddy never forgot him.

"Last night they were celebrating a contract Buddy signed late yesterday afternoon with Spencer Sporting Goods. I was keeping a low profile, leaving Buddy as the glamorous 'bachelor' golfer. We were selling him as the next hot commodity in the endorsement marketplace. Buddy hated it, my not being there, our deception by silence. I told him two more days, and we were coming out of the closet. His future was now guaranteed. He could concentrate on the last two rounds of the Open. Play golf, as he always had, for the love of it. God, I wish I had been driving on that bridge and not him."

She's sincere, or she's Sarah Bernhardt, Morris thought. He'd never met Paul Mitchell. He'd never even heard of him.

"Why was Tenney Bidwell at the party? Why did Buddy agree to drive her home?" asked the sheriff.

"She'd been hanging around, lusting after Buddy—

her sexual distraction of the week, I expect," said Jerry. "Not an unusual circumstance for Buddy, even among young socialites. But he was a marvel at deflecting them—*after* I got their pictures in the newspapers. She picked up on the party. Buddy said her family knew the Spencers. She didn't understand that she was wasting her time. Buddy was a faithful guy. Maybe he always wanted a home. He'd grown up alone and had had plenty of . . . female adventures.

"Now he had his agent and his first big contract. He didn't need any more photo opportunities. He called me," said Martin. "You can check the phone records at the Spencers' beach house. Buddy said he was driving her home. He said she could barely stand, after what she'd been drinking and smoking at the party. He said she lived in Southampton."

"What time did he call?" the sheriff asked.

"It was about ten after eleven. I'd nodded off. I looked at the clock."

Morris knew that he and Sullivan had come on the scene of the accident at 11:50 P.M. The car had gone off the bridge not twenty minutes before they got there. The girl was still dripping wet after being pulled out of the canal.

"So you knew he would be crossing the Shinnecock Bridge," the sheriff said.

She nodded, yes.

"Where were you, exactly, when he called?" the sheriff asked. His voice had lost its sympathetic tone.

Morris knew that all over the world, even in the most lavish mansions of Long Island, behind the highest hedges, husbands, if murdered at all, are most often murdered by wives and lovers.

"I was in our condo in West Tiana."

"West of the bridge, and a few minutes away?"

"Yes," she said in a small voice.

"Did you have a second car?"

"I *did*," Martin said.

"What do you mean?"

"After he called, I kept waiting for Buddy to come home. I finally called the Spencer house in Westhampton Beach. The party was still going. But they couldn't find Buddy. I thought he must have gotten hung up talking future contracts with Paul Mitchell."

"You didn't imagine he had gone home with Tenney Bidwell?" the sheriff said bluntly.

"No. Not in the way you mean. I thought maybe he'd gotten lost looking for her house. Or they'd had a flat—" She paused, her mouth open, as if it could not close around the magnitude of the *collision* that had killed him.

"You say you *did* have a second car," Sullivan interrupted. "What did you mean?"

"I was exhausted from fighting the crowd on the golf course and from so much mental strain, and I'd had a couple of drinks and no dinner," said Martin by way of explanation. "I dozed off again. The late, late news came on the television. And suddenly they were saying Buddy's name on TV. It was like a terrible dream. I put on my shoes—I hadn't taken off my slacks—and I ran outside. My rental vehicle was *gone*. I couldn't believe it. I rushed around. Maybe it's still in the parking lot, and I was too hysterical to find it. A young man was getting in his car. He could see I was distraught. He asked if he could help. I asked if he knew how to find the Southampton Hospital. The TV announcer had mentioned it. The young man said yes, he did. He asked, was I ill? I said please take me there. He did. A very young man. I didn't catch his name. I wept all the way."

The words rushed out of her mouth as if she were still in the terrible dream headed for the hospital.

"What kind of rental vehicle couldn't you find?" Haggard asked without expression.

Morris closed his eyes, knowing what she would say,

as if he and Sullivan had been part of her nightmare—
and in truth, they had been.

"A Ford. A sports utility vehicle, I think they call it.
An Explorer. A red one."

Of course it's red, Morris thought, catching the eye of
Sullivan, who shook her head silently but adamantly.

Haggard said to Martin, "I want you to go with my
deputy to your condo. See if you can find the Explorer.
Before we list it as stolen."

Martin looked at Sullivan, *as if for support or for legal
advice,* Morris thought.

"Do you think you had better warn her of her rights,
sheriff?" Sullivan said, as if reading Morris's mind.

"Maybe so. Understand"—he looked directly at
Jerry Martin—"anything you say can and will be held
against you."

Martin grasped her own right hand as if it might lash
out and slap the sheriff. "What are you talking about?
It's my husband they killed."

"Why do you say *they killed*?" Haggard asked.

"Buddy drank very little. And never more than a beer
or two during a golf tournament. He was a gifted driver.
He'd driven in jungles and on autobahns. He'd never
had a moving accident. And *this* was no accident. Let's
go look for the goddamned vehicle. I'll worry about my
rights."

The sheriff stepped outside and came back with a
deputy Morris recognized, Perry Angle, of the classic
profile. He was young enough for his face not to show
that he had been up all night.

The sheriff told his deputy to drive Ms. Martin to
her condo and look for her *missing* rental vehicle. If they
found it, he was to call for a deputy to stay with it. And
to keep it untouched. And to let him, the sheriff, know
they'd found it. Then to accompany Ms. Martin to their
Suffolk County office so that she could make and sign a
full statement of her activities of last night.

Morris knew he was speaking to Jerry Martin as much as to the deputy. She seemed entirely unimpressed.

When they'd gone, Haggard said, "A *red* sports utility vehicle. What do you think of that, Morris?"

"Trouble."

"You two don't go making a fantasy arrest," Sullivan said, "you'll be making a large mistake."

"You don't believe she was a woman wronged?" the sheriff said.

"No."

"How do you explain the young woman in the next room? You buyin' that just-drivin'-her-home shit?" The sheriff sounded more down-home Mississippi than he would have imagined.

"I believe her," Sullivan said.

The sheriff looked at her skeptically, then at Morris.

"Otis"—Morris spoke his first name for the second time—"arrest whomever you have to. But don't bet even a plug of tobacco with Julia Sullivan. Trust me."

The sheriff laughed. "Can't you see me chewing Redman, like my daddy, up here in Southampton?" Then he was deadly serious, "I'm putting my money on the red vehicle. We'll see who was drivin' it."

The nurse stepped through the door from the bedroom. She looked to Sullivan. "Miss Bidwell is awake and asking for you."

"Calm her down as much as you can," said the sheriff. "Then I want to come in and talk with her."

"I'll see how she is," Sullivan said, promising nothing.

Sweat had popped out under Haggard's eyes. Miss Bidwell's family owned a great swath of Southampton. But family influence stopped where murder began. Of course, the influence would stay long after the murder was past tense.

* * *

Sullivan took the young woman's outstretched hand, remembering how small it was. Her large gray eyes were strangely alive.

"I remember . . . your holding me," Tenney Bidwell said in a whispery voice. "I thank you. What's your name?"

"Julia Sullivan. My friends call me Sullivan."

"Thank you again, *Sullivan*." She tried to smile and could not. Her mouth turned down. Her eyes closed. But she seemed remarkably in control of herself.

"Your parents?" Sullivan said.

Tenney waved off the idea of her parents. "They're somewhere in Europe. I don't want to see them until this is all over."

"How did you first meet Buddy Morrow?" Sullivan asked, unsure if she would answer.

"At the golf course, yesterday," Tenney said in a voice that wavered with emotion.

"How did you meet him?"

"A member of Shinnecock Hills, a friend of mine, introduced us. I asked him to," she admitted, almost smiled. Remembering seemed necessary to her. As did talking, so long as she could avoid the crash on the bridge.

"He—Buddy—was on the practice putting green," she said.

"Was he . . . friendly?" asked Sullivan.

"Yes. Oh, yes. A photographer from the *Times* asked to take our picture. He was very good about it. We even had a beer in the clubhouse."

"Did he ask you to the party last night?"

"No. No," she said. "In fact, I asked *him* to a party. At a friend's. He said he couldn't go. He had a previous commitment."

"How did you wind up at his party?" There was no accusation in Sullivan's voice.

"I overheard Mr. Spencer—Edgar Spencer, a friend

of my father's for years—speak of the party he was having for Buddy Morrow. I invited myself. Mr. Spencer said, 'By all means come.' So I did."

"You found Buddy appealing?"

"Yes. I don't know the first thing about golf. But he was damned handsome"—her voice faltered, let a moment pass, then said—"and approachable. I'm not one to sit by shyly if someone appeals to me. It's not like he was married." She ground her small white teeth. "Not to say that has bothered me in the past," she admitted, not looking Sullivan in the eye.

"You saw him at the party?"

"Yes. He remembered me. He was surprised to see me."

"How did he come to drive you home?"

Tenney took deep breaths, as if preparing herself for the ordeal ahead. "I asked him if he would. I'm afraid the bartender was mixing the drinks a bit strong. I didn't trust myself to drive my own car. One more moving violation, and I lose my license." She closed her eyes. "I don't know if I will ever be able to drive a car across a bridge."

Sullivan kept her voice neutral. "What time did you ask him?"

"I don't know. I wasn't thinking too clearly."

"Was it midnight?"

"No. It wasn't that late. I remember"—she closed her large eyes—"looking at my watch at some point and seeing ten o'clock. I thought the night was still young, but I was already a bit woozy."

"Buddy agreed to drive you home?"

"Yes. But he had to speak again to Mr. Spencer and to his agent, I forget his name, and say his good nights. It took a while."

"Did he use the telephone?" Sullivan asked quietly.

"Yes. I saw him across the room on the telephone. Not long before we left."

"Did he say who he was talking to?"

"No. I didn't ask him. I was only interested in spiriting him out of the room. I liked him. He had more than looks going for him. More than being young and famous. He was easy to be with."

"Do you remember what happened after that?" Sullivan asked, fairly sure she would not.

"Oh, God." She opened her eyes and hugged her chest with her arms, her composure leaking away. "It soaked into my mind. I'll never forget it."

"You'll have to talk about it with the sheriff. He's waiting to see you."

"Why? The sheriff? I'd been drinking. I—I'd even—"

"Careful what you say without a lawyer. You aren't being charged with anything," Sullivan warned.

"I wasn't driving," Tenney insisted. She seemed startled that her eyes were filled with tears.

Sullivan waited, not speaking, not touching her hand.

"He was . . . taking me home." She searched with her hands as if for a cigarette. "I wanted him," she said bluntly, careless of the line of tears down one cheek. "I'd fought with my date. Told him to get out of my life. We were in my car. I don't know how he got home. I'm a terrific person."

Sullivan handed her a nose tissue.

She closed her eyes again as if the words were visible and too painful to be seen. "Buddy wouldn't . . . he lifted my hand away from his lap just as we reached the bridge. Then came the terrible crash. I didn't know what happened . . . and then we were—falling."

She buried her head in Sullivan's arms. But kept talking between ragged breaths. "I've got to say it all. . . . I can't live with it inside me. We hit, and my seat belt . . . cut off my breath. I didn't know we'd hit water." She trembled at the word *water*.

"When I could finally breathe, I couldn't stop screaming."

Tenney raised her head, the terror of it in her eyes. "At first the lights on the dash didn't go out, and I could see Buddy fighting to get out from under the steering wheel. But he couldn't. He was stuck and the water kept coming in. . . ." She closed her eyes again. "Buddy suddenly quit struggling, and reached over to undo my seat belt. He grabbed me with hands like iron, shook me, '*Shut up!*' he yelled, '*shut up!*' He shook me. '*Hold your breath,*' he yelled in the dark, lights all out, he yelled: '*Window! Push you out! Hold your breath!*' He shouted two words: One of them, '*Jerry!*' . . . I couldn't make out the other. It was like all of it was happening to somebody else, but he grabbed me, pulled me, pushed me, and then somehow I was breathing air and trying to scream. Somebody grabbed me, but all I remember is trying to scream and choking."

Sullivan held her as she wept. Finally Tenney Bidwell could sit up and breathe without sobbing. "I'm a terrific person," she said again, hating herself. "I left him down there to die. All because I wanted him for one night. He wouldn't have me. But he saved me anyhow. Who could Jerry be?" she asked, as if it had just occurred to her.

"His wife," Sullivan said, without cruelty.

"Oh, God." She tried to weep but could only shake her head at the absence of tears.

"It was not your fault," Sullivan said. "Someone killed him and nearly killed you. Did you see the vehicle that struck you on the bridge?"

"On purpose? Someone meant to crash into us? Why?"

"That's the question," Sullivan said. "What did you see on the bridge?"

"I hadn't thought." Tenney put both balled fists at the sides of her head. "I saw lights, coming up from behind. Then banging into us. All noise. Couldn't think, or see."

"Was there a car, or truck, following you before you got to the bridge?"

She pressed her fists into the sides of her head. She could only shake her head. "I don't know. I was only thinking of making out with him." She dropped her hands in her lap. "Right now I want to change my life. Tomorrow?" Her eyes were suddenly chilly and unblinking. "Tomorrow I'll want something else. Or somebody—maybe for the night. I'm a terrific person."

"And maybe you are, or will be," Sullivan said. "A dance with oblivion has a way of changing us, however much we resist it."

"I don't believe he would ever have left me down there alone," Tenney said. "Just another reason to hate myself."

"You owe him a few things," Sullivan said.

"What?" There was true alarm in her eyes.

"That's mostly for you to figure out."

"God, I hate to see this sheriff."

"That's the first thing you owe Buddy Morrow. A chance to catch the person who killed him. Best to be truthful. Tell the sheriff what you remember. You might be surprised what else comes back to you. But," Sullivan warned, "you can have a family lawyer here, if you feel you need one, to protect your best interest. It wouldn't mean you were guilty of anything."

"Save me from daddy's lawyers."

"After the sheriff there'll be dozens of reporters and cameras."

"Do I have to speak to them?" There was panic in her voice.

"No. But you can't escape them forever. They won't give up."

"Later. I'll think about them later."

"Then I'll bring the sheriff in?" said Sullivan.

"Will you stay with me?"

"Of course."

Sullivan motioned Sheriff Otis Haggard inside. Morris knew from the look on her face to stay away.

Coming out of the bedroom ahead of the sheriff, Sullivan felt as if she'd given blood. She needed the arm that John Morris was circling around her. The memory of their own terrible crash in the car with Monty Sullivan was suddenly too much alive in her mind.

"You were a big help in there, Sullivan. I thank you," Otis Haggard told her. "I would never have gotten half that much out of the girl."

"Sullivan has a way with a witness," Morris said. "Be glad she won't be with the defense team in the courtroom when this thing goes to trial." It was a remark Morris would not forget.

"*If* it goes to trial," said a skeptical Sullivan.

"Hell, yes, it will. Some sonofabitch will answer for what happened on that bridge," Haggard said.

"*If* you can place him in the vehicle that hit them," Sullivan said.

"We'll place him—or *her*, believe me," Haggard said.

"I hope you do," Sullivan said, "so long as it's the true driver."

"Some guts this guy Morrow showed," said the sheriff. "Bad luck she didn't see the driver of the vehicle that hit them."

Tenney Bidwell hadn't remembered anything different from what she'd told Sullivan. Sullivan gave Morris one of his own shorthand versions of her narrative. Enough to chill his blood. She'd save the specific details until later. They'd go down better in a glass with Mr. Vodka.

"He was a lovely man, Buddy Morrow," Morris said. "We can't let him drown alone in the dark and not have justice done."

"You put your mind back on the U.S. Open," Sheriff Haggard said. "I'll see that justice is served in Suffolk County."

Sullivan winced. Justice could be an elusive thing.

The sheriff answered his cellular phone.

Morris knew what had happened from his end of the conversation.

Haggard made no secret of it. "They found Ms. Martin's vehicle. A red Ford Explorer. In the driveway behind her condo. There's no question it's been in a collision. Its right fender panel and door panel are bashed in. My deputy is taking her in for further questioning." With that, the sheriff left to meet them.

Sullivan felt her skin grow cold. "Morris, do you know any Long Island lawyers?"

"Let me think. Yes. One, an old friend of Willie's. Ed Higgins is his name. I haven't seen him in years. I have no idea if he still practices in Bridgehampton."

"We'll check the Yellow Pages. Jerry never killed Buddy Morrow. She loved him. But she's in a bad spot. She wouldn't be the first innocent person found guilty in New York State."

"Let's see—Julia Sullivan as acting judge and jury in this case," Morris said.

"Do you believe Jerry?"

"Sure," Morris said, and meant it. "But I don't vote in this state. Put your working duds on. I think Jerry Martin needs you now more than Tenney Bidwell does. I'll see if I can reach Ed Higgins—if he's still practicing law in Bridgehampton. You work the jailhouse. I'll work Higgins and the golf course. If you need me, leave a message at the press tent."

"I'm afraid for Jerry," Sullivan said, touching his arm.

"With damned good reason. But she would have to be mentally ill to wreck the vehicle killing her husband, then leave it in the parking lot at her condo, catch a ride to the hospital, and take the deputy back to find it sitting there all bashed in."

"Someone stole it. Crashed it. And brought it back."

"Splendid. If he hot-wired it, the cops will know it instantly. She's off the hook. If not? How did the thief start it? Then how did he know where Buddy Morrow would be last night? Or when he would leave the party? Or that the girl would be there—and too drunk and doped up and horny to drive—or that Buddy would drive her home across the Shinnecock Canal? Since he was renting a place in West Tiana, Buddy had no prior reason to cross the bridge at all."

"Minor questions," Sullivan said, knowing how deadly they were. "Obviously she left the keys in the ignition of the Explorer. I do it all the time in Colorado. Obviously the killer *knew* where the party would be and was invited, or crashed it. He *stole* the Explorer. Perhaps he meant to run Buddy down in the street, or in the parking lot outside Edgar Spencer's house in Westhampton Beach. He saw the girl at the party. Drunk and doped out. He *heard* her ask Buddy to drive her home. He *knew* where she lived. He took his chances in Jerry's Explorer. And he was lucky as hell."

"He would have to be desperate as hell. And/or crazy. It might have been *him* going off the bridge. Then to wait until Jerry Martin heard the news on TV and left the house to put the Explorer back in the lot? Desperate, angry, greedy, maybe a tad suicidal, and/or crazy. Somebody who lost out in the Buddy Morrow *Sweepstakes*—an agent, a sporting goods rep, a manufacturer . . ."

"That's our man, Morris. We'll smoke him out before the weekend is over."

"Let's not get carried away. It could have been a terrible coincidence: some kid borrows the Explorer for kicks and loses it on the bridge, has no idea who he had killed, then sobers up and drops it back where he got it."

"Just happened to kill the husband of the driver of the vehicle he stole? That's more coincidence than one island can hold."

"Maybe so. There seem to be plenty of losers in the Buddy Morrow Sweepstakes. First one comes to mind is J.C. Stroud. Our Nashville country boy–agent has lost his main client, Roy Bream. The only dollar he hasn't divorced or gambled away is the gold dollar-sign belt-buckle that holds his pants up over his big gut."

Morris said, "Then there's J.C.'s Yale Law School counterpart, Jason Everett. Never trust an agent, Sullivan, in a blue blazer and linen trousers traveling in his own jet plane. You can believe he bought it all off the torn anterior cruciate ligaments of broken-down athletes. Not to forget that Everett's erstwhile partner hanged himself two years ago, one week after Jason dissolved their partnership, taking most of their clients with him. Everett flew Buddy from Houston to Long Island. He meant to add Buddy to his string of athletes, even hinted that if Buddy signed with him, he could soon afford to buy his own jet plane. Such a man would not be a gracious loser."

Morris tapped the floor with his cane. "Not to forget Jack 'Speed' Wallace, the macho erstwhile tight end for the New York Giants. And now vice-president of Wargo Golf, Inc. Ol' Speed's thick chest has slid down into his pants. But he's still strong as Octagon soap, with a temper that also has eight sides. Once threw a competitor through a Wargo golf display at a trade show. Sweet guy. Told me he was ready to write Buddy a check for 'seb'en zeros.' Ol' Speed is a Chapel Hill man. I expect he could count the zeroes. You get the idea—the good sheriff is not going to be short of disappointed suspects. Unhappily, the sheriff has his antenna tuned to the comely widow."

Sullivan, her working duds on her arm, nodded her understanding, in truth pleased that Jerry Martin was not alone as a logical suspect. "I'll brief Sheriff Haggard on the backgrounds of those worthy gentlemen," she said. "All we want is for him to catch the true felon."

Sullivan thought awhile before admitting, "Unless somebody saw the killer steal the vehicle, or saw him bring it back to the condo, or unless he did something foolish and left his prints on the steering wheel with those of a hundred others who've rented it—unless he was seen in the night or made a mistake, I worry about ever *placing* him behind the wheel."

"Which puts our fair Texan, Jerry Martin, squarely in the sheriff's crosshairs."

"I'm not buying 'we always kill the one we love,' " Sullivan said.

"Maybe not. But one day soon the sheriff may be selling it to a jury of her peers. You better get to the jailhouse, lover."

Sullivan looked at him, astonished, certain he had never called her by that noun, even under the influence of single-malt scotch. "John Morris, the latent romantic."

The cushion off the couch struck her squarely in the rear.

CHAPTER THIRTEEN

Ed Higgins still practiced law in Bridgehampton. His deep courtroom voice sounded nothing like he looked, an unkempt, roly-poly little bachelor whose shirt was always trying to escape his trousers. But John Morris remembered he had a degree from Harvard Law hanging on his picture-crowded office wall.

Higgins also remembered him. "What do you hear from Willie?" he asked of their mutual friend.

"He's happily married, well published, his Ole Miss Rebels are on a rampage. I think he's running for King of Mississippi," Morris said. "One of his lawyer-friends has done pretty well as a novelist; you might have heard the name: Grisham."

"Tell Willie I'm taking typing lessons."

John Morris then explained what had happened to the golfer Buddy Morrow and the awkward position in which his widow, Jerry Martin, found herself. As they spoke, the fatal hit-and-run vehicle rented to her was still sitting in her condo's parking lot.

"Most of my about-to-be-divorced clients here on Long Island prefer to *run-and-sue*," Higgins said. "Where was the widow at the time of the crash?"

"Alone in the rented condo with the television for company."

"Where are the keys to her vehicle?" Higgins asked.

"Good question. I don't know."

"But we both know Sheriff Haggard. He's a master of the obvious. This Jerry Martin has to account for those keys—with a plenty strong story."

"Failing that, a plenty strong lawyer," Morris said. "What's the drill?"

"You remember Julia Sullivan?"

"We Harvard men are short on much, sometimes including stature, but we never forget a beautiful woman." This response seemed to be endemic to Long Island.

"She's gone down to the Suffolk County sheriff's office to see what's up. She'll know if Jerry needs help. Expect a ring."

"Unless somebody hot-wired that Ford Explorer, she'll need all the help she can get."

"She's not alone among potential suspects," Morris said. He ran down a short list of disappointed agents and at least one sure-to-be-hostile manufacturer's rep. "There might be others I know not of," he said.

"Okay, Prince Hamlet, tell me, who's going to win the Open?"

"Lord, I'd almost forgotten they were playing it. This *is* Saturday? So much happened last night, it seems like we ought to be in the middle of next week. Today is moving day. Nineteen guys are within no more than six shots of the leader, Greg Norman. All twenty guys can put themselves in position to win it—or shoot themselves out of it, today. Maybe this is the year Norman flies home with the trophy in his personal jet plane. But I wouldn't bet the law practice on it. In fact, I'm headed to Shinnecock Hills to see for myself."

"While the rest of us are stuck with life and/or death."

"What did somebody say: 'Life is a six-foot sidehill putt.' I'll be checking in with Sullivan. And thanks."

"What's a Harvard man for?" Higgins said.

Morris stepped out of his rental Ford to catch the twenty-miles-an-hour wind off the Atlantic straight in his face.

"Scotland come to Long Island," he said to himself. Plenty of high hopes would be blown into Peconic Bay.

He avoided the press tent. It would be knee-deep in the aftermath of the death of Buddy Morrow. Most of the leaders wouldn't be teeing off until after lunch. He had time for a bite to eat, thanks to Julia Sullivan's magical clubhouse pass.

"Mind if I sit, Morris?"

Edgar Spencer IV looked as if he might collapse if he didn't sit—coat, tie, buttoned-down shirt, and all.

"A terrible thing, Morris," Spencer said.

"For Buddy Morrow, or Spencer Sporting Goods?" Morris made no effort to soften his cynicism.

"To tell you the truth, for us both."

"I understand you'd signed a large contract with Buddy."

"Two million dollars. Up front."

"Can you take the hit?"

"Most of it's insured. We can swallow the rest. But frankly we needed the kid's name on our line. We needed a boost. The big guys are stepping on us with their huge advertising budgets. They intend to kill us off or buy us out. I don't know how long we can hold on."

It was obvious that Edgar Spencer hadn't gotten the word. Buddy Morrow was no *kid*. Morris knew that his own story for the AP would be stirring up the boys in the press tent.

"How can I help you?" he asked, truly puzzled. He'd never known Edgar as well as he'd known his old grandfather, who would have been concerned about the death of Buddy Morrow and not the threat to his line of sporting goods.

"I'd like your opinion. The kid dying young? Do you think it might create a following?"

"You mean a sort of James Dean thing?" Morris said, unable to hold down the anger that rose up inside him. Buddy wasn't even in his grave—he was lying on a metal slab in the Southampton morgue.

"Yes. A young man killed—perhaps murdered—in the prime of his life." There was a hopeful quality in Spencer's voice.

"Don't know if a deceased forty-one-year-old golfer would inspire a cult following," Morris said, putting down his sandwich, his appetite suddenly dead on the plate.

"What the devil do you mean, forty-one-year-old?" Spencer's Princeton formality was seriously fractured.

Morris gave him cold-blooded minibiographies of Clarence Noland James "Buddy" Morrow and his widow, Jerry Martin.

"I don't believe it." Spencer's mouth opened and shut like that of a beached perch.

"Check with one of the boys in the press tent," Morris said, picking up his sandwich again; Spencer's shocked disbelief brought back his appetite.

"I've been defrauded. My lawyer—I'll annul the goddamned agreement." He looked at his watch. "It's too late to stop the check, not that that means a damned thing." Spencer was still sitting there, but his self-interest had already walked out the door and down the steps toward the courthouse.

"Be an unusual contract that guaranteed the signee's *age*," Morris couldn't resist saying. "I thought the government frowned on age discrimination. What the hell do I know about contracts? Let me ask you something, Edgar."

Spencer was too shocked to stand up and leave the table.

"Did you see Buddy when he left the party last night?"

Answering the question seemed more comforting than his own silence. "Yes. No. He shook hands. He *told* me he was leaving. I saw him start for the door."

"Tenney Bidwell left with him?"

"Terrible thing. Lucky she's alive. Her family will be shocked."

"I doubt anything Tenney Bidwell could do—that she hasn't already done—would shock her family," Morris said. "Did anyone else leave the party at the same time as Buddy?"

"Good Lord, how could I know? There were dozens of people. The party went on long after I went to bed."

"Buddy's new agent, Paul Mitchell, was your co-host?"

"Yes. Bright young man. Went down to Princeton. I've known him, his family, for years. He bought the liquor, the food, I furnished the beach house." Spencer's expression darkened as if it had just come to him—that he had been royally screwed by a young friend. "But the son of a bitch misled me on Buddy Morrow's age and background. Why would he do it? God knows he doesn't need the money. His family could buy and sell every golfer alive."

"I doubt this Mitchell had any idea of Buddy's true age, or his former name, or anything that's happened to him in the last fifteen years. What law says he has to know? Were there any other agents at the party?"

Spencer seemed to have aged in his chair. He was too weary not to answer. "Of course. A number of them have contracts with us." He named several, pronouncing each name with a certain distaste.

"Jason Everett?" Morris asked.

"Oh, yes. Not very happy about losing Morrow as a client. I expect he's laughing today. It would have been no great loss to that greedy young bastard." Spencer's contempt spilled onto the table. "He owns enough high-profile clients to bleed the sporting goods business bloodless. Not that he gives a flying damn."

"J.C. Stroud?" Morris asked.

"That hillbilly barbarian! He damned well was *not* invited. Loud. Drunk. Made a typical ass of himself. He actually threw up in the kitchen sink. Disgusting!"

"When did he leave the party?" Morris asked.

"He didn't leave. I had him thrown out. My gardener and my driver showed him to the door."

"What time was that?"

"I don't know. It wasn't so late, maybe ten P.M. It wasn't early enough. God, what a mess."

"Did he make a scene with Buddy and his agent, Paul Mitchell?"

"He's a walking, drinking scene. Buddy quietly told him to mind his manners. He has no manners."

"Any of your competitors drop by?"

"Sure. Some of the old guard. To offer congratulations. Not many of them left. The big chains have hot-eyed young sales managers for every sport. They know nothing about the traditions of the business, not to mention of the sports themselves; they work slave labor all over Asia."

Morris didn't imagine the workforce building Spencer Sporting Goods would stand the light of day.

The stricken look on the face of Edgar Spencer made

Morris remember his old grandfather and what a sweet guy he had been.

"Look," Morris said, "I could have it all wrong, how the golfing public might respond to the story of Buddy Morrow. It reads like a major motion picture. Every man's fantasy become reality. From tending bar in Mexico to leading the Godamighty United States Open. Then—sudden death."

Spencer responded to the words as if he'd been given a blood transfusion. "No question, it'll be sensational news all around the world."

"In whatever language they stick a flagpole in a golf green," Morris said.

"I want to meet this Jerry Martin, the widow. She'll control the estate." Spencer stood up with a newfound vitality.

"You'll like her. She'll be around, I'm sure. Before the weekend is over, I'll introduce you," said Morris, who only hoped she wouldn't be locked away without bail by the sheriff of Suffolk County.

The gallery in its enthusiasm. The wind in his face. The high grasses in the rough bending with false humility. The fairways and greens cut as formally as an English garden, with a stricter discipline. The players and caddies moving across the rolling landscape as if on some silent religious retreat. The scores flashing on leader boards, counting triumph and misfortune without distinction. All of it gradually turned John Morris's thoughts from death to golf.

His left knee swollen from two days of hiking up and down the hills and from one night of faint sleep, Morris floated in a tight circle among the 13th, 16th, 9th, and 18th greens, making one extended march to the high terrors of the 10th green. With way-stops in the clubhouse to catch the far-flung action on television over the rim of a nourishing mug of imported beer.

The winds threatened to blow the field entirely away. One exception: Tom Lehman. The man who couldn't make a three-foot putt to win The Masters dominated the raw winds with his low draw and fiercely struck irons. Four times he nailed the ball to the flag for birdies in scoring the low round of the day, a 67. It was one of only three rounds in the 60s, while four golfers scored in the 80s, including former Open champion Tom Kite.

Lehman even escaped the 10th hole with a rare par, stopping his approach shot on that high, slick, precarious green. One wag wrote that it was "like driving your ball down Wall Street and stopping it on a manhole cover." Only at No. 15 did Lehman falter, chipping the ball entirely over the green, but he chipped it back within a foot of the hole for a bogey 5.

Greg Norman told the press after his own round that Lehman scoring a 67 in the winds blowing over Shinnecock Hills was like a man "shooting a 59" under ordinary conditions.

Norman himself battled the winds and the course and his own errant long game to fashion a 74 and a tie for the lead with Lehman at 209. Norman managed to hit but nine fairways off the tee and only *five greens* in regulation strokes. He saved par *ten times* from off the green, including twice from greenside bunkers.

One of the ten saves did not come at the 10th green. Morris watched as Norman's approach shot backed off the elevated green and far down the incline. His first pitch shot back to the green experienced the same disheartening fate. Norman finally got it up and down in a double-bogey 6.

Norman's drives and approach shots were windblown and errant, but his putting was masterful. Through eighteen holes he required only *twenty-five* putts. He did miss a short one of five feet on the 18th hole to lose the sole lead in the tournament.

Norman told the press afterward, "My 74 felt like a 62. Unless you played, you have no idea how difficult Shinnecock Hills played today. I can't ever remember seeing so many great players humbled. Today was a day that tested your character and your intestinal fortitude. I enjoyed it. It finished off your learning curve about yourself and the game of golf."

Morris, standing in the back of the press tent, could not put it out of his mind that going into the last day in 1986, Norman had led the Open at Shinnecock Hills, only to suffer a closing round of 75. He'd finished tied for twelfth while Raymond Floyd, who teed off in the fourth-from-last pairing, shot a 66 to come from far off the lead to win the tournament.

By Sunday's final round, there were *twenty* players within six shots of the two leaders, including the resurgent Roy Bream, erstwhile client of J.C. Stroud, country boy–agent. Anything could happen to any one of them on any hole. As happened Saturday.

Morris huddled out of the wind on No. 18, as Jumbo Ozaki, who started the day two shots out of the lead, lost eleven strokes on the last twelve holes to shoot a fat 80. He watched as Tom Kite shot his age—forty-five—on the back nine. Kite's Austin, Texas, colleague, Ben Crenshaw, two-time Masters champion, absorbed a 79, having seen *two* pitch shots on No. 10 roll back down the hill between his feet as he scored a triple-bogey 7.

The masterful left-hander, Phil Mickelson, played more wildly than the twenty-five-mile-an-hour winds. He sprayed drives into the knee-high rough, scoring seven bogeys, but he rallied with brilliant putts for five birdies. "The birdies came when I was trying to play the holes smartly," Mickelson told the press. "The bogeys came when I was trying to make birdies."

Mickelson and Bob Tway finished at even-par 210, two shots behind the leaders. Two shots behind them were Englishman Ian Woosnam, Steve Stricker, Scott

Verplank, Nick Price, and Corey Pavin, who still bore the burden of being the greatest living golfer not to have won a major tournament.

No point in trying to brave the crowd making its escape from Shinnecock Hills up and down Highway 27, the third round of play having exhausted itself. Many of the wiser thousands were walking to the Southampton College station of the Long Island Rail Road. Morris headed to the press tent to see again if Julia Sullivan had left a phone message. The life and death of Buddy Morrow blew again into his mind as if on the gusty winds off the Atlantic. He was eager to talk with the sheriff, with the widow, and with Sullivan, who would be sure to know everything that had been learned.

A huge familiar paunch, contained by a gold dollar sign of a belt buckle, rounded the clubhouse. J.C. Stroud spotted Morris and stopped, as if he owed him money. But it was too late to turn back. J.C. put on his best shit-eating, country-boy grin.

"What's happenin', Morris?"

"A little golf. A little murder." Morris did not smile or offer to shake hands.

"I heard yore boy got his ass run off the Shinnecock Bridge. Too bad. Leastwise he didn't have to go out today and choke to death like he was born to do."

"Where were *you* last night, J.C.?" Morris leaned on his cane, his voice as even and deadly as he could make it.

"Same as I tole the sheriff. Got liquored up on Edgar Spencer's free booze. Spent the rest of the night at my new favorite joint, Buckley's Irish Pub, snakin' on the waitress."

"I thought you'd been thrown out of there for life," Morris said.

"I'm born again. From now on it's the Christian life

for me." Stroud rubbed his belly lasciviously, with both big hands.

Morris looked up at the clear sky as if he expected lightning to strike the ground they stood on. "I hear you threw your Christian guts up in the kitchen sink. Before Edgar threw your ass out on the street."

J.C. swelled up until his huge paunch threatened to break through the gold belt buckle. "His two hired sapsuckers showed me out. But I left on my own. I coulda squished one in each hand. Edgar hisself couldn't blow out a kerosene light."

"Did you kill Buddy Morrow?" Morris said it as coldly as the grave.

The grin popped back on J.C.'s face. "Ast the sheriff, if you want to know. I don't believe you're toting a police license in New York State."

"Whoever stole the Explorer and ran him off the bridge was a low-rent, ignorant, gutless piece of filth," Morris said, aiming each word carefully down into J.C.'s wide face.

J.C. inflated both big cheeks with his fury, but Morris—no drunken Speed Wallace waiting to be suckerpunched—leaned down over him, and he chose to widen his grin. "That boy could do it all, they say, but dudn't seem like he could breathe under water."

Morris looked into Stroud's flat, pale-blue eyes—suddenly sure beyond a reasonable doubt and to a moral certainty, without a speck of evidence, that Buddy Morrow's killer was looking back at him. It was a cold, silent moment that passed over the earth like some ancient airborne disease.

Morris did not speak again or turn his head until J.C. Stroud looked down and shifted his feet in his scuffed boots and gradually disappeared into the colorful moving crowd, the last visible aspect of him, his flyaway red hair, blowing in the wind, a faint remnant of the true country boy he once was.

Morris turned toward the press tent. Speed Wallace appeared in front of him as if he'd heard his name called. In fact, Morris was sure he'd been watching from a few steps away.

"Damn if you won't talk to anybody, Morris," said Wallace, the bruise over his left eye turning a deep yellow like some unwell autumn.

"A dangerous man, I think," Morris said.

"I kept back. I don't need any jailhouse doors slammin' in my face. I get close enough to touch him, and I know I'll kill him."

"There's been enough killing."

"It's a damned shame what happened to Buddy Morrow. There's no doubt he was killed?"

"No doubt," Morris said. "Were you at Edgar's party last night?"

Wallace nodded and put his right hand over his thick chest as if about to make the pledge of allegiance to the flag. "I wasn't the last drunk thrown out. I usually am. I didn't—I was off my feed. I left early, I admit it. But I went straight to my motel room."

"Have you talked to Sheriff Haggard?"

"Not yet. He called out at the Wargo tent. I'm goin' in now. Morris, I never killed the bastard," Wallace said.

"I doubt you did." Morris felt only a flicker of a doubt. Speed Wallace, the old Giant tight end, was going to fat. But you didn't have to be in shape to steal a Ford Explorer. And his nasty temper had always gotten the best of him. Until now. Not like Speed to back away from J.C. Stroud, who'd hit him in the head with a beer bottle. No way he'd go to jail in New York State for kicking J.C.'s sorry ass. Unless he feared more trouble on top of murder and attempted murder.

"Is that sheriff gonna believe me, Morris?"

"I don't know. Can anybody vouch for where you were?"

"I didn't see anybody." Wallace perked up. "I did talk to my daughter on the phone."

"From your room?"

"From my car phone," Wallace admitted.

"What time?"

He hesitated. "I don't know. I was ridin' around."

Wallace made a terrible liar. First he went straight to his room. Now he was riding around—and the phone call could prove it. Morris saw the fear creep into his eyes. He was also lying about not remembering the *time* of his phone call.

"I couldn't sleep," Speed said, compounding his lies. "Do I have to tell the sheriff about the call?"

"You better tell him. He wouldn't like finding out about it on his own. Speed," Morris said, "you better tell him the straight truth about everything you did."

Wallace closed his eyes for a moment as if trying to remember his assignment on some long-ago pass pattern. He decided what he needed was a change of subject. "Buddy Morrow turned down my three million dollars," he said, not realizing that such a snub put him, Speed, in an even more precarious position.

Morris didn't believe Wargo had offered Morrow $3 million. No way he would have turned it down to sign for $2 million. But Speed was a talker; he'd be saying he'd offered $5 million by the time the British Open rolled around. Assuming he wasn't being tried for killing the man.

Wallace had regained his false confidence. "I bet the check from Spencer Sporting Goods bounced like that car off the bridge," he said. He corrected himself into Morris's silence, "Not somethin' I ought to be sayin'."

"No," Morris agreed.

"Was Buddy Morrow really forty-one years old?" Wallace said.

"Yes."

"By God, he coulda fooled me. And he did. Just as

well that hotshot Princeton bastard Spencer has to eat
his own millions. They'd have been down the tube anyway. No forty-one-year-old rookie was gonna sell any
golf clubs to anybody."

"I guess there go *old* Jack's and *old* Arnie's endorse-
ments," Morris said, unable not to laugh. "Who can
say? Buddy's remarkable story might still stir up interest
in the marketplace."

"You think?" Speed Wallace didn't seem pleased.

"Maybe." Morris enjoyed his discomfort, but he
couldn't get the flat, pale-blue eyes and shit-eating
smile of J.C. Stroud out of his memory. J.C. was not
just a liar, he was a killer. *And how the hell was anybody
going to prove it?* Morris wondered. He jammed his cane
into the soft ground as if to bury any sliver of doubt.

He looked up, and Speed Wallace was gone, taking
his improbable story to the sheriff. That ought to cloud
the cold waters of Shinnecock Canal.

There was a note from Sullivan pinned to the message wall of the press tent: "Call me." Morris recognized the number of their rented beach house.

"Speak," Sullivan said.

Morris could imagine her lying down, her eyes
closed, with the phone in one hand as if only it were
awake.

"What's up?" he said.

"Our girl is up the river. Isn't that how they said it in
the old James Cagney movies? Otis is holding her overnight as a material witness. He hasn't charged her. But
he's going to. With murder. I'm sure of it. Can you
believe it?" Sullivan could imagine Morris leaning on
his cane, the phone shrunk inside his big mitt of a hand.

"I can believe it. But she didn't kill him," Morris
said. "So now the sheriff is *Otis*?"

"I'm trying to make him feel as badly as possible. He
likes Jerry. But Otis is married to his job—and to the
next election. Jerry's too heartbroken to understand the

terrible position she's in. Or even, really, to care. It's obvious how bright and appealing she is. But the sheriff is hung up on the 'woman scorned' theory of the murder. Not a bad theory, as theories go. Remember that, Morris." She said seriously, "Why are you so positive she didn't kill him?"

"Because J.C. Stroud killed him," Morris said.

Now Sullivan was sitting up as if she'd been kissed awake by the true prince. "Tell me."

Morris recreated his encounter with J.C. Stroud, down to the last sight of his flyaway red hair disappearing into the crowd.

"You could be right, Morris. A killer–country boy. Or maybe I just *want* to believe it. Remember, we've been awfully sure and awfully wrong before, about other murders."

Morris closed his eyes, but no doubts entered his mind. "You know how sure you are when you place a bet," he said. Sullivan had never been known to lose a serious bet.

She nodded her head into the telephone as if the motion could be heard.

"That's how sure I am," said Morris.

"Tell me again what he said about 'under water.'" The phrase made her flesh crawl inside her blouse.

"Oh, yes. The comment of a *sensitive* man. He said 'That boy could do it all, they say, but dudn't seem like he could breathe under water.'"

"That hillbilly son of a bitch," Sullivan said, "I hope you hit him with your cane."

"I won't need a cane when it comes time to hit him," Morris said. "I don't know how the hell we can ever prove what happened."

"Maybe fibers off his clothes, or one of his red hairs will turn up in the Explorer."

"Wouldn't want to bet your life on it—or Jerry Martin's life. J.C. is dumb like a hyena. He'd be *dead* careful."

"Indeed. Who else have you seen?"

"Edgar Spencer. He was weeping over his lost two-million-dollar advance. Most of it covered by insurance. That's two million reasons the sheriff will hold against your pal Jerry Martin. I'm betting she and Buddy had a joint bank account."

"Lovely," Sullivan said. "Who else have you seen?"

"Speed Wallace. He lied all over Long Island about where he was and what he did last night. Admitted he left Edgar Spencer's party early. Said he drove 'straight home.' Then said he called his daughter on the car phone while he was 'driving around.' Denies he remembers when he called. I'm betting it was near the time our boy was run off the Shinnecock Bridge. Speed might have killed him with his bare hands after Buddy turned down Wargo's offer. But I don't believe he ran Buddy off the bridge. Don't ask me why I don't believe it."

"Who needs evidence? The sheriff is ready to hang Jerry on circumstances alone. I'm glad ol' Speed is lying. At least it muddies the legal water. Morris, I like your lawyer-buddy Ed Higgins. He showed up at the sheriff's office like an untidy little boy who jumped into his clothes and left the house before his mama woke up. He's making Otis put up an indictment or shut up. Only I'm sure Otis is ready to put up."

"I'll see if I can talk some sense into him," Morris said.

"Let's change the subject," Sullivan said, closing her eyes again and taking deep breaths to escape for a minute the subject of murder. "Who's leading my golf tournament?"

Morris was glad to tell her and to reinvent all the moments and images he'd snatched from time.

"I only wish you'd been here," he said. "The play

didn't seem quite real without you cheering some putt into the cup."

"Maybe it won't count, and they'll throw the round out and play thirty-six holes tomorrow. I'm not missing tomorrow," she said.

"Indeed not."

"Go to the bar and have a drink before you try to leave. Have two," Sullivan said. "You'll never get out of the parking lot alive for at least another hour. But careful who you drink with—and who you leave with. Remember the 'woman scorned' murder theory. That canal could hold another car."

Morris was glad to hear himself laughing.

A very small young man set a fresh glass of white wine on the bar beside Morris.

"You are Mr. John Morris," he said, sticking out a very small right hand.

Morris's own hand swallowed it. He'd seen the young man around but had never met him. "You can hold the 'Mr.' and the 'John,' " he said. "They call me—"

"Morris . . . I know."

"And you are . . ."

"Paul Mitchell."

"Buddy Morrow's—"

"Agent."

"We might as well be married, we're finishing each other's sentences," Morris said. "You lost a helluva client."

"And a good friend, I think. I mean, I believe we would have been good friends. I liked him. And he was married to a damned fine woman." Mitchell, in his smallness and his perfect profile, would remind you of Michael J. Fox, the actor.

"Did you guess his age?"

"No. Absolutely not," Mitchell said. "I was amazed

to hear it on television. I thought Buddy and Jerry were a May-December twosome. I very much envied him. She's an impressive woman. I was sure she was at least fifteen years older than Buddy."

"How did you meet Buddy?"

"I first saw him in South Africa. But I actually only met Jerry Martin. I must've been the only one who knew they were an official twosome. Jerry called me after he won the tournament in Houston. I'd forgotten her name. I almost didn't take the call. But she'd done her homework. She knew more about me than my mother. She'd even spoken to one of my professors at Princeton. Thank God she didn't catch a couple of them who flunked me."

"Did you know they were married?" Morris asked.

"I found out later, when we drew up a golfer-agent contract. And when he signed with Spencer Sporting Goods, their money went into a joint brokerage account at Merrill Lynch."

"Whose decision was it to sign with Spencer?"

"Oh, theirs. Jerry had researched the company and knew all of its financial problems. As well as its possibilities—with a hot new name in its golf lineup. To be truthful, I recommended he sign with Wargo. Their offer was quite a bit less, but they have the muscle these days in the marketplace."

"Speed Wallace said they offered a three-million-dollar advance."

"Do you know Speed?"

"Well."

"Enough said."

"Speed and J.C. Stroud at the same party?" said Morris. "I'm surprised they didn't break up the furniture."

"They walked around opposite sides of the same rooms, like two aging bull elephants." Mitchell smiled a perfect smile. "I heard about their fight. I would've paid good money to see it."

"Stick around. There'll be a rematch, sooner or later," Morris said, himself smiling at the prospect. "You were saying Buddy and Jerry made the decision as to which company's offer to accept."

Mitchell lifted his wineglass with both hands like a small boy finishing his milk. "I listened to Jerry's assessment of Spencer Sporting Goods. And I had to agree, Buddy could be a larger player in their plans. *If* they didn't go belly-up. They were offering two million dollars up front. So we really couldn't lose. Don't ask me where Edgar got the money. But I deposited it with Merrill Lynch—minus my fee, of course."

"Of course," Morris said, lifting his scotch to the negotiable fact of a $2 million advance. "When did you hear that Buddy had been killed?"

"This morning. Early. On television. I've tried to reach Jerry all day. But I can't find her. She doesn't answer the phone at their—her—condo. I thought you might know where she is."

"She's in the Suffolk County jail on Highway 24, just across the Shinnecock Canal, if you like irony," Morris said, lifting his own glass more solemnly.

"What the hell is she doing there?" Mitchell said, standing up out of his seat at the bar but actually lowering himself on his short legs.

"Awaiting a charge of murder, which is sure to come."

"That's insane."

"I believe she will plead innocent—and not by way of insanity," Morris said, lowering his empty glass and signaling the bartender for a refill.

"Of course she's innocent. What the hell is happening, Morris?"

Morris told him all that he knew, including the name of Ed Higgins.

"I've got to get to the jail myself," Mitchell said, looking at his watch as if it had betrayed him.

"Might as well have another glass of white wine. You can't beat this crowd for the better part of another hour. I'm buying."

Morris signaled the waiter for another white wine, which was the nearest thing you could have to not drinking. "What makes you so sure Jerry didn't kill him? Plenty of wives have killed husbands for a lot less than two million dollars."

"She was crazy about him. And she didn't have to kill him. All of their accounts were in both of their names. She could have taken off anytime she pleased with everything they had. Remember, he'd won nearly half a million dollars in the last two weeks. That woman has no business in jail. I'm telling you, the sheriff must be insane."

"Otis Haggard insane?" Morris said. "No, he's the most practical man alive. A Mississippi boy doesn't get elected sheriff of Suffolk County, Long Island, every day. Otis knows what's good for Otis. And there is no shortage of circumstantial evidence against Jerry."

Morris went over it, including her damaged Ford Explorer, which was used to run Buddy Morrow and the young socialite off the bridge.

"Somebody stole the Ford," said Mitchell, now back in his seat.

"Had to," Morris agreed, dropping his facade as a neutral observer. He did not say that his money was on J.C. Stroud. He did say, "How did the other agents take Buddy Morrow's signing with you?"

Mitchell turned up his hands, "Business as usual. Win some, lose some. J.C. Stroud made a nasty remark to me last night at the party, after crashing it and drinking himself sick and throwing up in the kitchen sink."

"He's a beauty," Morris said. "What crack did he make?"

"That he'd seen his share of 'pheenoms come and go, and this one could kiss his fat ass on the way to nowhere.' "

"A sweet guy, J.C. How did Speed Wallace take Buddy's signing with Spencer?"

"Hard. You know Speed. What could you expect? He told me, 'Buddy better keep winning if he means to keep eating—because Spencer Sporting Goods is going down for good.' I told him I didn't think Buddy would be standing in any breadlines. He backed off. But not because he wanted to. I have other high-profile athletes who represent Wargo. Speed wasn't burning any bridges. He left the party last night maybe an hour before Buddy. He was a long way from sober. And plenty angry."

"Angry enough to steal an Explorer and run Buddy off the Shinnecock Bridge?"

"Hey. I'm not making any accusations. But I'm glad I didn't meet him last night in the middle of a bridge. I'm making a run for it, Morris, traffic or no traffic. I've got to see Jerry Martin. And tell her I believe in her." Mitchell drained his wineglass.

Morris said, "I'll catch you later. Probably at the jail. Sullivan's been there all day. She's resting at the moment. Tell Jerry not to give up. Something will turn up. It's bound to."

Morris wished that he could believe it himself.

Easing his way to the press tent, Morris reached out and touched the arm of the very thin Jimmy Pitts, erstwhile caddy to Buddy Morrow.

"Terrible happenings, my young friend," Morris said.

Pitts was not ashamed of the tears in his brown eyes. "It's unfair. It's unfair, Morris," he said.

"Believe it," Morris said.

"Who would do such a thing?"

"The world has never suffered a shortage of low-rent cowards."

"Do you think they'll catch him?" Pitts clenched his thin fists.

"A matter of time. A matter of time." Morris wished he believed it. "Jimmy, you stood six feet from every shot he played. Do you think Buddy might have won it all?"

"Yes. He was born to play this course. And he was fearless. I don't think it occurred to him to be afraid. He laughed, he loved it when I was so tight I couldn't get my breath."

Morris suddenly remembered to ask, "The first time I met you, you said you'd 'read all the things they were writing about Buddy, but they were wrong.' About what?"

"I was sure he was older than they were writing. I saw him with his shirt off. I was surprised myself. He had the upper body of a middle-aged man—but one in top condition."

"Now we know you were right," said Morris. "Whatever his age, time won't forget him. His un-played final rounds will become the most famous in the history of the game—like an unfinished melody."

"Yes," said Pitts, "but he'll never fade another golf shot into the heart of a green."

"No," Morris said, his arm around the thin shoulders of Jimmy Pitts, "the hell of it is, he never will."

CHAPTER FOURTEEN

The traffic had all but vanished, the forty thousands fled to their separate destinies. Morris found the Southampton beach house after turning down six wrong lanes of fifteen-foot hedges.

Sullivan lay on the couch still in her trousers, absolutely asleep. He didn't have the heart to wake her. The tinkling sound of ice cubes in a glass did it for him.

"Bartender, I'll have a scotch on the lips."

Morris knew she said it without opening her eyes.

"Oh, my, that's better than scotch," she said, returning the favor, then opening her eyes and taking the glass.

Morris lifted his own, "To the cause: 'Free Jerry Martin.' "

Sullivan drank to that. "She needs all the help she can get. Our lawyer buddy, Ed Higgins, just called. Sheriff Haggard has gotten his warrant. She's under official arrest."

"Otis, the dumb bastard, just stepped in it," Morris said.

"Maybe so. But Jerry won't be the first innocent prisoner of the state of New York. Unless we come up with something. Or somebody."

"The kid," Morris said, "the 'very young man' who gave Jerry a lift last night to the Southampton hospital. We need to find him."

"I know," Sullivan said. She checked her watch. It was just before 5 P.M. She flicked on the television set.

Morris knew the look and knew better than to say anything.

At the stroke of five, after the opening ads, a talking-head male anchor, with a bushel of permed hair, came on to say that Jerry Martin had been charged with the murder of her husband—the golfer Buddy Morrow—killed last night on the Shinnecock Canal bridge while sharing the lead for the U.S. Open. There followed a tight close-up of a very distraught Jerry Martin, making no attempt to hide her face or her tears.

The talking head's female co-anchor chimed in to say that the lawyer for the accused, Ed Higgins of Bridgehampton, was asking for the young man who had given Jerry Martin a ride late last night from a condo in West Tiana to the Southampton Hospital to please come forward.

On the screen was a face shot of a more composed Jerry Martin. The female anchor repeated her request for the unknown young man to please come forward.

"You're way ahead of me, Sullivan—as always," Morris said.

"Higgins and I called every television and radio station on the island, and the newspapers, of course," said Sullivan. "I realize if the young man comes forward, it won't clear her. He picked her up hours after the crash. But he would confirm part of her story. And we don't know what, or who, he might have seen in the parking lot."

"Maybe he saw someone else in the red Ford Explorer."

"Or maybe he can verify that the Explorer was *not* in the parking lot at that time. Which would mean someone else left it there after Jerry was gone."

"Or maybe the young man just gave a weeping lady a ride to the hospital. A 'very guilt-ridden' lady, the sheriff might say."

"To hell with your buddy the sheriff," Sullivan said.

"May he perish in the next election."

"I've had my scotch transfusion. Let's go to the jailhouse, Morris."

"Let me hit the shower. I'm carrying twenty pounds of Shinnecock Hills in my trouser cuffs."

Morris gave her his best wire-service roundup of Saturday's third round of golf. Her eyes followed his lips, but her heart wasn't in it.

Sheriff Otis Haggard had his jaw out, just waiting for Morris to rattle his cage. Morris didn't disappoint him.

"You're giving the golf world a free shot at you, Otis," Morris said. "And the golf world only owns and runs Long Island."

"Tell me about it." Otis sat behind his big desk, crossing his long legs, as if his office were inviolate. "I'll tell *you* about it: the golfer is makin' out with a younger woman. And his wife loses it on the Shinnecock Bridge. I'll go for manslaughter. She'll be out in less than five years."

"She'll be out tomorrow morning, sheriff," Sullivan said, in her most dangerous polite voice.

"Not until somebody puts up a half-million-dollar bond. That dame has lived all over Asia and Europe and Africa. She could disappear into thin air. But she won't do it with blood money she killed for. The court won't let her touch it."

"I expect *somebody's* prepared to sign the bond, sheriff. The same somebody is ready to finance your opponent in the next election." Sullivan's voice was as dead-level as her gaze.

"That threat will get you thrown out of this office." Haggard sat up, settling his big boots on the floor.

"That *promise* may get *you* thrown out of this office." Sullivan never took her eyes off his.

"Here, here," said Morris, as fraudulent peacemaker. "We all want the same thing—the guilty party behind bars."

"The guilty party *is* behind bars," Haggard said.

"Maybe. Maybe not. They still have trial by jury on Long Island."

"We've got enough evidence to go for capital murder—and the district attorney agrees. The widow woman better ·jump all over voluntary manslaughter. That Ford Explorer didn't wait by itself in the night for Buddy Morrow, or get across that bridge by itself." The sheriff ran his tongue around his gums as if feeling for any holes in his case.

"Let me ask you a question, Otis." Morris used the tone of voice of an old-time friend. "Did you find the key in the ignition of the Explorer?"

Haggard hesitated, as if unwilling to reveal any facts against Jerry Martin. Then he decided to go ahead and say, "No. In fact, we did not."

"Jerry didn't have the keys with her—and they weren't in the condo?" Morris said.

"No." Otis wasn't sure where this was going.

"They just . . . disappeared."

"If they're anywhere around that condo or parking lot, we'll find 'em," Haggard said. "Of course, she could have thrown them in the ocean or off the road anywhere in Southampton."

"You mean, *after* her husband had been killed in the night—and *after* the young man found her crying and without her missing vehicle in the parking lot—and *after* he gave her a ride to the hospital—if she hadn't thrown the keys in the ocean, she threw them out of the young man's car window?"

"You're assuming there was a young man. And that Ford Explorer was still *in* the parking lot six hours later. It was never missing. Are you sure, Morris, she doesn't have a young lover of her own out there? Who drove her to the hospital? If she does have, we mean to find him and try him for murder."

"Imagine this, Otis: Someone steals the Explorer to commit murder. Jerry has left the keys in it. An awkward habit the killer doesn't miss. Maybe he means to run down Buddy Morrow in front of Edgar Spencer's beach house. Misses him there. Catches up with him on the Shinnecock Bridge. But now the killer has a problem. *His* fingerprints will be on the keys. Or he wore gloves and *nobody's* prints will be on them. Certainly not Jerry Martin's. So he has to lose the keys."

"*She* has to lose the keys. Only *her* prints are on them." Otis was back, running his tongue around his gums.

"Are you looking for the young man who gave her a ride?" Morris asked.

"We don't have to. The killer's face is on every telecast on the island, askin' for a young man who never existed to come forward." Haggard looked angrily at Sullivan.

"Somebody has to do your job, sheriff," Sullivan said.

"That's it. I've had enough. Out of here," he said, rising to his booted feet with a one-man show of force.

Morris put away the mask of peacemaker. "You've stepped in it, Otis. Not too late to pull one boot out. It'll stink, but not as badly as arresting and *persecuting* an innocent widow of a popular golfer, a woman who's done nothing but weep for her dead husband."

"Out!" Haggard said, his eyes squeezed narrow with anger and fatigue.

"A sweet man, your friend Otis," Sullivan said.

"Always fear a man with his tail in a crack," Morris said, "especially if he's carrying a gun and wearing a badge."

Ed Higgins, his shirttail sagging in his trousers, waited below for them both at the entrance to the Suffolk County Jail. Luckily he was on good terms with the night jail-keeper, who was married to a woman Higgins had successfully defended in a shoplifting case.

"We can see Jerry for a few minutes," Higgins cautioned Morris and Sullivan. "Special permission after visiting hours."

"*Ten* minutes," the older jail-keeper said, looking over his shoulder to be sure the sheriff himself didn't have him on the clock.

Jerry Martin looked abandoned by the human race in a formless blue dress. Her eyes turned away from the world and all of its vicissitudes.

Sullivan didn't bother to speak before hugging her like a lost sister. Martin managed the tiniest of smiles but did not speak, no tears rose in her eyes.

"Mrs. Martin, we'll have you out of here tomorrow by nine-oh-one A.M.," said Higgins.

"Absolutely," Sullivan said.

Morris sat on the edge of her bunk so that he wouldn't tower over her. He rested both hands on his cane. He didn't like the absence of fight in Jerry's face.

"We'll pick you up in the morning," Sullivan said. "You can't yet get in your condo. So you'll stay with us. We have enough room in our rented beach house for the Macy's Thanksgiving Day Parade. You can pick up some new clothes. You can rest. And then we'll prepare to kick this sheriff in his dumb ass, where he keeps what few brains he sits on."

Sullivan paused to look into the glazed blankness of Jerry's eyes.

"I know," Sullivan said, holding her like a younger sister. "I once lost a man I loved in a car wreck. And the world kept turning as if he'd never existed. But no damned fool accused me of murder. So I don't know how terrible that feels. Take this," Sullivan insisted on placing the small capsule in Jerry's mouth. "You'll sleep—I promise. You won't remember the one night you spent in this place. Tomorrow we kick ass in every newspaper in North America and most of the bigger papers in the world."

"I promise," said Morris. "Did Paul Mitchell come by to see you? And tell you he's in your corner?"

Jerry only nodded, no animation in her face.

"Jerry, help me here," Higgins said, his clothes as tortured on his lumpy frame as the expression on his face. "Do you remember any other thing about the young man who gave you a ride to the hospital? Anything?"

The words washed over Martin's expressionless face to no effect.

"Any stickers on his car windows?" Sullivan asked.

To her surprise, Jerry nodded, a hint of light in her hazel eyes. "My window." Her voice came from far inside her. "Blue and white. A shield. A dog on his hind legs. I couldn't even smile at him." And now tears did well up in her eyes.

Oh, hell, Sullivan thought, *a shield, a dog on his hind legs, blue and white . . . some college guy for sure. . . .*

"Oh, hell, yes! My nephew in law school—a Yalie!" she shouted. "By God, this boy is found! He just doesn't know it yet."

Morris remembered the Yale Law School sweatshirt

her nephew had sent her with the small dog walking on his hind legs. Sullivan wore it everywhere but in the shower.

The old jail-keeper stuck his head in the cell. "Time's up," he said.

Sullivan held on to Jerry as if they would be parted forever. "In the morning. I'll be here."

Martin sat on her bunk, looking at her feet, then lifted her head, even tortured up a faint smile. She spoke in the same faraway voice: "You two barely know me. I could be a terrible person. I'm not," she said, the first hint of fight in her eyes, but it quickly flickered out. "I have no way to thank you . . . for your help."

She seemed to run out of strength, then said, "I'll come to your beach house. But only if you leave a key with Mr. Higgins. And go on to the golf course. It's the last place where Buddy was truly alive. Tell me about it. Then I can try to think about his death."

Jerry put her face in her hands as if she could no longer hold up her head.

"A promise," Sullivan said.

Morris and Sullivan and Higgins stood outside the huge Suffolk County sheriff's office and jail compound. Night traffic was heavy on Highway 24.

"Get me to a phone, Morris. I'm calling every radio and television station on Long Island. I've just got time before the ten P.M. newscast. Somebody at that party last night in West Tiana is sure to see or hear the news and know the Yalie who drove Jerry to the hospital. If he doesn't see it himself. In fact, we're going to knock on every door in Jerry's condominium complex."

"What about her bond?" Higgins asked.

Sullivan reached into her purse and handed him a check. "I've already dated it and signed it. You fill in the amount."

"Think about this," Higgins said, holding the check

as if to blow on it to dry the ink. "You've only known her for one weekend. She *might* have killed him, however improbable the act. She *might* have money not also in her husband's name. She *might* skip the country. You'd be out a considerable amount of money."

"The sheriff *might* have one brain in his country head—but it's empty as the Mississippi Delta after dark. Give 'em the goddamned check and hush, Ed Higgins."

He made an elaborate bow.

"You know the courts on this island," Morris said. "What do you think the state's chances are of getting a conviction, if nothing changes with the evidence."

Higgins said, "It'll be nasty. The young rich girl in the car with the husband. The wife's rented Explorer the other vehicle in the crash. The wife home alone without an alibi. We can't deny any of that. But if she gets her will back—to be free—she'd make a powerful witness for herself. And *his* money was already in his *and her* names. She didn't have to kill him to take it and leave him."

Higgins filled his fat cheeks and blew his breath into the hot June air. "It'll be a near thing, Morris. I can't promise you she'll walk. But we might make a plea for criminal negligent homicide—a misdemeanor. In which case she serves little or no time. I wouldn't plead any worse than *involuntary* manslaughter. In which case she could serve a few months of a year's sentence, or possibly no time at all. She couldn't have predicted her vehicle would knock his off the bridge or that he would drown. *She* might have been killed instead."

"Then you think she was on the bridge," Morris said.

"I just can't prove she wasn't."

"Since when did the defendant have to *prove* anything?" asked Sullivan.

"Since her rented vehicle killed her husband," Higgins said. "I know, I know, the burden of proof is on the

state. They've got the dead man, and they've got the
vehicle that killed him—*her's*—not to mention a sexy
socialite who was on the front seat with him when he
drowned. Circumstances will convict you sooner than
eyewitnesses. Hell, witnesses lie and can be impeached;
they even die off. Hard to cross-examine a wrecked
Ford Explorer."

"Come on, Morris. We're knocking on doors.
They'll think it's Halloween."

First Sullivan rang up radio and television stations all
over Long Island. They recognized her name this time.
It was easy getting through. The stations already knew
Jerry Martin was charged with her husband's murder,
and it was Saturday night's big noise on the newscast.
All of them promised to put out an appeal for the young
Yalie who drove Jerry to the Southampton Hospital in
the wee hours of Saturday morning—asking him to
identify himself to defense lawyer Ed Higgins or to
Sheriff Otis Haggard.

Sullivan's only problem was getting off the phone.

"I don't think I'll come back in my next life as a
publicity flack," Sullivan said to Morris, having hung up
for the last time.

"Good thinking. Not that you don't have a gift for
it."

"It's all those years hanging around the Associated
Press. Some baked baloney was bound to rub off on
me."

They found Jerry Martin's condominium in West
Tiana. With Morris navigating, it was as easy as Amelia
Earhart's first flight across the Atlantic.

"You knock," Morris said outside the first ground-
level front door, nervous that the time was nearing 10
P.M.

A tall, skinny, aged man reluctantly opened the door,

while cranking up his hearing aide. *What? What? What?* was mainly what he said. Until he finally denied having hosted a Friday night party. He never did get it straight about Yale and kept checking the lock on his front door as if it needed repair.

They next raised a very attractive, very drunk young woman who invited them in with open lungs. "Let's have a party *now*," she kept saying, while Sullivan held on to Morris to keep him from falling into temptation once he spotted the upright piano in the front room.

Finally on the top floor a priest still in his clerical collar answered the knock.

"Sorry, father," Morris said.

"It's past office hours, too late for confession," said the priest, a small, slender man with mischief in his eyes. He identified himself as Reverend Anthony Powell of St. Mary's of West Tiana.

Sullivan told him who they were and who they were looking for.

"Terrible thing," the priest said. "I saw Buddy Morrow play the back nine at Shinnecock Hills on Thursday. He was quite brilliant. A marvelous swing. No doubt inspired by Hogan himself. A most appealing young man, though not so young as we might have imagined, I understand. You're telling me that his widow did not run him off the bridge."

"Absolutely not," Sullivan said.

The priest nodded, still with his smile, neither doubting nor accepting, having heard a lifetime of confessions and disclaimers.

Sullivan was astonished to hear him add, "You've come to the right door. I'm sure you must be looking for my nephew, Cecil Jordan, a senior at Yale Law School. He had a bit of a *do* here for some of his classmates Friday, and I'm sure it ran late into the single-digit hours. If I know my nephew. I was careful to be in the city. I didn't get back until today. It took me all afternoon to set the place straight—as straight as it gets." He opened the door, inviting them in.

The priest waved them to have a seat among a great gathering of books covering the walls and dripping onto the tables.

"How can we reach your nephew?" Sullivan asked.

"You can't tonight, I don't imagine," the priest said. "Cecil left a note. He's staying on the island with a *friend.* And heading back to Yale Sunday night. He's also here for the golf. He wouldn't miss Sunday's final round."

"Does he have that many friends?" Morris asked.

"I'm afraid so. This friend is very likely a girlfriend. I understand he's never short of girlfriends. I haven't met any of them this mating season." The priest flashed his best political smile.

"Maybe one of his classmates would know her," Morris said.

"Possibly."

He disappeared and reappeared with a short list of five names, with their New Haven telephone numbers.

"These young men have been guests here. I have no idea if any of them will be in their rooms on a Saturday night," he said.

"Not likely," Sullivan said, "unless they're fearfully behind in their research."

The priest lent them a quickie snapshot of his nephew, Cecil Jordan, in the event they stumbled across him tomorrow at Shinnecock Hills.

"Hardly probable among the forty thousands," Morris said, pocketing the snapshot and promising to mail it back.

"I hope my nephew can help clear Mrs. Martin's name," the priest said. "It's a terrible enough thing, losing a husband, without being charged with his murder."

"In truth, father," Sullivan said, "she is inconsolable."

"Ah, perhaps in need of a priest—who loves golf," Reverend Powell said, showing them to the door with his professional smile carefully in place. "I'll pray for her," he said seriously and with a solemn face.

At that moment Sullivan liked him.

Back at the beach house, Sullivan—aiming for the late news broadcasts—again rang up the radio and television stations, giving them the name of Cecil Jordan, Yale student and good Samaritan Friday night to Jerry Martin.

She collapsed onto the couch, hardly able to speak.

"Something tells me our boy, spending the night with his *friend*, is not likely to be listening to the radio or watching television," Morris said.

"Maybe sooner or later," Sullivan croaked. "These law students have a rough road to hoe and tire readily."

"Unlike we resolute journalists, who thrive on pressure and deadlines and *long hours* at play."

"You wish," Sullivan rasped, laughing in spite of her aching throat.

They were unable to raise a single one of Jordan's five classmates in New Haven.

"Good to know the next generation's lawyers have less on their minds than making their grades," Morris said.

"Of course they could be lost in the library stacks," Sullivan whispered.

"Then there's no hope for the law in the next century."

Morris alerted Ed Higgins and even rang Otis Haggard at home, earning no points with the good sheriff. Haggard did take down the Yalie's name and the names and phone numbers of the classmates and of the uncle the priest. But he promised nothing.

"Enough," Morris said as he put down the phone. "We'll smoke Cecil Jordan out tomorrow. There's no guarantee his story will help Jerry that much. At least the sheriff will know it wasn't some 'younger lover' who drove her to the hospital. And we'll know what Cecil Jordan did or didn't see in the condo parking lot."

Sullivan, rasping, sounding for all the world like a female godfather, said, "Now tell me, how are we going to hang J.C. Stroud, country boy–killer?"

"There's the question," Morris said.

CHAPTER FIFTEEN

Sullivan left a note to Jerry Martin in the middle of the kitchen table: *Ham and beer in the fridge; coffee in the pot; shampoo in the shower; feather pillows on the bed; rest easy. Keys to the second Ford out front if you hunger for some fresh air. See you a.g. (after golf). Be thinking about you. Love J.S. & J.M.*

With the sun roof open and the wind whistling past, the deadly toxins of "murder most foul" seeped away into the June air.

"So who is going to win the bloody tournament?" Morris looked at her as if the answer were written in her eyes, which cut from his own to the suddenly stalled traffic on Highway 27.

"Remember, I wrote it down for the cook. It would spoil all the fun if I told you," Sullivan said.

"If we could just announce who you've bet on, we could save the tortuous playing of the last round. Give me a hint. What state does the future Open champion come from?"

"That's for me to know—and us to cash in on," Sullivan said, easing the Ford forward amongst the horrendous traffic to Shinnecock Hills.

Her rare parking pass worked like a religious miracle.

Sullivan locked the Ford, and they leaned into the path winding between the practice putting green and the pro shop.

"A Bloody Mary would get the heart started, don't you think?" Morris said.

"I think."

They took the four steps up onto the steamboatlike wooden deck of the Shinnecock Hills Clubhouse and found their way through the favored membership seated in the main room into the bar. The wind off the Atlantic rattled the floor-to-ceiling glass looking out over the steep 9th green.

The Times of London had beat them to the bar. Tom Rowe stood and pulled out two of the iron Chinese Chippendale chairs, as if waiting tables were his true profession. He lifted his hand without saying a word, and their two Bloody Marys were on the way.

"Expecting us, I think," Morris said.

"As the night expects morning," Rowe said.

The three of them touched glasses.

"Loves . . . tell me everything," said Rowe.

"A simple truth," Sullivan said. "She didn't kill him."

Morris nodded like a justice of the Supreme Court confirming the simple truth.

"The sheriff—" Rowe began.

"Is a country-boy fool," Sullivan said.

Morris offering his confirming nod.

"Then who—"

"Best not ask," Morris said. "The sad truth is not a

pretty one, and I have no evidence against the man who killed Buddy Morrow."

"You know then?"

"Sure. Of course, the Fates could be toying with my imagination. It wouldn't be the first time."

"Will anyone ever prove who did it?" asked Rowe.

"I doubt it," Morris said. "Unless a witness comes forward, or the forensic lab stumbles onto something."

"What about the Yalie who's said to have given Jerry Martin a ride to the hospital?"

"Could be the deciding witness," Morris said. "Cecil Jordan is his name, a Yale law student. He's likely here on the grounds as we speak. We know he gave Jerry a ride. We don't know who else or what else he saw in her condo parking lot, if anything."

Morris pulled out the photograph of Cecil Jordan he'd borrowed from his uncle the priest.

"What will happen to Jerry Martin?" Rowe asked.

"Good question. *Her* rental vehicle kills *her* husband, who is with another, younger woman, while *she* is at home with no alibi, about to claim the better part of *his* two-million-dollar signing bonus."

"Maybe the sheriff has a point," Rowe said.

"He's wrong as rain indoors," Morris said.

"Jerry worries me, her lack of fight," Sullivan said. "She's still in shock over Buddy's death. Or she was last night. She's out on bail this morning, resting, I hope, at our place. She agreed to stay there only if we came on to the golf tournament."

"Ah, the golf tournament. There's that. You're the punter, Sullivan, who are you backing?" asked Rowe, well aware of her gambling prowess.

"Oh, no. I'll only say . . . I have some grand odds."

"Not one of the co-leaders, then?"

"Grand odds," Sullivan repeated, offering nothing else.

"Better dodge the press tent, Morris," said Rowe.

"They'll bury you with questions about the *'husband-killer'* Jerry Martin."

"I know that heartless breed," Morris said, "having been one of them most of my adult life. We're going to bury ourselves in the grand old game."

"Luck then," said Rowe, sitting back, the absolute English gentleman.

Morris and Sullivan took a seat on the low clubhouse steps and waited for the leaders to tee off in the 95th playing of the U.S. Open.

"Let's drift among 'em," Morris said, struggling to stand, "until fate has made its choice."

Sullivan smiled, having chosen while fate napped.

Two strong men stood tee-to-tee, the Saturday co-leaders, Greg Norman and Tom Lehman, each thirsting for his first U.S. Open title.

Fate cleared its throat on the 2nd hole, a par 3 of 223 yards to an elevated green. Norman, his blond hair blowing around his handsome forehead, tested the wind, tossing grass like hope into the swirling currents off the Atlantic. His long iron suffered from indecision and failed to find the narrow green. His chip left him five slippery feet from the hole. He gathered himself over the putt, gripping and regripping the club, his hands and eyes groping for the speed and line. His ball slid over the grass and into but *around* the cup, spinning 350 degrees back in the direction from which it was struck.

"Oh, my," whispered Sullivan, at the heartbreaking bogey.

"Maybe we're crowding his luck," said Morris.

"He's too beautiful, the gods are envious," Sullivan repeated from times past. "He has no luck."

And yet Norman endured for the first nine holes, scrambling on every green, holding a one-shot lead over the field at a desperate even-par.

Lehman, ever the grinder, his face a blank sheet of resolution beneath his unflattering baseball-style cap, lingered one shot back after the windswept front nine.

Davis Love, in command of his great length off the tee, also hung one shot off the lead, as did Bob Tway, who once stole the PGA championship from Norman, holing a bunker shot at Inverness of Toledo, Ohio, on the last green.

Two shots behind Norman today was wee Corey Pavin, still the greatest American player at age thirty-five, never to win a major tournament. God, Pavin was sick of that descriptive phrase.

Three shots off Norman's even-par lead was the left-hander Phil Mickelson, teetering between birdie and bogey on every windblown hole.

All six players—Norman, Lehman, Love, Tway, Pavin, Mickelson—were within sight of their names engraved on the championship cup. But there was the matter of the nine remaining holes.

Unknown to the leaders and most of the gallery was the play of journeyman Neal Lancaster, who birdied four holes in a row, while shooting an Open record 29 on the back side for a final-round 65. He was never a threat to take the lead but finished the tournament in a tie for fourth place.

Old Raymond Floyd also stole anonymously home with a 67, one shot off the closing round that had won him the 1986 Open at Shinnecock Hills. The defending Senior Open champion finished a respectable nine shots off the winning score.

The 95th Open turned on the 12th hole, a brutal par 4 of 472 yards that ran sharply downhill and then uphill, bending in its middle yards around Thom's Elbow. Not a hole for the faint of heart.

Morris and Sullivan struggled ahead of the leaders to wait in the crowd around the 12th green, like voyeurs anticipating a moving catastrophe.

Morris, with his binoculars, could see the tiny 150-pound Pavin take his weirdly flat practice swing, as if he were knocking pecans off a low limb of a tree. Now he turned into his more orthodox swing and sent his drive, a low fade, into the fairway. The downhill flight gave him an extra twenty-five yards but left him easily the shortest drive among the Open field.

Only 125 players enjoyed exempt status on the PGA tour. Pavin ranked number 150 in driving distance—the entire tour plus twenty-five nonexempt players easily flying their tee shots past his own. Accuracy and intelligence? Two separate matters altogether, both heavily in Pavin's favor, as was his deadly short game, allowing him to win twelve PGA tournaments in the last eleven years. In the majors he had come as near winning as third in the 1993 Masters, fourth in the 1993 British Open, and second in the 1994 PGA.

Pavin, at 2 over par, stood in the 12th fairway two shots off Norman's lead with seven and a half holes to play.

Sullivan, as was her habit, lifted Morris's binoculars, and he was unable to see what club Pavin pulled for his second shot. But it must have been a fairway wood screaming to the 12th green, where it rolled stiff to the pin, a remarkable shot that resulted in a rare birdie on the 472-yard hole and reversed the course of the tournament, only to be upstaged by Pavin's great approach shot to the 18th green. The birdie 3 on No. 12 dropped the wee Pavin to 1 over par, a bare stroke behind the leader, Greg Norman.

"There he stands, on the 12th tee," Sullivan said, her eyes draining the sight of the Great White Shark through the overheated lenses of her binoculars. She followed the flight of Greg Norman's ball for an astonishing distance.

"Oh, my," she said.

"Please concentrate on the ball and not the blond hair," Morris said.

"He's only delicious," Sullivan admitted, still welded to the glasses.

Norman's approach shot was not so tasty. His iron shot from 175 yards ran over the green and into the high rough. After the round he told the writers, hungry for his Open epitaph, "If I had one shot to play over, that would be the one. When the ball rolled into the heavy rough, I wasn't that far from the hole, but I had no green to work with. If I had it to do over, I would hit the iron a little lower so the wind wouldn't grab it."

Norman stormed up the steep incline to the 12th green like an angry young Palmer, though he himself was pushing past forty. He frowned deep creases into his sun-shattered face at his ball, settled in the high grass. His chip shot deepened the frown and the creases, the ball dying a full eight feet past the hole.

Again, Norman's hands gripped and regripped the club as if he could squeeze the putter into obedience. But the putt itself never found the hole. A bogey 5 after a monstrous drive.

Vintage Greg Norman, thought Morris, retrieving his binoculars and turning them on the scoreboard. At that instant in time, Norman was tied for the lead with his playing partner Lehman, who himself drained a heroic putt to birdie the lethal 12th hole, as well as with Corey Pavin, Bob Tway, and Davis Love. A five-man race to immortality.

Sullivan hurried Morris down the 13th fairway, he pausing just long enough to see Norman pull his tee shot into the heavy rough, assuring him of a second consecutive bogey and the loss of the Open lead.

"Come along, Morris," Sullivan insisted, dragging him up the dunes through the alarmed thousands, never stopping until they were panting on the tee of the par-4

15th hole, which fell away downhill to an elevated green 415 yards in the distance.

Morris managed, in passing, to see the failed eight-foot putt on the 13th green that dropped the gifted Davis Love out of the tie for the lead. Then came a missed four-footer at No. 16 and a ghastly double-bogey 6 on the last hole, to insure Love's *'labor lost'* in another major tournament.

Meanwhile Phil Mickelson dropped one of his heart-attack putts on the 14th green to pull within a shot of the lead—only to undo himself again on the par-5 16th hole, taking a bloody seven like an overdose of agony. For the tournament, he played the 16th hole *6 over par*, else he would have been the Open champion by two full strokes. Meanwhile Tway missed the 14th green and bogeyed the hole, also bogeying the 16th, to shatter his own hopes with 40 blows on the back nine.

There was plenty of wind but very little oxygen blowing over Shinnecock Hills.

Far down the 15th fairway, Corey Pavin made a small boylike figure, even in the strong binoculars. After his curious flat trademark practice swing, Pavin bent an iron shot onto the elevated 15th green, some twelve feet from the flag. He barely hesitated over the putt before rapping it directly into the cup. At long last Pavin stood even-par with Shinnecock Hills and in the lead of the Open by one stroke—Morris could see on the scoreboard—over Tom Lehman, Norman having fallen to 2 over par with his consecutive bogeys. But then Norman dropped his own birdie putt on No. 15—his first and only birdie all day—and lay one shot off the lead with three holes to play. The game was on.

Pavin told the writers after the tournament, "The wind was so strong, the course was playing so tough, I just concentrated on striking each shot solidly. I thought par would be a good score on any of the difficult closing holes."

Morris and Sullivan watched him wrestle a par 5 from the treacherous 544-yard 16th hole, which played into a twenty-five-mile-an-hour wind, and waited to see if Norman or Lehman could birdie it.

Lehman did not birdie it. He did not even survive it. His second shot landed in the high fescue, forcing him to simply pitch the ball back into the fairway. The wind knocked his fourth shot down into the rough at the edge of the green. Spooked, Lehman struck what he called a "fluffy chip" that rolled back off the green, and two putts later he had recorded a double-bogey 7, his Open chances dead in the grass.

Norman, still one shot behind Pavin, failed to land his wedge anywhere near the 16th hole and took a par 5, which must have felt like a bogey. His great length had failed him on a hole he might have dominated, even into the wind.

Up ahead, Pavin braced his slight frame against the stiff breeze and drained a tricky five-foot putt to par the 17th hole, which played 181 yards to a tricky pin placement.

Greg Norman was not up to the par-3 challenge. His iron shot missed the green, his chip was errant, and his putt never found the hole, for a bogey 4, leaving him two shots off Pavin's lead with only the 18th hole to play.

Only disaster could prevent Corey Pavin from his first major championship. But disaster had often struck on the last hole of the U.S. Open. The great Sam Snead once cost himself the only major title he never won with an *8* on the 72nd hole.

Pavin attacked the 450-yard par-4 finishing hole—the most difficult hole at Shinnecock Hills—with a modest drive of 241 yards. Which left him a 209-yard carry uphill to a blind green.

Morris and Sullivan, standing along the 18th fairway, heard Pavin ask his caddy, Eric Schwarz, "Do you think

I'm close enough to hit this club to the green?" He fingered what seemed to be his two-iron. They could not hear Schwarz's answer, but there was no doubt he was shaking his head.

Pavin pulled the cover off his four-wood. Took his baseball-like practice swing. And turned it into the most important shot of his life. The ball flew from his clubface with a slight right-to-left draw and landed just short of the blind green, rolling toward the flag, the top of which was barely visible below the Shinnecock clubhouse.

Pavin ran after the shot, hoping to see where the ball stopped. It stopped a bare five feet from the hole, very possibly the greatest closing shot in U.S. Open history. A huge roar rose up from the crowd around the green, which organized itself into a chant: *Corey! Corey! Corey!* His name resounded over the course as if he were being summoned by the golfing gods themselves.

A dead-spent Pavin later told the writers, "The last shot was the most pressure I've ever felt on a golf course. I just tried to gather myself and make a good swing. I was trying to hit a low draw, and I knew I'd hit a good shot. I just took off running then because I wanted to see it."

Pavin missed the five-foot putt. But he won the tournament by two strokes over Greg Norman, who was all generosity in defeat and who had now finished second seven times in major championships.

The photograph sped around the world, of a dead-spent Pavin holding the Open cup with his son Ryan, while hugging his wife Shannon, who held their younger son Austin. It was an exceedingly popular photograph in the wide world of golf.

As the thousands in the gallery made their separate ways off the Long Island peninsula or to fashionable parties the length of it, Sullivan stood looking over the now-empty course, catching a glimpse of Peconic Bay, shining in the late afternoon. Morris, who had stopped off to say good-bye to Tom Rowe, came on her standing there.

"Wouldn't it have been fun to see him finish?" Sullivan said without turning her head.

She didn't have to identify the *him*.

"We know one thing," Morris said. "Buddy Morrow would never have lost his nerve."

"We know that," Sullivan said.

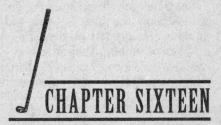

CHAPTER SIXTEEN

A young man, thin as a swizzle stick, touched Morris's sleeve, then pulled his hand back as if it had been burned.

"Excuse me," he said, almost swallowing his voice, "are you Mr. John Morris?"

"Absolutely," Morris said.

"I'm Cecil Jordan." He said his name as if confessing to a felony.

"Are you now?"

Sullivan touched Morris's arm.

"This is Julia Sullivan," Morris said.

She and Morris shook the young man's hand. It was cold as winter on a June afternoon.

"I was just in the clubhouse with a friend whose— father is a member. And I heard my name on the television. And that the sheriff of Suffolk County wanted to see me. I . . . ." He ran out of words or the air to speak them with.

Then he rallied, saying, "My friend's father is an officer with the USGA. He suggested I speak with you. He pointed you out."

"Did the television say why the sheriff wanted to see you?" Morris asked.

"No, just that it concerned the death of Buddy Morrow. Who I swear I never met in my life. I did see him hit practice balls and play the back nine on Friday. I never spoke to him. I swear it."

"This isn't a court of law," Morris said. "You aren't under oath. Did you give a distraught woman a ride to the Southampton Hospital late Friday night?"

"I"—Jordan faltered, the mind of an apprentice lawyer sorting through any possible misconduct on his part—"I did. I never met her before in my life. I don't even know her name. She was terribly upset. But she wouldn't talk about it. Why—"

"What time was that?" Morris asked.

Jordan closed his eyes as if consulting some internal clock. "It was late. I was going to get ice—we'd used it all. The party was still going in my uncle's condo. It must have been one-thirty A.M., or a little after."

"Describe the woman," Morris said.

Jordan described a weeping woman who could only be Jerry Martin. "Who was she?" he asked.

"Jerry Martin. Buddy Morrow's wife—his widow, by then," Morris said.

"Good Lord. I had no idea." Jordan closed his eyes again as if consulting an inner memory. "She seemed quite a bit older than Buddy Morrow."

"She wasn't," said Morris. "You must not have seen today's newspaper or watched much weekend television. But Buddy's age is another story. Tell me, when you came out of your uncle's condo late Friday night, did you see a red Ford Explorer in the condo parking lot?"

"I . . ." Jordan again seemed to be editing his memory for any awkward self-involvement. "No," he said, "not then. I'm sure of it. I'd forgotten where I'd parked my own Honda. I had to circle the entire parking lot."

"Did Ms. Martin say that her Explorer was missing?"

"No. She was too upset to say anything. She was crying. No wonder. She asked if I knew how to find Southampton Hospital. I said I did. She asked me to take her there. I asked if she were ill. She only shook her head. I figured some relative or friend had been in an accident. I never thought—I didn't even know Buddy Morrow was dead. The television . . . how did they get my name?"

"Actually, from us. We spoke with your uncle, the priest, Reverend Powell," Morris said. "Jerry Martin remembered the decal on your car window. Sullivan knew that the dog on its hind legs, and the blue and white colors, were Yale trademarks."

Sullivan said, "Just now you said you didn't see a red Ford Explorer 'not then.' What did you mean 'not then'?"

"No, I didn't see one early Saturday morning," Jordan said. "But I did pass a red sports utility vehicle—I'm pretty sure it was a Ford. I want one if I ever get out of law school alive. I passed one leaving the parking lot as I pulled in. Must have been ten P.M. I was late to my own party. I caught hell about that. A fellow law student was sharing notes for a lecture I missed Thursday. Try that on an old girlfriend."

"Who was driving the Explorer?" Sullivan kept her voice as steady as possible, while her nerves were screaming through her anxious hands.

"I don't know. I didn't get much of a look at him. His lights were in my eyes. I was just turning into the parking lot and was in a hurry. Is it important?"

"Yes," Morris said. "Think carefully. You said *him*. You're sure it was a man driving?"

Jordan closed his eyes and pressed both palms over

them for extra emphasis. "I saw an *outline* of a man—
I'm sure it was a man. I didn't see his full face."

Morris waited, then said, "Was he wearing a hat?"

"I don't know. I don't think so. I didn't see it if he
was."

"Was he wearing glasses?"

"No. Maybe. I don't think so." Jordan closed his
eyes again. "I caught just a glimpse of him."

"But you're sure it was a man."

"Yes." He said it with his eyes open.

"Was he a big man?"

He shut both eyes. "Yes. I mean . . . I think—the
outline of him seemed to fill up the window . . . but
he was above me, and moving, and the lights were in my
eyes . . . and I was looking to turn in. But I'm sure it
was a man driving."

"Damned sure?" Sullivan said.

"Yes."

"It's a matter of a person's life," Sullivan said, "Jerry
Martin's life. The sheriff has accused her of using the
Explorer to run Buddy Morrow's car off the bridge at
eleven-thirty P.M. Friday night and killing him."

"Impossible," Jordan said. He might have been
launching a closing argument in defense of his client.
"The woman I picked up *was not driving that vehicle at
ten* P.M. I didn't see a face. But it damned sure wasn't her
outline sitting up that high in the Explorer."

Sullivan kissed him square on the lips. "Young man,
you just won your first murder case."

"Get your Yale ass to the Suffolk County sheriff's
office," Morris said. "Do you know where it is—on
Highway 24—just across the Shinnecock Canal? Take
the same bridge on Highway 80 where Buddy Morrow
was killed. If you like irony."

"You two believe I saw the killer drive away in the
red Explorer?" Jordan was more excited than shocked.

"I don't think there's any doubt," Morris said. "The

sheriff of Suffolk County is about to eat one large un-cooked crow. I wouldn't miss it."

"After we break the news to Jerry Martin," Sullivan said. "Come on, Morris, shake a leg—shake both legs."

Morris turned for a last look at Stanford White's old clubhouse. It still sailed like a steamboat on a green sea. Shinnecock Hills had outlasted every golfer but wee Corey Pavin, and the new U.S. Open champion himself could only equal par over the 72 holes. *Well done*, thought Morris, before turning his mind to Jerry Martin.

The second rental Ford was not in the driveway. Sullivan knew the beach house was empty before she opened the front door.

Morris took to the kitchen to pour a pair of twin scotches. He never got past the note lying on the kitchen table. He carried it, resting on the palm of one hand as if it might take flight, into the bedroom to Sullivan.

She could read the apprehension in his face before picking up the note: *I miss my brown-eyed boy. Sorry, J.M.*

"What has she done, Morris?" Sullivan knew without asking. She wanted to break something with her bare hands.

"Maybe she changed her mind." Morris didn't think so for a minute.

"We should have stayed with her," Sullivan said, cupping the note in her two hands, as if in apology.

"She made us promise to see the golf. She'd never have come by with us here. Maybe she changed her mind," he said again but without belief.

He made the twin scotches. Then rang for Sheriff Otis Haggard, identifying himself to a deputy. Haggard came on the line full of himself, not waiting for Morris to speak.

"Yeah," he said, "I talked to the Yale kid. All he

knows is what he *thinks he didn't see.* A crock of Yale shit. It's gone way past that, Morris."

Morris leaned on his cane, feeling old as dirt.

"We found her," Haggard said, not bothering to keep the satisfaction out of his voice.

"Where?"

Sullivan needed only to hear the word *where* to know what had happened. The tears in her eyes might have been wept in older days for other friends.

"Drove her goddamned Ford damned near through a oak tree on Sag Harbor Road. Musta been doing ninety miles an hour. No seat belt. Then the car half-burned. Not enough left of her to know. Lucky she was carryin' identification. And the red hair. The same as a confession signed in blood," the sheriff said.

Morris said, "Otis, Jerry Martin never killed anybody but herself. She didn't need Buddy Morrow's money. She already had it. What about the bastards who lusted after his name on a contract: J.C. Stroud and Speed Wallace and Jason Everett? Where were they at eleven-thirty P.M. Friday night?"

"You know damned good and well this Stroud left the Spencer party and was drinking at Buckley's Irish Pub. This Wallace and Everett were making the party rounds on the island. And the goddamned island was drunk with parties. Nobody remembers seeing any of the bastards come or go."

"So why aren't your people out there triple-checking their stories? You expect the killer to come in on his hands and knees and ask forgiveness?"

"I expect the killer to be buried in her home state of Texas, if her people will come forward and claim the body."

Morris said, "Otis, all your father-in-law's lucky millions can't cure what ails you—a terminal case of ignorance."

"Let this greedy suicidal bitch come up out of the

grave and sell that to *my voters* and your fancy golf friends. This case is closed!" Sheriff Otis Haggard slammed down the telephone.

"And maybe it is," Morris said, now more sick at heart than angry.

Sullivan, who easily followed the conversation from hearing only his end of it, buried her face in Morris's wide chest.

He rang the AP news desk in Manhattan. The story broke all over America and around the world. Morris had only the satisfaction of Cecil Jordan's statement in the fourth paragraph of the AP lead, swearing that Jerry Martin was not the driver at the wheel of the Explorer an hour and a half before Buddy Morrow was killed.

But with the sheriff declaring the case closed, Jordan's statement fell a lifetime short of clearing Jerry Martin's name of murder.

Their things were packed. The 1995 U.S. Open was as surely in the past as the Open won at Shinnecock Hills by James Foulis in 1895.

The beach house telephone rang again. Morris could not have been more surprised. Calling was Jack "Speed" Wallace of Wargo Golf, Inc.

He said, "I felt like killin' him myself, Morris. When he signed with wore-out Spencer Sporting Goods. His stuff woulda died on the shelf soon enough. Too bad I didn't kill him. His woman would still be alive. I saw her on the golf course. Didn't hit me as a bimbo. Didn't know she was his wife. A helluva way to go. Dead into a tree, and cold sober. You knew 'em both. Do you think it was her killed him?"

"Might have been you, Speed. Nobody ever said you were anything but a rotten loser."

"You got that right, losin' is for losers."

"Might have been the boy agent Everett who killed him," said Morris. "You know how he loves losing the chance at a million-dollar client. Remind you of any-body named Wallace?"

"Jason, that little turd," Wallace said, "he couldn't kill fish in a bucket."

And yet Everett's partner had killed himself, Morris remembered. He said, "Might have been some rogue golfer with a grudge we don't know about. Might have been some rich kid in the bag drunk who lost it on the bridge. Might have been J.C. Stroud. Damned well might have been your drinking buddy J.C.," said Morris, any hint of speculation drained out of his voice.

"My buddy, my ass. I won't need a beer bottle for what I'm gonna do to his thick head. He's dodgin' me like I was one of his bookies. Well, he owes me, all right. I'm gonna take it out of his red-headed hide. J.C.'s just about smart enough to run somebody off a bridge—but, Morris, it was the wife who killed herself."

"And that's the only one she killed," Morris said. It irritated him how hollow that sounded.

"But the sheriff's closed the case, Morris. What do you know he dudn't know?"

"Not a thing. He knows some guy stole her vehicle and was seen driving it not two hours before Buddy Morrow was killed with it. The sheriff doesn't give a damn. His slate's clean for the next election."

"Then why do you care?" Speed said. "What—were you diddling this wife Jerry Martin?"

"No, I'm not slinking along at your speed, Wallace. So tell me, why the phone call? Never knew you to make sympathy calls."

"So I want to know, who was her closest kin? This boy dead is gonna have a following. The golfing James Dean. And the poor bastard might not have signed all his rights away to Wargo. These contracts have holes you could—"

"Drive a hearse through," Morris said. "I'm glad to know the world is still in its orbit, Wallace. That you are the same greedy bastard I met twenty years ago. If I knew her next of kin, I'd warn them against you and your bloodsucking kind. Nothing personal, you understand."

"To hell with you, Morris. A man has gotta take care of business."

"Yeah, I believe it. Somebody gets paid when they dig a hole for the corpse." Morris felt his attack of indignation subsiding. "The holy truth: Buddy Morrow and his wife were out to get all they could. Why the hell am I blaming you for trying to do the same thing, old man?"

"Goddamn, Morris. You sound almost like a human being."

"One thing," Morris said. "The bastard did love the game."

"You think I didn't love knocking the dog shit out of them Chicago Bears?" said Speed Wallace, his voice overflowing the telephone into the fake warmth of the beachhouse living room.

Morris couldn't help laughing, truly laughing, as if they were all going to live forever. "God help the Chicago Bears. Martin's folks are dead, but they lived on a sheep ranch in Texas. Somewhere near New Braunfels, not far from San Antonio. I don't know if she had any brothers or sisters. Try the *San Antonio News & Observer*. They ought to know, or be able to find out."

"Listen, Morris. I owe you," Wallace said.

"Yes. And the gods owe us all," Morris said, hanging up the telephone, having no idea what he meant.

"John Morris," Sullivan said, having overheard his end of the conversation, "will you please answer the phone when it's my time to be dead and gone?"

"Oh, no. It'll be you trying to bribe six pallbearers to carry me. Better make that ten or twelve. They won't be carrying Mickey Rooney."

"The sheriff took the coward's way out. Just close

the case and let it fade away. I knew he was a politician, Morris, but I thought he had some honest Yazoo County topsoil buried under his fingernails."

"Oh, no. Faulkner was wrong. The past *is* past. And the sheriff of Suffolk County is happy to shovel the dirt in the grave. He knows the dead aren't talking."

"What'll we do, Morris?"

"Not a damned thing we can do."

"You still believe J.C. Stroud ran him off the bridge?"

"Oh, yes."

"He's crude. Less than honest. Cheated on every wife he ever married—God knows why they lined up to marry him. He took a beer bottle to a drunken man. But you always had a weakness for him," Sullivan said.

"It's true. I wouldn't trust J.C. with the dust off the wings of a moth. But he could make you laugh, just the sight of him behind that belt buckle. And the bastard could promote. Usually himself. I never thought him to be murderous."

"Can he live with it?"

"I think maybe he could have kidnapped the Lindbergh baby and had a beer and laughed it off. What did he say, 'That boy could do it all . . . but dudn't look like he could breathe under water.' Fate might not forget a man saying that. But I guess we'll have to," Morris said.

Sullivan should have suspected the incipient depression in his voice.

"So it's a long good-bye to Shinnecock Hills," she said.

No answer.

"We'll drink only the best stuff, Morris, so we can live long enough to see the old club host another U.S. Open."

No response.

"Here's to Corey Pavin," Sullivan said, pouring two hits of vintage scotch.

She and Morris drank to the wee champion.

But Morris kept his silence.

/CHAPTER SEVENTEEN

Julia Sullivan, wrapped in a long winter coat, stood on her deck breathing frozen vapors into the chill air. The mountain, thick with snow, fell away under her in silent contentment, a state that eluded Sullivan herself. Even the far lights of Denver with their promise of good friends and warm fires could not dislodge her unrest.

Another week had passed, and John Morris had not called. She knew that when she herself rang, he would answer. He would stir himself into a false enthusiasm. Promise to come and see her before Christmas and mean it. And fall back into the long apathy that had consumed him since the dark night on the Shinnecock Bridge.

The playing of the British Open and the PGA had stirred him only temporarily out of his funk. He was nowhere near finishing the book he was writing on the history of the women's golf tour, and the deadline had slid quite out from under him. He was making noises of returning his slim advance. Sullivan knew his editor at Dell had called, reminding him he had never missed a deadline. Old friends called Sullivan, worried about Morris's obvious depression. She could only share their concern, which mirrored her own.

Such thoughts lured her each evening to her deck to watch the sun sink behind the mountains, leaving her world to darkness and to silence.

It did not help that J.C. Stroud had prospered. His new young protégé from Australia had nearly won the British Open and had finished among the top ten at the PGA. Stroud had been full of himself at both tournaments, though careful not to approach John Morris, who avoided him at every opportunity.

All summer the vintage scotch hung listless in Morris's glass, and not once did he lift a barroom baritone in the late hours of the evening.

Something damned well had to be done. Sullivan's buddy was sinking gradually inside himself. He would wake up one day a lonely old man, and that wouldn't do.

Maybe it was the birds chirping at the feeder, or the lights rising in the distance over Denver, or the silence of the mountain that inspired the thought process growing in Sullivan's imagination.

She went directly inside and switched on her computer. She began to type out, in no particular order, everything that she had seen or heard or that Morris had ever told her that she could remember about the particular man and his life, from the first time she had been aware of him until this year's U.S. Open. Sullivan was surprised at how much she remembered.

She typed her thoughts into words without regard to shape or form or action. Until she hit on another name. Then her thoughts shaped themselves into a rather astonishing, improbable idea. It had never occurred to her not to act on it. If only to shake John Morris out of his all-consuming ennui.

Sullivan looked up to realize that she had forgotten supper entirely.

Money can't buy happiness, they say. Sullivan laughed to herself. *The hell it can't*, she thought. It had certainly bought the attention, not to mention the participation, of a world-class expert. It did not hurt that he was retired with time on his hands. She arranged to pick him up at the airport in St. Louis. He was an honest man who said she was throwing away her money. "So be it," she said, and agreed to pay for his time, however long it might take, and for any materials he might need to carry out his inspection. He was long retired but had no trouble arranging, by telephone, for copies of all documents from the original investigation. He wasn't surprised that there were very few.

Sullivan did not explain anything to Morris when she called him. She only said, "I need your help. Pack some warm outdoor things and a pair of boots. And a coat and tie. I'll come by your place to pick you up." She wouldn't listen to his mumbled objections or relieve his faintly concealed curiosity.

"Just be packed and ready Wednesday," Sullivan said. "That's December 20, Morris. Still shopping time until Christmas." She hung up before he could object or ask even one question.

Sullivan pulled into the parking lot of Morris's aging apartment house in old, and now swank, Ansley Park. Morris always insisted that no man could consider himself to be a native Atlantan who could not find his winding way in the night, quite in his cups, the length of The Prado.

Sullivan sounded the horn on her rented Ford Explorer, not venturing into Morris's second-story apartment. She knew he would invent a continent of excuses for not leaving his rooms.

Here he came, she could hear him grumbling to himself, carrying his old beat-up leather bag that had been scarred by careless handlers on six of the seven continents.

Henry Parker, a tall, thin man with a long sweep of gray hair spilling over his ears, had removed himself to the backseat of the Explorer without prompting from Sullivan. She introduced the two men, careful to leave off any description of Parker's former profession.

"What the hell's with the boots, Sullivan?" Morris said, lifting his own large booted foot and tapping the toe with his cane.

Sullivan was careful to shift the Explorer into forward gear before beginning her explanation, leaving no chance Morris could bolt for his apartment. She'd long constructed the narrative in her mind and only needed to say it aloud.

Sullivan concluded, "I'm like a friend of mine, famous for his musings about golf. I have no confidence whatsoever in coincidence—especially when it comes to sudden death."

"You're nuts, you know that," Morris said when she had finished.

She glanced at him, swinging the big Explorer north onto Interstate 85. She was pleased to see he could not subdue a certain eagerness in his eyes, however much fatigue dragged against his voice.

"I did my best to talk her out of it," said Parker, speaking for the first time from the backseat.

"Not your fault," Morris said, "no one ever won a bet or an argument with Julia Roberts Sullivan." There was almost a hint of satisfaction in his voice, which was much to be preferred to the long absence of animation.

"John Morris, you never said my middle name in your life. How do you even know it?"

"Oh, you'd be surprised what I know about you—and the games you play," said Morris, but without his old fake malice.

Sullivan would have spilled liquid gold to hear one of his iron objections, or an exegesis on the implausibility of her wild gambit. But he closed his eyes and went straight to sleep as she took the fork in the expressway toward Tallulah Falls and the Georgia mountains and then the North Carolina mountains.

Morris awoke as they finished the long, winding climb to the tony old resort town of Highlands, North Carolina. The light snow that had fallen in the night had custom-decorated the smart downtown shops with a veneer of Christmas. Morris's own spirits seemed to have been drawn irretrievably under by his long nap.

For the first time Sullivan was truly afraid. Maybe her old pal had crossed some divide from which there was no way back. *To hell and back with that.* She stepped more seriously on the accelerator as if defying the hairpin curves in the mountain road.

It was a short but equally twisted run to Cashiers, pronounced "Cashers" by the small band of locals who stayed on when the tourist season ended. The light dusting of snow gave the tiny village an antique look.

The High Hampton Inn was officially closed. It had been open briefly for Thanksgiving, then shut down for the winter. Sullivan and Morris had discovered the old inn years ago, and its mountain lake, and sporty George S. Cobb golf course with views from greens and tees to commit to memory, and walking trails, and tidy old Spartan cedar cabins with wood-burning fireplaces and no outlets for the wrath of television or telephone, and the inn itself with its dark, welcoming bar in the basement and open fires in the wide lobby, and long tables of food in the dining room, requiring a coat and tie at dinner and all of the help more like old friends pleased to see you.

Always there was a golf clinic, or a nature study, or a literary conference, or a landscape painting excursion on the grounds. Or you could rock untroubled in rocking chairs on the wraparound porch, where John Morris could often be found asleep in the daylight hours.

"It's like summer camp for adults," Sullivan always said. Families had been coming here from the South and from across the country for more than four generations. The land had been owned by, and the inn named after, the Confederate general Wade Hampton, who would have approved of the careful way the mountains and lake and grounds had been preserved and the inn had been run.

Young Will McKee, who operated the inn his family owned, was there himself to help them to their twin cabins, the other cabins and grounds entirely empty under the great trees. Even Morris was stirred out of his gloom at the moment of shaking hands and the recollection of good times past. It obviously excited Will to meet Henry Parker, having led his professional colleagues to the infamous site on Chimney Mountain some twelve years before.

Will was no amateur climber of these mountains, having once negotiated the sheer face of Rock Mountain, which rose over the grounds of the inn like the palm of a huge rock hand.

It was too late in the day to start out. Will and his wife Becky joined them at a local eatery that specialized in providing you with a round granite rock heated to an improbable temperature, on which you cooked your own steak or fish, careful not to drop it into your lap.

Parker asked many questions, which Will answered to the best of his recollection.

"I have a clear memory of the day it happened," Will said. "It was during the biggest snowstorm of the year.

And the temperature dropped, and we had ice in the mountains, making the rocks dangerously slick. We had a difficult time locating the site. And plenty of trouble bringing the bodies out. It'll be much easier tomorrow. We've had less than two inches of new snow and no icing to speak of."

"How intact is the crash site?" asked Parker, who'd investigated thousands of them in his thirty years with the Federal Aviation Administration.

"I haven't seen it in a couple of years," Will said, "but the last time I climbed down to it, it seemed very much as we left it twelve years ago. It's in rough terrain, not easy to get to. You'll see tomorrow."

The peak of Chimney Mountain was a two-hour hike from the inn. They could have made better time through the shallow snowdrifts, but Morris had to pole his way along the trail with his cane. Sullivan was pleased with the outrageous quality of his language. Nobody ever accused the last angry man of being depressed.

They were packing in Henry Parker's tools, which were not light, two small tents, and a couple days' supply of food and drink.

Sullivan was also pleased to see Morris taking every care of the bottle in his backpack.

"If you're on a fool's errand, you'd be a damned fool not to have along a single-malt scotch," Morris said, sounding exactly like his old self. Sullivan held her breath, not daring to break the mood.

Will McKee stepped off the trail to an almost level spot just below the top of the mountain. There was barely enough earth over the layers of rock in which to pound home the tent pegs. Sullivan was glad to have the inflatable mat for the floor of their tent. She laughed out loud to imagine John Morris taking to their bed in the tent on top of the snow-covered mountain.

"What are you laughing at?" Morris groused.

"My favorite outdoorsman." She couldn't stop snickering.

"The only tent fit for human habitation is a god-abandoned press tent," Morris said, "and I better not be reading about this farcical adventure in some third-rate sports column."

He glowered at Sullivan, who put her hand over her heart in a fraudulent pledge, while imagining how the excursion would read in a *first-rate* column, say by Tom Rowe in *The Times* of London. You wouldn't want to confine so rich a story to the fifty states.

Will said the best route to the wrecked plane would not be life-threatening.

"You could fool me," said Morris, looking down the steep mountain to the far valley, all of it covered in snow like a frozen sea.

"But you could take a nasty fall," Will admitted, while linking them each to a rope, with him on the front end and Henry Parker bringing up the rear, weighted down with his several tools.

Morris slipped and cursed his way behind the nimble Julia Sullivan, his stiff left knee threatening to spill him with every step.

They stopped as often as they moved forward, Will seeking out the most benign route possible for his unlikely band of climbers.

"Believe it or not, it'll be much easier on the climb back up," he said.

"Sell that to the bloody tourists," Morris said, looking back up at the height from which they'd descended. He'd never admit it, but it felt rather good to have made it this far down without killing himself or anybody else. The absurd intent of the venture—the four of them hanging off the mountain to get to a twelve-year-old plane wreck that hadn't revealed any hint of foul play the day after it crashed—made him smile. He knew damned good and well Sullivan had cobbled up the expedition—at a helluva expense—to get him out of his rooms and his dark funk. What the hell, maybe it was even working.

"It's going to be a bit tricky, this last descent," Will said.

"Imagine that," Morris said, looking over the ten-foot-high ledge. A piece of fuselage shone in the snow, bringing the disaster on the mountain alive to him for the first time; he closed his eyes and imagined the sound of the plane crashing in the night against the slanted rock face, and the dead silence that followed in the drifting snow, as if no more than a songbird had fallen and died, and in fact, it had.

Morris handed himself down the ledge, having no idea how he would lift his formidable self back up.

Julia Sullivan knew by the violence of his language that her money had been well spent. Her old pal had recovered his identity—if only they could get him back up the mountain alive. She laughed into both hands to see his powerful bulk hanging from the ledge, and he cursed the Fates until he dropped, undamaged, into a large, soft, innocent bush that would never be the same.

Henry Parker changed identities at the crash site. Tall and thin and gray like some oracle of the mountain, he motioned them all back, each of them sitting on a separate rock. He had passed around to the three of them the FAA file on the 1983 crash of the Cessna 210 that had killed Little Nell Lambert, her guitar picker, and her pilot.

Morris remembered that "High on whiskey and run out of gas," had been J.C. Stroud's account of his erstwhile client's sudden death.

The FAA file confirmed the pilot had radioed in: *I'm out of goddamned gas and can't believe it.*

And J.C. hadn't lied—at least about this fact: Little Nell was heard by the Asheville control tower to be singing Hank Williams's trademark, "Long Gone Lonesome Blues," when the radio went dead silent.

The FAA's Lawson McGee—whom Parker "knew to be a sound investigator but only in his second year on the job"—had found that the plane was "empty of gasoline when it struck the mountain." The heavy snowfall had precluded even a fire breaking out from the volatile fumes. McGee had found no reasonable explanation for the crash, other than the pilot's inexcusable error of running out of gas miles short of the Asheville airport in a heavy snowstorm that ought to have precluded the flight in the first place.

Little Nell had been trying to make a concert date she very much needed, her country music star having set a long way from the Grand Ole Opry. Morris and Sullivan knew that the "setting star" of her career had prompted her to fire her agent, J.C. Stroud, who had discovered her singing in the bush leagues of country music.

"Morris, I need your strong back," Parker said, and meant it, having been coached by Sullivan to involve him at the site as much as possible. He was pleased to see the large man had shaken off the silence that had consumed him on the drive up from Atlanta. Parker was sure it was the only positive result the venture would afford. But he did not deny the enthusiasm he saw in Morris's eyes at being again at the site of a plane crash, even one as small and old as this one.

Morris took the crowbar and forced open the pilot's door to the crumpled cabin. Wind and time must have closed it again over the years. He could see the marks of an original crowbar from the FAA investigation of twelve years ago.

Parker leaned into the tortured cabin and shined his powerful light on the instrument panel, which had been crushed by the impact. The force of the crash had ripped away the underbelly of the plane, which seemed, at the last instant, to have flown *up* the mountain more than directly into it.

Will said the bodies had been oddly intact for so violent a collision. It was not a happy memory.

Morris watched Parker probe for some time among the instruments and the plane's controls, which had been driven back by the force of the crash. He checked now and then with the technical entries in the original FAA file and could only nod his head in agreement.

"I feel like an archaeologist scrambling among ancient artifacts," said Parker to Morris, as if they were investigative equals.

Parker backed out of the cabin and walked to the opposite side of the plane, its wing nearly intact. He disappeared under it. In a very short time, an impromptu *goddamn!* rose from under the wing, as if Parker had torn a finger on a piece of metal. He said it again more deliberately, a sound of clear astonishment and not pain.

Morris worked his way around and leaned under the wing.

"What's up?" he said.

"Only what brought this baby down," Parker said quietly.

Morris felt a rush of blood through his own face.

"What do you mean?"

"Reach under here." Parker guided his thumb to a round, hollow, ungiving stub of metal, not unlike an air valve on a truck tire.

Morris pressed with much force. "Nothing happens," he said, almost losing his balance, leaning as he was under the wing.

"Nothing, indeed," Parker said, "and that's the hell of it."

"I don't understand," Morris said.

"It's a scupper drain. There's also one under the other wing. They're spring-loaded. You press them and drain away a bit of fuel before you take off. To be sure it's in there and circulating properly. You release the pressure, and the spring shuts off the drain. This drain is jammed open."

"That's not so surprising. It hit a mountain twelve years ago," Morris said, suddenly skeptical of Mr. Parker's sudden enthusiasm.

"It wasn't the mountain that jammed this drain." Parker shined his light directly at the small opening. "I believe it's a goddamned hairpin. I don't want to pull it out until I photograph it. And I'm betting there's a hairpin in the other drain."

Morris yelled for Sullivan to bring Parker's camera and tripod. She and Will McKee scrambled to the wing on the far side of the plane.

Parker explained what he was sure he had found.

Sullivan smiled the smile of Englishman Howard Carter and his Egyptologists breaking into the tomb of Tutankhamen. She kissed Morris dead on the lips.

Parker, using the tripod, photographed the jammed hairpin in the drain from one inch away. Then he had Morris take a sequence of shots as he slowly extracted the hairpin with a pair of metal tweezers.

"When was this pin placed?" Morris asked.

"Not until the pilot was at the controls. Someone jammed it in at the last minute. Actually, it would have taken a matter of seconds to jam both drains. The plane would have been bleeding fuel from that moment until it crashed."

"Why didn't the pilot notice he was losing gasoline?" Sullivan asked.

"He should have. I can only speculate. The fuel gauge may have been tampered with. The way it's crushed, it may be impossible to prove. We'll pull it out and have it taken apart. And the pilot was a kid, with little experience. He wasn't flying that far, from Nashville to Asheville. He knew how far he'd flown since he'd last refueled; he wasn't worried about his fuel. He was plenty worried about the snowstorm and the limited visibility."

Parker was glad to step from under the wing and straighten up. "The kid shouldn't have been up there. The Asheville airport was actually closed. Of course, they didn't turn him away after they learned he was running out of fuel. When the pilot himself realized it, it was too late. The Asheville tower was in contact with him until he hit the mountain. As you know, all they heard at the last was Little Nell Lambert singing "Long Gone Lonesome Blues." If she'd known what we just found out, she might have been cursing and not singing."

With a great deal of prying and propping, the three of them managed to get Parker under the other, collapsed wing. After much grunting and even sweating in the cold air, he came out with the other hairpin.

"Why didn't this investigator, McGee, discover the jammed drains?" Sullivan asked, a question Morris had been waiting to ask.

"I'm speculating again," Parker said. "McGee was a good man, but in those days he was young, like the pilot, who was a twenty-four-year-old kid named Barnes, Pete Barnes. He radioed he was out of fuel. McGee could see when the plane impacted that there was no fuel spillage and, of course, no fire. He figured it to be an open-and-shut case of pilot error. The pilot is always responsible that the plane carry adequate fuel."

"Wouldn't refueling records show that the plane should have had plenty of gasoline?" Morris said.

"In fact, no," said Parker. "If you look in the FAA file on the crash, you'll see—on the pilot's American Express receipt—the Cessna was last refueled *three weeks* before it crashed. The pilot had aborted a trip to St. Louis—Little Nell's concert was suddenly canceled because of bad weather—as ironic as that. There was no record to tell McGee how far the plane had gotten toward St. Louis before turning back. Or how much fuel should have been aboard."

Parker opened the FAA file and handed Morris the appropriate pages. "Of course, we now know the plane had plenty of fuel when it took off for Asheville. But it was bled away. And unfortunately the pilot was watching the weather and not the fuel gauge, which may have been sabotaged.

"McGee hung the responsibility for the crash on the pilot, and it was a logical conclusion. Don't forget, he was up on this freezing snow-laden mountain, and three bodies had to be carried out."

"It took us two days," Will remembered. "There was never anything said about sabotage. Just that the plane ran out of fuel. I do remember that the FAA later decided it was far too costly to remove the wreckage from the mountain and there was nothing to be learned from it."

"Only a small matter of first-degree murder," Morris said, striking the nearest rock with his steel-tipped cane, which was once Monty Sullivan's two-iron.

"Henry, I know you have to report this to the FAA," Sullivan said. "But after what we've found, they owe us a couple of days' head start in Nashville."

"I can live with that," Parker said. "McGee's a good man. And now an experienced one. This evidence is going to hit him plenty hard."

"Henry, who could have been in position to jam the scuppers?" Morris asked, knowing absolutely who was responsible for having it done—if he hadn't done it himself.

"Any ground crewman with the least bit of experience. Even a layman who'd been around planes. It had to be done at the last minute. The pilot, before he climbed in the cockpit, would have seen the fuel streaming out. Whoever did it almost surely pulled the chocks from under the tires before the plane taxied off. That would be your man, or woman."

"I know it's a sin, Sullivan, to pray that our boy didn't pull those chocks himself," Morris said. "If he did, he'll never admit it, and they'll never close a cell door on the son of a bitch."

"You think it's possible he had a co-conspirator?"

"Yes," Morris said, more in hope than in belief. "J.C. might have been some kind of shade tree mechanic, like any kid growing up around machinery on a farm. And maybe he tampered with the fuel gauge when the plane was sitting out by itself. I'm betting—you're betting, old pal, it's your money that has us on this mountain— you're betting he bought somebody's immortal soul to do the deed with the scuppers. He wouldn't want to be anywhere near the plane when it took off for the last time. Excuse me, God, but I hope he had a co-conspirator."

Sullivan said, "Buddy Morrow ignored J.C. And Little Nel dumped him. We know that. Maybe the postman does ring twice."

Parker and McKee understood enough not to ask any questions.

CHAPTER EIGHTEEN

Sullivan slipped her Gulfstream jet onto the runway at Nashville International Airport as if she'd been born to the left seat of the cockpit.

Morris toasted the Music City with the remains of his scotch miniature. He had long gotten over any white-knuckle reluctance to flying with Julia Sullivan at the controls.

It hadn't taken him an hour in the Atlanta public library to dig out the fact that twelve years ago Little Nell Lambert's Cessna had flown out of hangar one in Nashville on its doomed flight into the North Carolina mountains.

That hangar was precisely where Sullivan was taxiing her own plane now.

Guided to a stop by a young man with a red bandanna, she shut down the fierce engines. Into the sudden, absolute silence, she said, looking directly at him: "Morris. We know what J.C. did. Here and on Long

Island. We may never prove it. We have to live with that. We can't let him kill our own lives."

"No," Morris said, touching her wrist with his fingers, "I swear I'm up to it. I just had a sinking spell. Maybe it was a long time coming. Maybe J.C. Stroud had nothing to do with it. The person I owe, old pal, is *you*." He reached over the plane's controls to put his big arms around her in his best Robert Redford imitation.

"Well," said Sullivan.

"Now let's get after his anatomy."

Morris waited for her to step down and pat her plane as if it were alive and appreciated all the encouragement it could get.

She walked over to the young man with the bandanna in his back pocket. He said his name was Red. Red Walker. He came by his nickname naturally, thin flames of hair leaking from under his baseball cap.

"How long have you worked here?" Sullivan asked.

"Right onto five years," he said.

"Anybody at hangar one been here twelve years?"

"Sure," Red said, "the manager George Pugh. Been here twenty years. He ain't too happy, working on a Saturday. Couple of guys didn't show. Too much weekend." Red's crooked smile made it plain he was sorry he missed out on the action.

Morris recognized Pugh's name from the FAA crash file.

Sullivan arranged to have the plane refueled and stayed to see it done, as she always did.

Morris followed carefully behind Sullivan as she stepped inside the low office building, which had been recently redecorated. Somebody had stuck a heavy hand in the red paint bucket. But old maps at awkward angles on the walls, and a poster girl for aviation gasoline with politically incorrect cleavage, and sliding stacks of unclean magazines on the cheap furniture, and a crackle of a voice from a weather broadcast were reclaiming the room in their own image. Morris thought it looked very much like the inside of a small plane crash.

"Are you George Pugh?" Sullivan asked the older man, whose large stomach had slid into his lap.

"Yep, that's me." He put down his *Nashville Tennessean*, open at the sports pages.

Sullivan introduced herself, Morris carefully avoiding any eye contact.

"You were here twelve years ago?" she asked.

"Oh, yes. And a long time before that. Damned time gets up and runs out the door." He shook his balding head as if he might have stopped it if he'd been alert.

"Anybody else been here that long?"

"No. Just one dumb bastard here, that's me. They don't pay enough to keep anybody but an old fool bachelor on the job. Why? What's so important about twelve years ago?"

"The day Little Nell Lambert ran out of gas and flew into Chimney Mountain. Were you working that day?" Sullivan looked him directly in the eyes.

"Oh, shit," he said, flinching, crumpling his newspaper, "that was a long time ago. Nothing to be done for that. Why? Why do you want to know?"

"I'm writing a book about her life." Sullivan lied so smoothly, so wonderfully, Morris, who had slipped closer to the conversation, shook his head with envy.

"Be damned. She was a pistol, Little Nell. Always full of mischief," said Pugh, standing up to spit in a sorry wastebasket. "I was here that day."

"Did you service her plane?"

"Naw. Naw, wadn't me. Jake took care of it. Not much to do. Just pull the chocks."

Morris, standing now directly behind Sullivan, felt her entire body go stiff; it was a good thing Pugh kept talking and she didn't have to speak.

"She'd ordered three dinners, I remember that," said

Pugh. "Always got 'em from the same café—they didn't deliver, sent 'em out by taxicab. She loved a pastrami on rye. Don't know how a country gal came to love pastrami."

Sullivan relaxed her grip on her shoulder bag. She could feel Morris leaning against her. She didn't interrupt.

"Always up to some foolishness, Little Nell," Pugh said, now warmed to his subject. "One time she give the hangar manager then, a real bastard, JoJo Boggs, tickets to this concert—only they wuz a year old, and the dumb bastard had to pay at the door. Little Nell laughed at him—she loved it how hot old JoJo got. Dead now, killed in a car wreck seb'en years ago, old JoJo, dumb as they came."

"This Jake," Sullivan said, "what was his last name?"

"Reese. Jake Reese," Pugh said his name as if he hadn't heard it spoken aloud in years. "A good ol' boy. From up in the mountains. Now, he knew his way around the inside of an airplane engine, I can tell you that. Or a pickup truck. Didn't make no difference to Jake. Ah engine was ah engine. But the kinda man, if he didn't have sorry luck, wouldn't have had none a'tall. You gonna quote me up in this book about Little Nell?" Pugh looked over his drugstore reading glasses with every anticipation.

"Absolutely," Sullivan said. "What do you mean this Jake didn't have any luck?"

"His chillun always sick. His old folks at home dyin'. Wife left him, tired of him making what they paid here, took the two kids, went back to the mountains. Jake was the kinda guy without no tool in his hand was lost to the world."

"Had to shock you when Little Nell's plane ran out of fuel," Sullivan said.

"Oh, hell, yes. Ain't never no need of that. Wadn't no fault here at hangar one," Pugh hurried to say, as if he had been personally accused. "Damn fool pilot hadn't gassed it up in a month."

"What kind of fellow was he, the pilot?" Sullivan asked, careful not to say his name.

"A hot-shot. Pete Barnes. Nobody could tell him nothin'. Bad weather up in the Smokeys. He wadn't about to listen. They finally closed the goddamned airport in Asheville. He and Little Nell and the guitar man—now he could walk all over a guitar, I forget his name—was dead by then. All of 'em. That'll be a big thing in your book?"

"Oh, yes," Sullivan said. She had her pencil out taking notes. Morris was prepared to believe in the book himself.

"How long has Jake Reese been gone?" Sullivan asked.

"Lemme see"—Pugh closed his eyes, figuring—"ten years . . . naw, eleven. Ol' Jake."

"What happened to him?"

"Last I knew he was working down at the Midas shop. Helluva thing a man can make-a engine walk an' talk puttin' on new mufflers. But it'd be a couple of years since I seen him."

"Do you know a man named J.C. Stroud?" Sullivan asked, her pencil poised over her notepad.

"Who dudn't know J.C.?" Pugh spit again in the wastebasket. "I had to throw him out of here twicest. Hollerin' at Little Nell. She'd had enough of him by then—'livin' off of her,' she called it. 'Big-time agent,' to hear him tell it, waitin' on her plane to get in late some nights. To me a blowhard."

"Was he here twelve years ago when Little Nell took off?" asked Sullivan, forgetting her pencil.

"Yeah. Made a big fuss over Little Nell. Said 'not to forget the good old times,' I heard him. Little Nell even hugged his fat neck. He left the hangar, too drunk to drive. Then she was gone. Seen him a few times later, flyin' out of here with that golfer Bream—flies hisself that boy, and a good pilot I hear. He done left J.C., too, 'ccording to the *Tennessean*. I keep up with the sports, but that golf ain't nothin' but a rich man's game anyhow."

Sullivan folded away her notepad. "You've been one big help, George. I won't forget you."

Pugh smiled over the ruins of his newspaper. He never asked John Morris his name, and Sullivan was careful not to introduce them and break the mood.

Morris borrowed the Nashville phone directory at the rental car company. There was no Jake Reese listed. Not even a John Reese or a Jack Reese. Plenty of Midas shops. The third one he called, Jake worked there, but Saturday was his day off. It took minimal effort to worm Jake's apartment address out of the guy on the phone, who obviously had a shop full of unhappy customers waiting on a new muffler or maybe to have their brakes relined.

Sullivan drove, as always, piloting the Ford through downtown Nashville, nearly as frenetic with traffic as automobile-crazed Atlanta, toward the Woodland Street Bridge over the Cumberland River. For decades anyone crossing that bridge might have been lost to time and to the mainline folks of Nashville. The Old Guard had not lived in East Nashville since the '14–'18 War and found precious few reasons to cross the bridge and visit.

A few architectural gestures at restoration had been made among the old Victorian houses along the neglected streets. Most of the houses had been cannibalized into cheap apartments, with missing fragments among the wooden gingerbread.

Sullivan slowed several times until she found the correct address. It was a vast old frame house gone badly to ruin under twin oak trees of enormous age and apparent embarrassment.

Now Morris took the lead, poling his way up the unsteady steps, with Sullivan a half-step behind him.

"John Morris," she said, his full name putting him on full alert, "this may be a dangerous man. Use your best judgment. It should be in good repair—"

"Not having been used lately," he completed her sentence.

She couldn't resist a burst of laughter, more of nerves than wit.

Morris's smile compressed into anger, though he could barely remember the very country voice of Little Nell Lambert. It was the country-boy face and iron gut of J.C. Stroud that dominated his memory.

Jake Reese lived in apartment one. It had to be on the first floor. The lock to the front door of the house itself hung ruptured and useless.

Morris led the way to apartment one and rapped on the drab green door with the handle of his cane.

To Sullivan, the minutes seemed as long as some afternoons until the door opened.

Jake Reese stood in a long-sleeved flannel shirt and dirty dungarees—six feet tall, thin, almost consumptively thin, his long face unshaven, and his brown hair going entirely gray and as untrimmed as the old hedges in the neglected yard. His brown eyes, with flecks of black like tiny cinders, were sunk in his head with misery, as miserable as the cheap lapsed furniture behind him.

"So you are the son of a bitch who jammed the scupper drains on Little Nell Lambert's Cessna," Morris said, never calling on his carefully rationed judgment and restraint.

"Oh, God," Jake whispered, as if to the angel Gabriel at the door.

Whatever he had been, he was no dangerous man.

Sullivan thought only his unclean dungarees were holding him up.

Morris put a big hand in his thin chest and shoved him inside.

Sullivan was startled to see great tears rolling down Jake Reese's long face. He stumbled back and fell against the wall, with its wallpaper peeling around him like physical regret.

Morris charged brutally ahead, having kicked the worn door shut behind them all.

"How much did J.C. pay you? Did you get a bonus for also killing the pilot and the guitar player?" Morris looked down into his misery without any quality of mercy.

Jake whispered, his thin lips hardly moving, "I never meant to . . . kill nobody. Not . . . Little Nell. Nobody."

Jake swiveled his eyes, left and right, searching without hope for absolution. "He said 'Jus' mess up the concert . . . make 'em turn back . . . bad weather comin'. Pilot bound to see the gauge . . . ' Oh, God. He never told me he fooled with the gauge."

He whispered it all, a black prayer of hopeless atonement he'd rehearsed for a decade.

Morris waved it away.

"Bullshit! How much blood money did he pay you?"

Jake, trembling in his mouth and hands, turned toward an open door into a severe bedroom, with a battered bureau, an unmade iron army cot, and not one picture or image hanging on the dreary walls.

Morris stepped quickly behind him, a loaded handgun alive in his imagination.

Jake worked the reluctant top drawer open in the battered bureau. His hand came away with a thick envelope and not a handgun.

"I never . . . spent . . . the first dime," he said,

handing the envelope toward Morris, who let it fall untouched on the surprisingly clean floor.

"Sullivan, get us a plastic bag. I think from the kitchen. I don't want to touch this envelope." One of the bizarre facts that stuck uninvited in Morris's mind was that Egyptologists had taken the clear fingerprints of scribes off papyrus thousands of years old.

"How much in the envelope?" Morris asked. It lay on the bare floor like an obscene letter.

"Five thousand . . . dollars," Jake said.

"Jesus Christ, you killed *three people* for *five thousand dollars!*"

"He never paid me . . . the other five thousand," Jake said, his nervous hands seemingly out of touch with his long thin arms, tears again in his deep-set eyes. "He said he'd swear to any police I ruint the gauge. I never did."

"Good ol' J.C.," Morris said. "Just the man to stiff a killer."

A croak escaped from Jake Reese at the word *killer*.

Morris didn't know one cop in Nashville. Henry Parker had given him the name of a Lieutenant Fred Hicks he'd met working a small-plane crash in the Nashville city limits. Hicks was off duty, but in the phone book. Morris caught him at home watching Kentucky dismember Tennessee in basketball.

"Yeah," Hicks answered, more than a little annoyed. But he remembered Henry Parker, who had flown commercial to Nashville at Sullivan's expense and was holed up in the Hermitage Hotel.

Morris, calling from Sullivan's cellular phone, described again the sequence of events that had brought him and Julia Sullivan to apartment one in East Nashville.

Jake Reese sat unmoving, his long head in his hands, his eyes shut on his bleak past and bleaker future.

"The hell you say," Lieutenant Hicks said for the

third time. He'd been on the force when Little Nell's
plane went down but was no way involved in the brief
investigation of hangar one. Hicks knew of J.C. Stroud
and had even had a beer at one of his press deals for the
golfer Roy Bream. J.C. was still a Big Noise in town, his
latest client nearly winning the British Open. His arrest
for murder, and/or murder for hire, would be an international story.

"It's your case, lieutenant," Morris said. "Henry
Parker is registered in the Hermitage Hotel. He has the
hairpins and the film from the crash site. I can ring him
for you."

"No, I'm on my way. I'll pick him up. This Reese
isn't dangerous?"

"Maybe to himself," Morris said, "but not to worry.
We'll hang around."

Hicks looked nothing like his voice of authority. He
was short and round as a toy top. His deep voice now
shook with barely concealed ambition. He had no doubt
he was involved in the biggest case of his life.

Parker, as tall and thin as Hicks was round and fat,
reached past him to shake Morris's large hand and
openly hug Sullivan.

"Some fast work," he said.

Reese still did not look up, as if someone else's life
and liberty were at stake in the room.

"You Jake Reese?" the lieutenant said, his voice now
cop-tough.

Jake raised his eyes but not his head and nodded into
his hands.

"You jam the pins in the scupper drains?"

Jake closed his eyes but nodded, as if in his prayers.

"J.C. Stroud pay you?"

Jake kept nodding.

Sullivan handed the plastic bag with the envelope
and money inside to the lieutenant.

"I understand the money hasn't been out of the envelope, and the envelope has been in the same drawer for twelve years," Morris said. "You may still pick up J.C.'s prints, if he wasn't wearing gloves."

Lieutenant Hicks snapped the handcuffs on Reese, who made a small sound like an wounded animal in a trap.

Sullivan and Morris and Henry Parker waited their turn to make formal statements, while the lieutenant and the police chief, himself deposed Jake Reese, who signed his own statement with anguished relief. He'd taken the money, hoping to get back his wife and kids. They'd never returned to Nashville. He never spent the money. Finally he couldn't bear to put his hands on another airplane. He could change mufflers on old cars blindfolded. And that's how he lived his life, alone in his neglected rooms. He "never meant to kill nobody." He couldn't escape the three lives. He was "glad to go to jail."

Parker offered prints of the developed film, showing the crashed Cessna in the snow and tight images of his hands removing the hairpins from the scupper drains.

The envelope and the fifty-dollar bills inside were rampant with fingerprints, many quite clear after twelve years. It remained to be seen if any of them belonged to J.C. Stroud.

The lieutenant was given the privilege of bringing in Stroud, but as a material witness, not, as yet, as a murder suspect.

Sullivan followed the police cruiser to exclusive Belle Meade. Somehow, through all his failed marriages and gambling losses, J.C. had always held on to his expensive, imitation-Tudor digs not far from the country club. To J.C., it meant he had come an impossible way from the hardscrabble farm he'd been born to.

Sullivan stayed behind the wheel of the rental Ford. Morris propped himself against the front fender.

The lieutenant was not inside very long. J.C. came off the wide porch ahead of him, his freckled face redder than his untamed thatch of hair.

Morris could hear him cursing but could not make out the individual obscenities. Morris smiled as widely as he had since Jack Nicklaus, age forty-six, won the 1986 Masters.

"Hello, J.C.," Morris said, friendly as a neighborhood grocer.

Stroud stopped, the short, round lieutenant bumping slightly into his wide girth.

Morris could see the calculation in J.C.'s hard eyes.

"Fuck you, Morris. This don't mean nothin'," J.C. said.

"You're right, J.C.," Morris said. "*A boy like you can do it all . . . but dudn't look like you're gonna breathe your way out of the penitentiary.*"

J.C. spit. But he didn't say a damned thing.

EPILOGUE

Julia Sullivan, if she leaned just to her left, could see the lights of the boats on the Thames River.

"I'm not sure I'll ever love another stream of water," said John Morris.

"You can't live your life avoiding all the world's rivers."

"No. And we have to have the water to make the ice—"

"To put in the scotch." Sullivan touched her glass to his.

"I swear, looking back, we all seem like characters out of some preposterous drama."

"But the two of us were good characters, Morris."

"Damned right. Heroic and all that."

Sullivan couldn't hold back the laughter, glad of the noise in the crowded restaurant.

"What's so funny?" Morris had a suspicious idea.

"I can still see you hanging by your fingers on that

ledge on Chimney Mountain." Sullivan was laughing too hard to continue.

"I doubt Sir Edmund Hillary could have done better," Morris said, patting his chest with his wide hand.

"Like a great bear coming out of his cave." Sullivan tried to stop her laughter with her hand over her mouth.

Morris tried not to laugh but couldn't help himself.

"Waiter, these two Americans are making a terrible fuss."

They both looked up at the snow-swirl of gray hair and the long lean face of Tom Rowe, professional Englishman.

Sullivan spilled her drink standing to throw herself into his arms.

"Watch that, Rowe. This is a respectable restaurant." Morris offered his wide hand to the gentleman golf writer.

They all sat down in a flurry of words. A new set of drinks came, and Morris raised a quiet toast: "To Buddy Morrow, the last American hero."

They touched glasses. It was too dark to see if there were tears in any of their eyes.

"So the late Jerry Martin had an older brother," Rowe said.

"Yes," Sullivan said, "a very nice chap. Teaches school way out in El Paso."

"It seemed unnatural for the state of Texas to claim the inheritance. On the grounds that his sister killed her husband. And with the sister dead and unable to defend herself. Would never have happened in merry England."

"Blame it on the sheriff of Suffolk County," Morris said. "He wouldn't let go of his false accusations even unto death, the bastard. But he and Texas got what was coming to them—their noses bloodied in the courtroom."

"We even staffed the trial in San Antonio," Rowe said, of *The Times*. "Buddy Morrow has become a folk hero in these islands."

Morris said, "The Yale kid's testimony was powerful. And the little Long Island lawyer, Ed Higgins, put J.C. Stroud—convicted murderer—behind the steering wheel of that Ford Explorer, although the judge never allowed him to use J.C.'s God-abandoned name. Still, the judge's gavel seemed to drive Stroud's murder of Buddy Morrow into the souls of the jurors. It was a helluva feat."

"The verdict was unanimous on the first ballot," Sullivan said. "The late Jerry Martin was found absolutely innocent. We sent an eight-foot-long telegram to the Suffolk County sheriff's office and to every radio, television, and newspaper office on Long Island. It seems Otis Haggard will have some Democratic competition in the next election."

"What happened to the money?" Rowe said.

"There is a great deal of it, and more to come. Buddy Morrow golf clubs have taken on a life of their own. Jerry's brother is giving most of the royalty money to junior golf—not in Texas, believe that, but in towns and villages around the world where Buddy had played."

"And our old buddy J.C. Stroud caught life imprisonment in his own trial?"

"Without possibility of parole. Couldn't have happened to a nastier guy," Morris said. "I can't believe how I used to laugh at all his country sayings."

"Two good things came out of his trial," Sullivan said. "He was found guilty of first-degree murder, and it gave new life to the songs of Little Nell Lambert. Her murder has made her into a Nashville legend."

"Speaking of Nashville, you never met the airplane mechanic, Jake Reese," Morris said to Rowe. "A pitiful sort of guy. He seemed glad to plead guilty as an accessory to murder. He turned state's evidence and took his twenty-year sentence like an expiation. My guess he'll be out in seven or eight years."

"I hope so," said Sullivan. "J.C. bought the poor devil when his pitiful world was falling apart. He swore he didn't know Stroud had tampered with the fuel gauge before he jammed open the scuppers. He swore he thought the kid pilot would turn back and Little Nell would simply miss her concert."

"He swore it," Morris said, "but he had to know the ten thousand dollars was blood money."

"True enough," Sullivan admitted.

"I can't believe what you two amateurs discovered on that mountain," Rowe said.

"It was Sullivan," said Morris. "We both realized there would never be enough evidence to convict J.C. Stroud of killing Buddy Morrow, but Sullivan pulled the idea out of thin air that J.C. very likely had also killed Little Nell Lambert. It would never have occurred to me in a thousand years. If you are going to kill somebody's hero, don't kill Julia Sullivan's."

Tom Rowe shook his head. "All those years that plane wreck lay on the mountain, a silent witness."

"Which we didn't have on the Shinnecock Bridge," said Morris.

It was the only time they mentioned the bridge, while the dark waters of the Thames rolled inexorably on below them.

"How good do you truly think Buddy Morrow might have been?" Rowe asked Morris.

"You saw him play two rounds. I believe he could have been as good as they come—at least for a few years. Remember, Hogan was never his greatest until age forty. Could he have been Hogan? There was never but one Hogan. But Buddy Morrow would have made his mark—in fact, he did. He won twice against the best in golf and will always be a co-leader of the U.S. Open after two rounds. Not many golfers will ever say that."

"What about you two?" Rowe said. "You seem happy."

Sullivan looked over the top of her glass at Morris.

"If we were captive birds with the cage door open, we couldn't be happier," said Morris, looking over the top of his own glass.